C

The Raging Spirit

The Raging Spirit

June Gadsby

ROBERT HALE · LONDON

ISBN 978-0-7090-9228-5

Robert Hale Limited
Clerkenwell House
Clerkenwell Green
London EC1R 0HT

www.halebooks.com

2 4 6 8 10 9 7 5 3 1

Typeset in 10.5/14.5pt Sabon
Printed and bound in Great Britain by
the MPG Books Group, Bodmin and King's Lynn

For my husband, Brian, who has visited St Kilda and who inspired me to write this book.

CHAPTER 1

THE LONE FIGURE of a young woman was the only thing that moved across the moorland landscape. It was strangely at odds with the tranquillity of the early morning, for she moved not with grace, but with heartiness in her step, head held high and proud, arms swinging in time with her long, confident strides.

It was April, but the land was cloaked in a crisp hoarfrost, glistening and shining pale golden where the sun's rays gently caressed it. Now and then the young woman stopped, spun around as if in a trance, or perhaps it was a dance of her own invention to music playing in her head. Curling tendrils of corn-coloured hair escaped from the hood of her heavy woollen cloak. She unmindfully pushed them back into place, turned her face to the pale blue sky and gave a spontaneous smile that lit up the day even more.

It was not a beautiful face by any manner of means, but pleasant enough, full of vitality. But it was the eyes that drew the attention of any onlooker. They were large and of a hue more startlingly blue than the richest of sapphires and with a gaze so intense it took the breath away.

Regardless of the biting cold and the wind that raced through that isolated place, the young woman continued on her way, humming softly to herself. Within minutes she effortlessly climbed a hill and descended to the valley beyond. At the sight of tall, stone chimneys, sending up swirling plumes of grey smoke into the frosted atmosphere, her steps quickened considerably. By the time she reached the house and let herself in through the heavy oak door she was quite breathless, but glowing with health.

'Father!' she called out. 'Father, I'm back!'

She hurried down the wide hall, opening doors and peering inside. The interiors were dim because Daisy, the little housemaid, had not yet drawn back the curtains. It was Sunday and therefore the day took a little longer to get started.

'In here,' came her father's response from the study, together with a whiff of sweet Virginia pipe-smoke.

The room was warm and welcoming because of the flickering flames of a log fire. Her father kept it burning throughout the year because he liked the ambience it created. Here on the Northumberland moors the house could be cold even in the height of summer.

Dr Josiah Jolly was slumped in his favourite armchair close to the hearth, yet facing the large bay window. From here he could look out on to the garden that he and his wife had created during their long years of marriage. Hannah Jolly had died two years ago, so she could no longer share his passion for plants and flowers, but gazing upon the blooms that she so lovingly cared for kept her alive in her grieving husband's heart.

'Oh, dear!' Meredith felt a stabbing sadness as she noticed the glass of amber liquid on the small occasional table next to a vase of bright-yellow daffodils.

'Ah!' The doctor saw her expression of disapproval and pulled a wry face. 'You weren't supposed to see that. What are you doing back here so early? I thought you went to visit the Cummings sisters.'

'I did and they're fine,' Meredith said, wondering whether she dared remove the glass of whisky and hide the bottle, at least until her father had eaten a hearty breakfast. 'Dora sends her love and asks when you are going to propose marriage to her: Bessie needs your advice on how best to invest her life's savings, which I suspect she keeps under her mattress, and Eloise—'

'What did that little harridan have to say?'

'She asked me if we'd had Christmas yet and was I going to bake them a cake.'

The good doctor lowered his wiry grey eyebrows and shook his head.

'They're crazy, all three of them,' he said, then he smiled genially. 'But if you can't be a little crazy when you're in your nineties, when can you? So, they're all right, are they?'

'Full of complaints as usual, and squabbling among themselves.'

Dr Jolly gave a chuckle. 'They're fine, then. It's when they stop complaining that I'll start to worry about them. But why are you back so soon, Meredith? Were you hoping to catch me out having a secret tipple? In which case, you succeeded. *Mea culpa*, I'm afraid.'

'Not at all.' Meredith dimpled and searched among the items in her capacious bag, which accompanied her everywhere. 'The postman delivered a letter to the sisters by mistake. It's addressed to you, Father, and it looks important.'

She found the stiff vellum envelope and handed it to him. Dr Jolly took it to the window and inspected it back and front, frowning over the official stamp.

'Goodness me, it's from the Royal Society,' he said and set his pipe aside. 'I wonder what they want with me?'

He continued to stare at it, puzzled, showing no real desire to open the thing. His daughter shifted from one foot to the other, impatient to know the contents. They were not accustomed to receiving mail of such importance and she did hope dearly that it might contain something that would reignite her father's old vigour.

'Well, aren't you going to open it?' she asked, her curiosity getting the better of her. 'Would you like me to open it for you?'

Meredith held out her hand, which he ignored; he slid his thumb under the seal before drawing out a single sheet of vellum paper.

'Who is it from, Father?' Meredith felt a rise of excitement beneath her ribcage as she saw her father's perplexed expression.

'Good Lord!' Josiah Jolly exclaimed and reached for his pince nez that dangled from his neck on a black ribbon. Drawing a deep breath, he skimmed again more closely the words written there as if he couldn't quite believe his eyes. 'What extraordinary handwriting! So bold, and yet ... quite disturbing in some odd way that I can't explain.'

'Oh, Father, do put me out of my misery and tell me what it's all about,' Meredith cried, her patience finally snapping.

'Here, read it for yourself,' her father said, passing her the letter; there was a discernible shake in his hand.

'Professor Fergus Macaulay!' Meredith read out aloud. 'Isn't he quite famous? Do you know him?'

'Who doesn't know him, my dear? He's one of the most illustrious naturalists of our time and has written definitive papers on many of the far-flung corners of the earth. Specializes in islands and the people who live on them. I used to attend his lectures. He was, to say the least, spellbinding. His name is revered all over the world.'

Meredith returned her attention to the letter, studying it closely for it wasn't easy to read. It had been written by an erratic hand, letters sloping this way and that, with wild loops and crossings-out, all in thick black ink that had splotched across the page as the writer had written in obvious haste.

'He ought to get himself a writing machine,' she mused. 'What does he say? I can't make it out. Something to do with an invitation...?'

She heard her father's long, indrawn breath. 'I'm invited to accompany him on a long research trip to the archipelago of St Kilda. It's one of the world's most important sites for seabirds. The Royal Society seems to think that I can be of valuable help in writing a definitive book on the islands.'

'But that's wonderful!' Meredith bent low and gave her father a hug. 'Congratulations, Father.'

He patted her cheek tenderly and reached for his glass, taking a long sip. With vaguely troubled eyes he contemplated the flames roaring up the chimney.

'It's an honour to be asked, of course,' he said eventually, 'but I shan't go. There are others, younger and fitter than I am, and with just as much expertise. I'm only a small fish in a very big pond.'

Meredith couldn't believe what she was hearing. Her father was a great naturalist. Perhaps not so well-known as this Professor Fergus Macaulay, but he had been honoured by naturalist societies the length and breadth of Britain. He had gone against his father's wishes that he should study medicine and had followed his greater passion for the natural world. And Meredith had shown the same tendencies from the time she could walk, trotting after him on unsteady legs. She had shown herself to be an excellent artist and had illustrated much of his work. Now, she was earning a modest living with pen and brush as a free-lance illustrator. Her income was small, but it gave her a modicum of independence, which she valued greatly.

'Father, you can't turn down an opportunity such as this,' she said. 'It's just what you need to get you out of yourself. You've mourned for Mother too long already.'

He smiled and she saw great sadness shadowing his eyes. 'I shall never stop mourning for your mother, Meredith. She was the love of my life.'

'She wouldn't want you to be like this. Remember how she used to encourage you, how happy she was just listening to what you had discovered? Is this how you want to remember her, sitting miserable, drowning your sorrow in whisky?'

He stared down into the now empty glass, turned it in his hands, then remorsefully let her take it from him.

'You're right, of course, Meredith. I owe my poor dear Hannah more than that. But today the first daffodils flowered and I remembered how she used to love them and fill the house with them.' His voice broke slightly. 'I picked six this morning and had to stop. It was too painful.'

'Tell this professor that you will accept his invitation. It will be the best medicine for you, I'm sure.'

Dr Jolly gave it some thought, then heaved a sigh of resignation.

'Yes, perhaps I will. He asks if I will travel to Edinburgh to meet him. Will you accompany me, Meredith? It's a long time since we enjoyed an outing together.'

'That's the spirit. I'll write your reply on my machine. Let's show the professor how efficient we are.'

The doctor smiled at his daughter's ardour, which was so like her mother's.

'Don't you think we should discuss it first with your Aunt Agnes?'

Meredith's enthusiasm crumbled into a dark frown. Her mother's sister never found favour with anything or anyone. A maiden lady in her late fifties, Agnes had lived under their roof for two decades. Meredith thought it was like living with a threatening storm cloud. It was difficult to be fond of someone who lived in constant misery and self-pity. Aunt Agnes had donned the black of mourning when her fiancé jilted her and had never come out of it. She even went so far as to wear black ribbon trimmings on her nightwear and kept the curtains of her room closed so that the sun could not penetrate with a cheery glow. She deigned to join her brother-in-law and her niece for meals and accompanied them to church on Sundays, but that was the extent of her social life. Agnes preferred solitude and prayer and her Bible was so well-read that it was falling apart.

'What is it that you should discuss with me first?'

They looked up sharply at the sound of Agnes Dawson's haughty voice. The excitement over the letter had been such that they hadn't heard the rustle of her crisp taffeta skirts. She was standing stiffly erect in the doorway, her small pinprick eyes surveying the scene and, Meredith thought, already preparing herself for the worst.

Dr Jolly jumped self-consciously to his feet, fingering his cravat and Meredith quickly hid the whisky glass behind her back. What Aunt Agnes didn't see she could not dwell upon.

'We'll discuss it over breakfast, Agnes,' Dr Jolly said, cocking an eyebrow at Meredith. 'Come along. I do believe Daisy is doing kippers and scrambled eggs – your favourite.'

'That girl should go,' Aunt Agnes commented uncharitably. 'She always burns my toast.'

'Mm.' The doctor made an unintelligible sound. 'I think it's muffins this morning.'

'Toast or muffins,' Agnes said with a disgruntled pout, 'burnt is burnt.'

As luck would have it, Daisy did not burn the muffins that morning, but tripped as she entered the breakfast room and sent one of the buns rolling across the polished parquet. Aunt Agnes, fortunately, did not see what happened and Meredith deftly caught the offending muffin under her foot. She hated to see Daisy cower terrified beneath the stern gaze of her aunt. The girl was perfectly adequate, but Agnes had a way of turning her into a nervous wreck.

'Kipper, Agnes?' Dr Jolly asked, proffering the server and placing two of the golden-coloured fish on her plate.

'Do have a muffin while they're still hot, Aunt Agnes,' Meredith said.

'I can sense something in the air,' Agnes announced and looked from one to the other of them. 'There's bad news, isn't there? Has someone died?'

'Nobody has died, Agnes.' Dr Jolly patted her hand and glanced at his daughter in such a way that she suspected he was suddenly lacking in courage. He had never been any good at dealing with his sister-in-law's emotions.

'Father's had a very important invitation from the Royal Society,' Meredith blurted out. 'They want him to be part of a research team going to ... where is it, Father?'

'St Kilda,' he said quickly, staring at the table in front of him rather than meet Agnes's sharp eyes. 'It's a remote group of islands off the Hebridean coast in the Atlantic Ocean. It looks like being a big project.'

'And a lot of kudos for Father....'

'You are not taking it up, I hope,' was Aunt Agnes's response as she picked delicately at her kippers like a practised surgeon, separating the flesh from the fine bones.

'Well, I—'

'Of course he must take it up. It will make him famous and rich and—'

Dr Jolly held up his hands and shook his head at his daughter. 'Now, now, Meredith, it says nothing like that in the letter. At best it will get my name on the publication and perhaps some acknowledge-ment in the world of natural history explorers.'

'Father!' Meredith tapped her foot impatiently. 'You are far too modest!'

'You can't possibly go, Josiah.' Agnes left the kippers and started moving lumps of scrambled egg about her plate, peering at them suspiciously. 'That is final. Now, Meredith, I've been thinking that it is high time you found yourself a husband. It was your mother's dearest wish to see you settled down. This young man you've been seeing for so long ... what's he called again?'

Meredith's face twitched and her eyes lost some of their brightness. 'Arthur,' she said. 'Arthur Graham.'

'He seems a respectable young man and, being the son of a banker, he undoubtedly has good prospects for the future. You must set a date before you lose him to another.'

Meredith felt a hot, angry flush burn her cheeks, but before she could utter a syllable her father gave a warning jerk of his hand and her mouth snapped shut.

'I think Meredith is old enough and wise enough, Agnes, to make decisions for herself,' he said.

'How old are you now, girl?'

'I'm twenty-four, Aunt Agnes.'

Agnes scowled. 'Most girls of your age are already married with babies. Don't put off any longer. You don't want to end up ...' Was she about to say *like me?*

'No, Aunt Agnes,' Meredith said. 'I'll get married when the time is right, if the occasion arises. However, I'm not sure that Arthur is the man I want to spend the rest of my life with.'

'You cannot afford to pick and choose, Meredith. Not at your age. Northumberland is not exactly the heart of English society. We live in isolation here on the edge of the moors. Where would you meet another young man suitable for a girl of your station? You must invite Arthur and his parents to afternoon tea on Sunday.'

Meredith's jaws tightened with indignation and, ignoring another warning from her father to tread carefully, she blurted out: 'I would rather live alone than marry a man I don't love, just for the sake of being married. Besides, I will be accompanying my father when he goes to St Kilda. He will need an assistant and I'm very good now on the typewriting machine.' She eyed lovingly the Remington machine that weighed down the small desk at the window where she spent many an hour tapping away in sheer delight. A wealthy cousin had sent it to her from America so she could transcribe her father's work more easily. It was such an exciting invention and saved the cramped and ink-stained fingers she suffered by gripping a pen.

She thought she heard her father groan, but it was smothered by the rustle of Aunt Agnes's stiff petticoats as she pushed herself up from the table.

'Foolish girl! You're just like your father! Headstrong and foolhardy.' Agnes stepped back and looked down her nose at her brother-in-law. 'And just how do you propose to get to this island of yours?'

'By boat. It's a long journey by all accounts. I've heard of some people taking forty hours to reach it in stormy seas.'

Agnes closed her eyes and clutched at her throat. 'Dear God, you'll both be killed and then what shall I do?' With that she marched stiffly from the room, leaving Meredith and Dr Jolly staring blankly at one another.

They listened to the tap-tap of her small feet on the floor above as she mounted the stairs and the distinct click of her door closing. Meredith glanced sheepishly at her father and bit down on her lip to stifle a laugh that was determined to be out.

'Well, that's put the cat among the pigeons,' said Dr Jolly with a dramatic roll of his eyes. 'At this moment she is probably writing out an order for a new bolt of bombazine so she can mourn us in style.'

Meredith's laugh finally escaped and she was relieved to see that her father joined in. But then the mirth ceased. He became serious and took her hand in his, gripping it tightly.

'Now, young lady, what's all this about you coming with me, eh?'

'Well, I thought it might be exhilarating. Something of an adventure.'

'An adventure, you think? The isles of St Kilda are reported to be inhospitable, surrounded by a wild and dangerous sea. The only contact they have with the mainland is through the few boats that dare to put in to Hirta, which is the main island in the archipelago. Even then, the landing is so difficult there's a risk to life and limb.'

'Are there people living on the islands?'

'Ay, lass. A few crofters, but they're not like ordinary people. They're tough and fearless and spend their lives scrambling up and down the sheer cliff faces, catching sea birds and harvesting their eggs for food.'

'Are there women, Father?'

'Of course, and children too, but—'

'Then I shall be in good company.' Meredith gave a decisive nod. 'Besides, you can't possibly leave me here alone with Aunt Agnes. Cruelty to your only child has never been your style.'

Dr Jolly suppressed a smile of amusement. 'Professor Macaulay might not allow you to go,' he said.

'That is something we shall have to find out, won't we? Now, what would you like me to say to the famous man?'

'Ach, heaven help me.' Dr Jolly shook his head and ran his fingers through his shock of curly, steel-grey hair. 'All these years when I wished for a son I never realized that my sweet little daughter would turn out to have the mind and the constitution of a man. Are you sure, then, that you don't want to stay behind and marry Arthur?'

'Positive,' she told him. 'If I marry any man at all, he will have to be more interesting than Arthur Graham.'

'I think I shall pity any man who takes you on, Meredith. He will have to be very special indeed.'

'I'll settle for nothing less,' she told him, biting lustily into a muffin and getting melted butter dribbling down her chin.

Meredith kissed her father's cheek and sauntered out of the room, muffin in hand, her steps light, her hips swaying. Her father watched her go, his heart swelling with love for this wayward girl of his, who had been such a disappointment to her mother. He, on the other hand, would never be disappointed in anything Meredith chose to do. She was strong-willed and independent, and he was convinced that she would always do the right thing in the end, even if the journey taken was a perilous one.

And she was right, of course. It was time to stop mourning his beloved wife and get back to the work he enjoyed. Being a part of Professor Macaulay's team might be the perfect answer and, if the project was successful, his name would indeed shine alongside that of a man who had been his hero for many years.

Professor Fergus Macaulay was on top form. He was always at his best when entertaining. His dinner guests would listen to his anecdotes and short, impromptu lectures with rapt attention. After all, it wasn't every day they had the opportunity to dine with someone so illustrious.

'... and blow me if the fellow didn't come up to me and offer me the shrunken head of Perkins, my assistant, who had wandered off into the bush and never come back, the oaf.'

'Oh, dear me!' exclaimed a bejewelled lady on his right as she fanned herself with her napkin. 'I never knew such things existed. I mean, how do they…? Oh, no, don't tell me, I really couldn't bear to hear how they do it.'

'My wife has a rather delicate constitution,' said an elderly gentleman with military bearing. 'She couldn't stand India, you know. Had to send her back to Blighty, what?'

'I hear you're about to go off on your travels again, Professor Macaulay,' said a young man with long eyelashes and the complexion of a young girl. 'Where's it to be this time?'

'What's your name, boy?'

The young man blinked and his Adam's apple wobbled up and down as he swallowed. 'Davidson, sir. John Davidson. I'm—'

'Ah, yes, I remember now. You're one of my final-year students, aren't you?' The professor studied the young man through half-closed eyes. 'What was your question again?'

'I … I …' the student stuttered nervously.

'He asked you where you were going on your next trip, dear,' said Mrs Macaulay, who was looking charming and doing her usual best to be a good hostess, though she hated these dinner parties where she knew no one and felt largely invisible in the enormous presence of her husband.

Professor Macaulay refilled his glass with claret from a decanter and gave a sign to his butler to fill up the other glasses around the table.

'It's a place not many people have heard of,' he said slowly, liking to stir up the curiosity of his listeners before divulging the information they sought.

'Somewhere exotic, no doubt,' said another young man who had spent the last half-hour trying to have a conversation with the professor's daughter, without success.

'Alas no, Lewis,' Macaulay turned a jaundiced eye on the second student. 'Not this time. But interesting, very interesting. I've been there before, five years ago, and I swore I would never go back, but the Royal Society has persuaded me that it's necessary. They were going to ask some nondescript biologist, but I wouldn't have it. I had done the original work, so I demanded that it should be me leading the second expedition. However, they insisted on my inviting this fellow Jolly to come along. He's published some papers that impressed them and backs them up with fancy illustrations. And now, I believe, he's taken to photography, would you believe? His reply to me was written on one of those infernal typewriting machines.'

'Quite a modern chap, then, Professor,' Peter Lewis said. 'Forward thinking.'

'Hmm.' The professor scowled. 'You can say what you like, but I don't trust all this new technology.'

'So where is it you are actually going, sir?' Peter Lewis leaned forward eagerly.

'I'm going back to St Kilda.'

Mrs Macaulay gave a gasp; her wine glass fell from her hand and broke, spilling its contents over the starched white-damask cloth. She dropped her gaze and fixed it on the spreading stain as if it were blood.

A silly young woman at the other end of the table gave a hoot of nasal laughter.

'Goodness, can it be that bad? Poor Mrs Macaulay's gone as white as a sheet. Whatever happened the last time you were there, Professor?'

Someone hushed her, but it was too late. All attention was riveted on Ann Macaulay's ashen face and the professor's solemn expression.

'It was where our son died,' the professor said flatly and an uncomfortable silence fell around the table like an icy shroud. 'We left the island in stormy weather. He was washed overboard.'

'How sad,' muttered the silly girl, who began to nibble at a fingernail, obviously wishing she had never voiced the question.

'Please ... excuse me!' Marion Macaulay rose, stumbling against her chair which scraped noisily over the floor, and virtually ran from the room.

Mrs Macaulay started to rise, obviously thinking to go after her daughter, but a sharp look from her husband made her change her mind.

'It's all right,' she said in a small voice. 'It's just that ... Marion was very close to her brother. It always upsets her when ... well, you understand.'

There were nods all round and someone tried to change the subject, but the professor was still in the chair and not about to end the discussion there. Within seconds, he had their attention again as he plunged into a detailed account of his stay on St Kilda. He painted a bleak picture of the place: so much so that the women in the party shuddered in horror and the men agreed it was perhaps only fit for hermits and sub-human species.

'So, Johnny and Peter,' Professor Macaulay said at the end of his lecture. 'Can I count on you two boys to come with me, eh?'

The two boys in question looked taken aback, then their faces broke into eager smiles as they uttered their thanks and gratitude. It was an honour, they considered, to be asked to take part in the great naturalist's research programme. It would mean taking time off from their studies, but the experience gained on the trip would be priceless. An impressive addition to any curriculum vitae and a guarantee of a place in any scientific institution to which they applied.

'That's settled, then,' the professor said, getting to his feet and giving a formal bow. 'I bid you all goodnight.'

The dinner guests looked a little startled, but it was not unknown for the professor to curtail things in the middle of a meal if he chose to do so. He was famous for many things, but not for politeness. There were a few murmured responses aimed at his back, then, one by one, they went in search of their waiting carriages with mixed feelings, the uppermost of which was disappointment.

The dinner party already gone from his mind, Fergus Macaulay went looking for his gillie to instruct the man to prepare for the forthcoming expedition.

Gregory Frazier had worked for the professor as gillie on the Macaulay estate ever since he'd killed a man in a bare knuckle fight when he was eighteen. He was an unlikely-looking character with a misshapen, scarred face. He was big and ungainly with a low intellect and people often wondered why the professor should employ a man who was better fitted to a life of crime in the backstreets of

Edinburgh. But Frazier was worth his weight in gold. The professor had saved him from the gallows, in return for which, the fellow would do anything asked of him. No task was too great, or too dirty. To refuse would risk being turned over to the authorities. Not even Frazier was stupid enough to tempt fate. He knew on which side his bread was buttered and knew also that he needed to tread warily.

'Frazier!' Professor Macaulay rapped his knuckles sharply on the gillie's cottage door. It opened immediately and Frazier stood there, bleary-eyed and smelling of liquor. 'I want you to prepare for a long stay abroad.'

'Aye, all right,' the gillie said, rubbing at his eyes and smothering a yawn. 'Where's it to be this time?'

'St Kilda.'

The gillie stared at him, open-mouthed. 'Ye canna mean it?'

'I mean it, all right, Frazier. And this time we'll be on the islands for a whole year.'

'But …' The gillie didn't finish his sentence. He looked dumbfounded. He also looked scared.

'No questions, man! It'll be all right. The people on the islands are close-mouthed. It's been five years. I doubt they'll even remember, and if they do, who'd believe their stories? They're just natives, for want of a better word, with not an ounce of intelligence between them.'

'When do we leave, sir?'

'Just as soon as I've assembled my team. Perhaps in a week or two. We'll need to charter a boat, one of the steamships perhaps. Something big enough to carry us and any equipment we might have. I've already sent word ahead that we will be coming and that accommodation is to be made ready for us. Thank God they have proper cottages now and don't still live in cleats. I have no fancy to spend a twelve-month living in a hole in the ground.'

Giving a short, sharp nod the professor walked slowly back to the house, which was now empty of guests and silent. Rivers, the butler, appeared with a lighted candle to see him upstairs, then quietly disappeared to his own premises at the back of the house.

The professor opened the door to his bedchamber. He held the candle up high so that it illuminated the great four-poster bed and its occupant. Anne Macaulay, in lace-edged bed-cap, lay facing away from him. He knew she was still awake by the way she quickly tugged the bedclothes up to her chin and curled into a foetal position.

'Why do you always do that, woman?' he addressed her sternly. 'You should know by now that I won't touch you.' Silence met him; the woman was holding her breath, probably biting down on a corner of the sheet. 'I get my pleasures elsewhere, as well you know.'

Without a further word he closed the door and moved down the broad landing, trying the door to another room. As he half-expected, it was locked. It was a long time since Marion had started locking herself in, and him out: ever since her sister had been put in an asylum for the mentally insane, an illegitimate child in her belly. As a father, he had not been blessed with children of great fortitude. The daughters were weak, like their mother. The son, too, had turned against him and was now, thankfully, gone for ever.

The streets of Edinburgh glistened as if oiled by the fine misty rain that fell on the cobbles. Professor Fergus Macaulay rode his horse through the back alleys where no lights shone. He needed no light, for he and his mount knew their way blindfolded. He stopped outside a shabby building that showed chinks of yellow gaslight through crumbling shutters. There was a muffled sound of raucous laughter and conversation from within.

He dismounted, tethered his horse and pulled the hood of his cape well down over his face before entering by a side door. In an alcove, a painted, bejewelled woman of uncertain age bent over some tatting, muttering to herself with every stitch. She looked up sharply as he approached.

'Ah, 'tis you, sir!' she said, leaning forward to reveal her low décolletage.

'You have something for me tonight, Bella?' the professor asked. 'Something extra good, I hope. I have a great hunger on me.'

'I think you'll be well pleased.' The painted woman, advanced in age and strung about with gaudy jewellery, passed him a large iron key. 'A new acquisition, pure and untried. Top of the stairs, third room on the left.'

He gripped the key in his sweating palm and pressed a sovereign into the woman's outstretched hand. She bit the edge of the coin; then, with a nod of satisfaction, slipped it into her tight bodice.

Macaulay mounted the stairs three at a time, found the room and entered. The young boy on the bed did not move. He simply stared at his first client with scared, saucer-like eyes, his long lashes making shadows on his high cheekbones.

'Indeed, the old madam was right,' the professor said, going over to the boy and tilting his face up so that he could see him more clearly in the glow of the oil lamp by the bed. 'I can see I shall not be disappointed.'

CHAPTER 2

MEREDITH'S FOOT KEPT tapping, much to the irritation of her father, but she was becoming restless. They had been waiting for the best part of an hour in the small reception room of Bracken Tor Hall, the home of the Macaulay family. An imposing grandfather clock ticked away the seconds and Meredith's eyes followed the mesmerizing swing of the pendulum. Twice, sleep had almost claimed her, with her chin sinking to her chest, then her head jerking upright as she emitted the tiniest of snorts.

They were both tired after the journey, first by train to Edinburgh, then by carriage from the station to the Macaulay estate. The train ride had been uneventful, but they had stopped frequently and the air was full of steam and oily soot.

'How can you sit there so calmly, Father?' Meredith asked, jumping up and pacing the floor in front of him, believing it to be the only way she could stay awake.

'Because I'm older, wiser and more tired than you, my dear,' Dr Jolly said with a weary sigh. 'Now do sit down and stop agitating.'

Meredith sat once more and stared grimly at her fingers interlaced in her lap. They were blotched with grime and her clothes were the same. It would take more than one washing to get it off.

'I was looking forward to seeing the Hall,' she said, wishing she could hypnotize the clock into silence, but it ignored the spell she tried to cast upon it. 'But from what I've seen so far it's quite dreary.'

'Mausoleum is the word, I think,' her father said with a twinkle in his blue eyes.

'It certainly doesn't look or feel lived in.'

Meredith thought of their own cosy home which was warmly decorated and where there were always signs of life, such as books and sketchpads and writing implements. When her mother had been alive there had always been evidence of her in every room. Unfinished knitting, tapestry, recipe books left open, the appetizing smell of baking wafting from the kitchen. Here, all was bare and smelled of stale polish and must, like a museum.

A sudden rattle of crockery made them draw up to attention. Footsteps pattered across the hall and the door opened to reveal a rather plain-faced but elegant lady, expensively clad, followed by a maid carrying a tea tray.

'I'm so sorry you've been kept waiting,' the lady said. 'My husband was delayed, but he will join us in a moment. I am Mrs Macaulay.'

'Dr Josiah Jolly,' the doctor said, rising and bowing over her outstretched hand. 'And this is my daughter, Meredith.'

'Charming,' the woman said with the smallest of smiles.

When Meredith took the woman's hand she couldn't help thinking that it was like shaking hands with something dead and limp. And although it was an uncharitable thought, the handshake went perfectly with Mrs Macaulay's whole demeanour.

A large figure now appeared in the doorway, almost filling the space. Meredith saw a swarthy man with black, penetrating eyes in a face that had once been handsome but was now truly weathered and ravaged by time and a life out of doors. It only took one glance to instil in Meredith a feeling of foreboding. If this was the great Professor Fergus Macaulay, she thought with a suppressed shudder, she had no wish to get to know him better.

'Jolly?' The two men clasped hands briefly. 'Come into the study and we'll talk business while the ladies take tea.'

Meredith caught her father's eye but was too polite to object at being left out of the discussion. No doubt the great professor saw her as a simple-minded female, interested only in domestic matters. Her father was forever telling her that she was ahead of her time, reminding her that it was not yet the twentieth century, when young women might expect some social change. She, however, was not prepared to wait the few years remaining of the eighteen-nineties.

'My daughter, Professor Macaulay, is also my assistant. You may have seen her illustrations. They are really very good, I'm sure you will agree.'

The professor's eyes drifted slowly over Meredith and she suppressed another shudder when he gave a broad, serpentine smile.

'Really? Well, I'm afraid there is no place for any female on this expedition. They're sickly creatures. We need strong young men to do the donkey work.'

'I'm as strong as an ox,' Meredith blurted out and heard a shocked gasp from Mrs Macaulay, who was trying to offer her a cucumber sandwich.

'And as stubborn as a mule, no doubt,' Professor Macaulay said, then ignored her as he drew the doctor out of the room, an arm firmly about the smaller man's shoulders.

'Come, my dear,' said Mrs Macaulay. 'Tell me all about yourself.'

There seemed to be no choice other than to do what was expected of her, but Meredith was not happy. She was not happy at all.

During the next two hours Meredith learned little more about the Macaulays. Ann Macaulay was not exactly a chatterbox and was obviously uncomfortable when faced with questions about her husband and his work. She seemed distracted and there were long silences when she became nervous and fidgety, glancing numerous times at the door as if willing the business discussion in the study to come to an end.

When the door did eventually open it was to admit a tall, dark-haired woman somewhat older than Meredith. The long, oval face bore an expression of melancholy and the eyes were sad and ringed as if she spent a lot of time weeping.

'I'm sorry, Mother,' she said, hovering in the doorway, her hand still on the doorknob. 'I didn't know you had company.'

'Come in, my dear, and meet Miss Jolly.' Mrs Macaulay's smile warmed slightly. 'This is my daughter, Marion, Miss Jolly.'

But Marion Macaulay, perhaps taking after her mother, was obviously not a sociable creature. She simply inclined her head and fixed her attention on Mrs Macaulay.

'Has there been any news?'

Ann Macaulay seemed disturbed at the question. She shook her head and touched her mouth with trembling fingers. 'I'm sure everything is just fine, dear.'

Marion's bosom rose and fell, then she backed out of the room and Meredith again found the plate of cucumber sandwiches under her nose.

'Do eat something, Miss Jolly,' Mrs Macaulay said. 'I'm sure no food has passed your lips since leaving home this morning.'

'It's very kind of you, Mrs Macaulay,' Meredith assured her hostess, 'but we did bring a picnic basket with us on the train.' She then pressed on, her curiosity getting the better of her. 'Have we perhaps arrived at a difficult time for you?'

'A difficult time? Why do you say that?'

'Your daughter seems distraught and eager for news of something … or someone.'

The professor's wife licked her lips and swallowed with difficulty. Her eyes were as troubled as her daughter's had been. 'Yes, well, Miss Jolly … it's my other daughter, you see. She has been quite unwell and …'

'I'm sorry to hear that. Is she in hospital?'

'Hospital? Well, yes, of a kind.' Mrs Macaulay looked flustered, then burst out: 'She is in an institution for … for people who are sick in their minds. We don't talk about it, so … so please don't mention it to my husband. Fergus never speaks of his children. It's far too hurtful for him.'

'You have only the two daughters?'

'Now, yes. We had a son, but he went with his father to St Kilda five years ago and … and perished on the homeward journey.'

'How sad for you.'

'It's worse for Fergus. I think he blames himself for Stuart's death. He drowned, you see, and my husband could do nothing to save him. Do have another sandwich, they'll only waste.'

The sandwiches left on the platter were dry and curling up their corners. Meredith declined graciously and was glad to hear a rumble of voices outside, heralding the return of her father with the professor. It had been the longest afternoon.

*

They had made the railway station with seconds to spare, tumbling into the last carriage as the whistle blew, the steam hissed and the wheels turned.

'Now will you tell me what you and the professor talked about?' Meredith insisted as they fell breathlessly into their seats.

'Let me get my breath back, girl,' Josiah Jolly said, chuckling at his daughter's eagerness to know all that had taken place.

He had refused to talk as they travelled to the station in the professor's brougham, for anything said and overheard by the footman or driver would undoubtedly be repeated and he wasn't sure he wanted his private thoughts transmitted back to the Macaulay household.

'What did you think of Professor Macaulay?' Meredith asked with a frown. 'I found him somewhat daunting. Those eyes of his! They seemed to penetrate right through me.'

'He's certainly an austere-looking chap and has changed considerably since I used to attend his lectures. Of course, we were both much younger then. It was rumoured that he had to fight off the ladies, they found him so attractive.'

Meredith gave a shudder and stared out at the dark landscape sliding by.

'He has the touch of the Devil in him, I'm thinking,' she said, conjuring up in her mind's eye the face of the professor and feeling an icy finger tracing a pattern up and down her spine.

'That's a little fanciful, Meredith,' her father said, patting her hand. 'He's a very important man, very serious about what he does. He won't suffer fools gladly, so I'm flattered that he wants me on this trip.'

'But you don't like him, do you, Father? You can't possibly like him.'

'That's not a prerequisite. I don't have to like the man to respect him and what he stands for.'

'That's true,' she conceded with a sigh. 'So, you're going then?'

'Yes. We set off during the first week in June. That gives us plenty of time to assemble the necessary provisions and equipment. We'll have to be thorough. A whole year on the islands is a long time and sometimes the boats can't land for months at a stretch.'

Meredith's mouth had opened wide. 'A whole year!'

'It's a daunting prospect. Do you think you're up for it, Meredith?'

She blinked furiously at him through the yellow gaslight glow of the railway carriage's lamps.

'I assumed he would refuse to take me,' she said eventually, her eyes big and round with the astonishment of it all.

'It took me two hours to persuade him,' Dr Jolly said. 'Of course, I will quite understand if you choose to stay at home with your Aunt Agnes and Daisy. In fact, Meredith, I would prefer it if you didn't go.'

'Why's that, Father? Do you think I won't be up to the journey?'

'No, girl. I know how hardy you are, and courageous, but …'

'But?'

'It's Macaulay.' The doctor pulled reflectively at his beard and reached for his pipe, though he sucked at it without lighting up. 'There's something about him that bothers me. Do you know, I have half a mind to turn him down after all.'

'I thought he was your mentor,' Meredith said, quite surprised to hear her father talk in this way about a man he had admired for so long.

'That's so, but …' He stared into the bowl of his cold pipe. 'Och, it's probably because I'm old and tired. Nothing seems the same any more since your poor mother died.'

'The expedition will give you renewed stimulus,' Meredith told him.

'Ay, you're right there, daughter. And …' The twinkle had returned to his eyes. 'A year away from your Aunt Agnes is not to be sniffed at, eh?'

Meredith gave a chuckle and affectionately linked arms with him. Her father might be almost sixty, but he would never seem old to her as long as he retained that youthful outlook on life for which he was well known. They had been companions for as long as she could remember. He was not just her father, he was also her best friend.

'So, we're going to St Kilda?' she said and he nodded.

'Aye, lass, if you're sure.'

'I can't wait.'

Meredith fell silent, breathing deeply, her brain churning one way, while her stomach churned the other. It was a little intimidating to spend twelve months on an isolated group of islands that were as wild and as untamed as the seas that raged around them. It was only when her thoughts turned to the professor, with his frightening regard, that she felt a vague shadow of doubt creeping over her. However, once they were on the train and chugging back to Northumberland, all doubts were pushed firmly away. She was facing the adventure of a lifetime. Nothing was going to stop her now.

On the main St Kildan island of Hirta the people's parliament was in session. It was a daily affair, with the exception of the Sabbath. The Parliament consisted of every man of the village, so, there being only one village in the whole of the archipelago, it seemed that life stood still while important decisions were taken. Some forty men and boys sat in a rough circle discussing the business of the day to come, from the cutting of peat for fuel to the baptism or, as was too often the case, the burial, of the latest newborn babe.

They had chosen the factor's house, which doubled as the school because a boat had come into the bay yesterday from Harris, bringing supplies and, most important of all, a batch of letters. Since most of the villagers were unable to read, Mr McEwan, a divinity student there on a year's sabbatical for the purpose of teaching the children, would have the honour of reading their contents out loud. In this way everybody knew everybody else's business. There was no room for secrets and indiscretions. All news, good or bad, was for public consumption.

But it was to Lachlan MacGregor, the village elder, that everybody looked for guidance. Old and nearly blind, he was still a commanding figure, revered among the islanders as a man honest and true. He was mild-mannered, but cross him and it would unleash a fury as mighty as the savage sea that battered the coastline. Leaving out the pastor, who more often than not appeared in their eyes as the Devil's advocate, Lachlan was the man whom they thought to be as near to God as any man on the island.

This morning, there being letters, every member of the parliament was bright-eyed and fidgety, anxious to receive news from the mainland and some from relatives who had emigrated to Australia. But they knew better than to show impatience. Lachlan would not be pushed. *All in good time*, would be his words if they tried to get ahead of him.

'Well now,' Lachlan said, having assured himself that all were present who needed to be. 'What have we today? Who will speak first?'

There was a clearing of throats and a shifting of eyes until everyone's gaze rested unwaveringly on Callum MacDonald. He gave a slight nod, wiped his hands down his shirt front and gave his report.

'The cattle are outfield now,' he said, speaking in the Gaelic that they used amongst themselves, though they all could speak English if they had to. 'There's still land to prepare and turf cutting to be done. Archie and Donald MacKinnon have been over on Boreray and will likely come back today with the gannets they have caught.'

'Ay, Mr MacGregor,' piped up a boy of not more than sixteen, who wore a Guernsey in tatters and no shoes on his feet, despite the weather being nippy. 'They've signalled already.'

'You've seen the black square, Neil?'

'Aye, Mr MacGregor, I have an' all.'

'Then prepare the boat and go over for them,' the elder instructed. 'Take Malcolm Gillies with you. The swell isn't so great today, the Lord be praised, so the two of you should manage fine.'

'What progress have the women made?' Callum MacDonald asked the gathering.

'The weaving is finished,' reported a man with a beard as white and as long as Lachlan's own proud facial adornment. 'The women are now pulling the cloth.'

'Good, good.' Lachlan nodded, his head bowing so low that his great hooked nose almost met the rough earth on which he sat.

'I have bad news.'

Heads turned towards the speaker, who was a man in his twenties. The fellow stood, rather than sat. His shoulders were slumped and he twisted his cloth cap in his hands as he spoke.

'Go on, Kenny. Tell us your bad news.'

'My wife gave birth just a week ago,' Kenny told them, then stopped to think of his next words. 'The babe died in this night. The nurse said it was lockjaw.'

There were murmurs of commiseration, then they passed on to other business. Deaths on the islands, especially neonatal ones, were not uncommon. Without proper medical aid, illness and death was at best avoided, at worst dealt with or ignored.

'If there is no more business we will ask Mr McEwan to read out the letters.'

Normally the meetings of the parliament went on for a good two hours or more as the men chewed over each detail and decided how best to tackle the work at hand. However, on a day when there were letters to be read, the meeting was cut short. The arrival of mail on the island was a rare and important occurrence and even those families who never received a word from abroad drew pleasure in hearing news of the world outside the islands.

There being no further pressing business, Mr McEwan placed a chair in their midst and began to read the letters in his possession. They were for the most part short, personal notes, yet the listeners latched on to every word as if it had been inscribed in gold. Mrs Harris's sister in Australia had given birth to twins; Hamish Cameron's brother had been in hospital with a burst appendix, but was now on the mend; Charlie Ferguson's cousin had died and left him a pocket watch and five guineas in silver.

'What am I to do with such a fortune?' Charlie wanted to know, spreading wide his calloused hands. 'There's nothing to spend it on here on Hirta.'

'Bury it,' came the response. 'You never know, it might turn to gold and you can buy the island.'

There was a burst of laughter till Lachlan held up his hands and begged for silence so that Mr McEwan could continue with his reading.

The mood continued to be light and gay, with excitement rising at each and every letter that was opened. Then came the very last, which was addressed to Lachlan MacGregor himself and looked highly official.

'What is that you've got there, Mr McEwan?' Lachlan asked curiously, squinting short-sightedly at the stiff envelope in the schoolteacher's hand.

Mr McEwan's great black bush of a moustache twitched as he turned the envelope over and read the printing on the back.

'It appears, Mr MacGregor, to have come by way of the factor, from an association that calls itself "The Royal Society" in the capital.'

'Edinburgh?'

'London, Mr MacGregor, and it has an impressive seal.'

On hearing his words the group fell silent. All attention was riveted on the letter. Above them there was a scream as a great herring gull swooped, turned, then planed away over the bay and on, out to sea, disappearing over the hazy horizon. Lachlan's short-sighted eyes followed the bird's flight, then he turned back to Mr McEwan.

'Would you be so good as to read it to me, Mr McEwan?' he said, and his voice sounded suddenly weak in his throat.

'It is a long letter,' Mr McEwan said, drawing out at least three sheets of paper covered in a heavy, erratic hand.

'What is it about?'

'The signature is a certain Professor Fergus Macaulay....'

There were one or two sharp intakes of breath as Mr McEwan gave the name of the writer of the letter. Lachlan's old parchment face creased with displeasure and he raised one hand, flapping gnarled, arthritic fingers in the air.

'Read it to yourself, man, and give me the sense of it,' he said in a low growl. 'I will read it properly for myself later with my eyeglasses.'

Mr McEwan's eyes skimmed the pages while everyone waited in silent anticipation. The atmosphere settled heavily among the men as if a black storm cloud had descended.

'Well,' Mr McEwan said as he came to the last sheet. 'It seems that there is to be a visitation in the month of June, weather permitting. An expedition by a group of naturalists who are charged by the Royal Society to look at all aspects of life on St Kilda, including flora and fauna ... and other inhabitants. You are requested to provide accommodation for the group and to co-operate fully with them. Some seven people in all.'

An expression of disgust exploded from Lachlan as he reached out and grabbed the letter from the schoolteacher's hand. He stared blankly at it and shook his head.

'What are they, these "naturalists"?' The question came from young Neil Stewart. Although he posed the question it seemed, by his dreadful expression, that he already suspected the answer to be displeasing.

'They are scientists, Neil,' Lachlan said. 'If you do not remember their first visit five years ago, then 'tis a blessing. Mr McEwan, do they say they are bringing anything with them other than themselves?'

'Yes, Mr MacGregor. There is a long list of supplies that will be very important to the village. Food and medicine and all manner of things.'

'Then we cannot afford to refuse them. Our lives depend on what the boats bring us and they come little enough.' He got up from his squatting position and straightened his stiff legs, rubbing them more vigorously than was necessary, for he was burning with anger. 'I declare the parliament ended for this day.'

The men also stood, exchanged curious glances, then drifted away to start the day's toil, every man knowing exactly what he was to do. Only Callum MacDonald remained, a deep frown darkening his features.

'Mr MacGregor, sir,' he said and the old man glanced sharply towards him. 'Someone will have to tell Logan.'

Lachlan nodded gravely. 'Aye. Don't you think I have already thought of that? He will have to know. Where is he?'

'Last seen heading towards Mullach Sgar. I don't know why.'

'Is there any one among us who knows what drives that man?'

''Tis doubtful, Mr McGregor, but best not to question his ways,' Callum MacDonald said and everyone nodded in agreement.

'True,' Lachlan said and stroked his beard thoughtfully, his gaze reaching to the far horizon. 'He is a man driven by the demons inside him, but he does much good for these islands all the same.'

'Will I send a boy out to tell him, then?'

Lachlan shook his head. 'No. He will take the news better from me. Have him come to see me.'

'Aye, that's better for sure.'

Lachlan turned to face the sea, looking across Village Bay, though his poor eyes could see only a steely blue blur of sea merging with sky on the distant horizon. Beyond lay Harris and then further on again, the mainland where the boats came from. It was not in Lachlan's nature to wish ill on anyone, but a part of him was praying for bad weather to visit in June so that Professor Macaulay and his team could not land on Hirta. He wished it with all his might, for if that man set foot on the island one more time, God help them all.

In Northumberland the atmosphere was just as oppressive, with Aunt Agnes turned to stone at one end of the dinner table and Arthur Graham, just as dour-faced, at the other. Meredith and her father had argued all the way back from Edinburgh over which one of them was to deliver the news to Agnes. In the end, it fell to Dr Jolly, and he managed to slip it into the conversation between the roast chicken and the trifle.

The sweetness of the dessert turned a little sour in Meredith's mouth when she saw how distraught Arthur was over the news. Her telling him that she was going away was bad enough, but when he heard it was to be for a whole year, and probably with no communication, she thought he was going to break down in tears. His plump jowls went very pink and wobbled as he looked from one to the other of them. There was shock and disbelief in his eyes as he clasped Meredith's hand in his thick, soft fingers.

'But Meredith, my dear,' he said, between gulps, 'I was just about to ask your father for your hand in marriage! You know how we've talked on a number of occasions about getting engaged.'

'No, Arthur,' she said as gently as she could. 'I think all that talk was on your side. I don't ever remember making you any promises. I'm very fond of you, of course, but—'

'A whole year, Meredith! It's a lifetime.'

'I don't expect you to wait for me, Arthur.'

'I see. So, the last three years have all been for nothing, have they?' He got to his feet and dabbed briskly at his mouth with his napkin. 'This is not the kind of behaviour I expected from the woman I chose to be my wife, Meredith. How can you even contemplate such an outlandish expedition?'

Meredith could see that he was in no mood to be reasoned with. She had no intention of entering into a vociferous argument with him, for she was likely to say things she would later regret. If truth be known, she had cooled considerably towards Arthur over the last few months, when he had started to display the same boring tendencies as his father. He obviously wanted a prim little wife who would serve him uncomplainingly and desire nothing more than to raise his children and bolster his self-esteem.

'I have nothing more to say, Arthur,' she said. 'I'm sorry, but this is something I must do. Before I settle down to marriage with *any* man, I must feel that I have accomplished something important in my life.'

'It's high time, Meredith, dare I say it, that this raging spirit you have inside you is quenched once and for all. Women are not expected to ...' At this point he threw up his hands, unable to go on.

Dr Jolly got up and went to the sideboard where there were wine decanters set out. He picked up the brandy and fixed Arthur with an inviting eye.

'Will you take a noggin with me before you go, Arthur?' he asked genially. 'I would hate us to part on bad terms.'

'Thank you, Dr Jolly, but no. I must now go and break the news to my parents that wedding plans are not, after all, to be made. They will be highly disappointed.'

'Better to be disappointed now than after the wedding, I'm thinking,' Dr Jolly said with the smallest of secret smiles at his daughter. 'Perhaps you should see Arthur out, my dear.'

When Meredith followed Arthur to the door Josiah Jolly sat down by his sister-in-law and rested his hand on hers, but she pulled away from him.

'Come, Agnes, stop all this nonsense,' he said gently. 'You know fine well that Meredith and I will always follow our hearts. Besides, I do believe it will do us all the world of good to be separated for a while.'

'Twelve months is not a *while*. It's an interminably long time. A lot can happen. I could fall ill and die and you wouldn't know about it.'

'And men might grow wings and fly to the moon! Och, Agnes,

where's *your* raging spirit, woman? I seem to remember that you were full of vitality when you were a young girl, just like Meredith is today. Did you bury it all when that silly fool of a fiancé of yours left you standing at the altar?'

He saw tears well up in Agnes's eyes, but still she did not move, other than to dab the end of her nose delicately with a black-edged handkerchief.

'If you go to St Kilda I will never see you again,' she said. 'Neither you nor Meredith. I know it's true. I feel it in my bones. There's danger lurking, you mark my words.'

When she quietly left the room, she looked suddenly old and through his irritation the doctor's soft heart went out to her. He didn't think she would ever realize that she was responsible for her own life and could change it if she wanted to. But no, it was too much to expect of Agnes. No doubt, as soon as they left, if not before, she would be ordering more black veils and bombazine from Madame Deville, the French couturière in Newcastle, convinced that they were all doomed.

For a fleeting second something deep inside his gut stirred uncomfortably. He pushed it aside, refusing to acknowledge that tiny glimmer of doubt. Being of a philosophical nature he firmly believed that whatever would be, would be. If there were dangers to be faced, he would not be facing them alone. Professor Macaulay had visited places more dangerous than St Kilda and would know how to deal with any untoward situation.

And there again was that gnawing deep down as he thought of his famous mentor, but he couldn't for the life of him decide why the man should now so suddenly instil in him this inexplicable doubt.

CHAPTER 3

THE WEEKS UP to the departure date dragged interminably. Meredith, in particular, thought she might burst with excitement if it did not come round soon. And then, suddenly, there were only a few days to go and not sufficient hours in the day to do all that was necessary.

Between the making out of copious lists and shopping for essentials in Hexham, she frantically packed and unpacked and repacked a trunk and various valises for herself and her father. And then, when all was ready to be transported, she went the rounds, paying farewell visits to friends and relations, all of whom were driven to tears as they kissed and hugged her and told her to look after her father for them.

The three Cummings sisters were the most emotional of all, stating that they weren't at all sure that they would still be on this earth by the time she returned. They gave her scented sachets of lavender to place among her underwear to keep it sweet-smelling and to remind her of them.

'I will write when I can,' she told them, 'but I fear there isn't a post office on the island, so letters must wait for a passing boat.'

It was all too much for the sisters to take in. They threw up their hands, covered their mouths and mopped up their tears and told her to make sure she ate well and not to drink the water in case it was poisoned. She did not dare tell them that there was no water on the island, except catchments of rainwater, and that the staple diet of the inhabitants was porridge and gannet, with eggs being a rare luxury.

At last the day dawned when Meredith and Dr Jolly set out on their adventure. By the time they reached Edinburgh it was a warm midsummer afternoon and Princes Street was bustling with people displaying themselves in their finery. Josiah and Meredith stood in awe, gazing at the sight of the imposing castle high on its volcanic rock, and again at the Waverley Hotel, where they were to put up for the night.

'It appears that Professor Macaulay has a generous budget,' Dr Jolly said, nodding to the liveried doorman as they walked through the vestibule. They approached the high desk in reception with its green electric light that gave a ghostly pallor to the face of the porter behind it. 'I'm glad we are not paying for all this.'

Before they could enquire about their rooms the booming voice of Professor Macaulay himself reached their ears. Already dressed for dinner and with his moustache waxed and cheeks powdered, he bore down on them, followed closely by three other gentlemen, one of whom looked somewhat out of place, for he was rough in his features as well as his dress.

'My dear Jolly!' the professor exclaimed, his face rosy with bonhomie, his eyes sparkling with hospitality. All, Meredith suspected, acquired from a bottle. 'Such a relief to see you here.'

He clasped the doctor's hand and shook it vigorously.

'How long will it take to reach the islands?' Meredith asked eagerly.

The professor seemed to notice her for the first time. His smile became cynical and he gave his answer to the doctor instead of responding to her.

'We'll make our way to Glasgow tomorrow, and then sail to Tarbert on the island of Harris. We can charter a fishing boat from there that will take us over to St Kilda. I estimate that we'll be setting foot on Hirta, weather permitting, in approximately seventy-two hours.'

Meredith now became aware of the two young men, who were peering at her with interest, from behind the bulk of the professor. She smiled back at them, hoping they were stronger than they looked. They were both too young to have experienced much of life. The fair one might well have been a girl with his pink cheeks and angelic expression. The darker and older of the two was more serious, with myopic eyes behind small eyeglasses, and a studious look. He dressed more drably than the other and was the very epitome of a young scientist.

'Hello,' she said, stepping around the professor, who was now deep in conversation with her father. 'I'm Meredith Jolly. I'm here as my father's assistant.'

'Goodness, Miss Jolly,' said the studious one. 'We didn't expect to have a woman … ah … I mean a lady on the team. Have you travelled widely?'

'I've been the length and breadth of Britain,' she told them proudly.

'How marvellous!' The fair-haired boy gave her an admiring glance. 'I'm Johnny, by the way, and this is Peter. We're Professor Macaulay's students … actually, we both hope to be fully fledged biologists after this trip, eh, Peter?'

Peter nodded shyly, but the conversation was cut short by Professor Macaulay inviting them all to dine with him in the grand dining hall of the hotel in an hour's time.

'Make the most of it,' he said, clamping his great plate of a hand on the doctor's shoulder. 'Once we're on St Kilda even normal everyday food will be scarce. I hope your daughter is not the fragile type of female, Jolly.'

Meredith felt her hackles rise, but her father was quick to respond.

'I think you'll find that Meredith has an excellent constitution,' he assured the professor, who gave a serpentine smile that, together with his hooded eyes, made him appear somewhat Satanic.

The last member of the team, whose name was Frazier, was taking charge of their luggage. He had little to say for himself and spoke only when spoken to. Meredith saw the professor slip him a handful of coins and warn him not to spend too much on alcohol.

'Your gillie won't be dining with us, then?' Dr Jolly said, watching the man's broad back disappear out into the street.

'I don't dine with the hired help,' Professor Macaulay said acidly. 'Don't worry about Frazier. He knows his place and can take care of himself.'

*

'I don't care for him, Father,' Meredith said later of the professor. 'He's a pompous ogre.'

'Now, now, Meredith.' Dr Jolly reprimanded her softly. 'You hardly know the man. It's not like you to make judgement so quickly.'

With a small, impatient sound, Meredith went to look out on the city with its lights and its busily moving traffic so late into the night.

'I don't like the way he ignores me, as if I'm not there,' she complained.

'I'm sure he means nothing by it,' her father said, trying to soothe her ruffled feathers. 'It's just his way. He's more used to dealing with men.'

'And when he does look at me, I don't like that either,' Meredith stated, hugging herself because a sudden chill had descended on her, making her shiver.

She heard her father's soft chuckle. She turned to face him, then realized how ridiculous she must sound. Her fierce expression relaxed and soon they were laughing together, the professor temporarily forgotten as they talked of more pleasant things.

'I'm for my bed,' the doctor said a few minutes later, stifling a yawn. 'Don't stay up too late, Meredith. We have an early start tomorrow, and for the next few days.'

'Yes, all right. Goodnight, Father.'

'Goodnight, my dear, and ...' He pointed a finger in her direction. '... I'm depending on you being civil to our illustrious leader. A year is a long time when there is disharmony in the ranks.'

Despite her promise to have an early night, Meredith found, to her consternation, that sleep evaded her. Her head was too occupied with thoughts of what lay before them. As if the excitement of the expedition wasn't enough, she found herself pondering on Arthur and what he and his parents must think of her for deserting him as she had done.

She thought of Aunt Agnes, wallowing in misery at being left alone, and of the three old sisters. Who would take them their medicines and their fresh eggs and butter and a cake now and then? But most of all, against all her will to the contrary, she thought of the professor, saw the wicked glint in his eye and his leering smile. Some women might find his roguish good looks attractive, but they simply made Meredith squirm inside and vow to keep a safe distance from the man.

She took a long, hard look at herself in the dressing-table mirror and heaved a sigh.

'Well, Meredith, my girl,' she said out loud, 'you've always fancied yourself as a bit of an actress. Now is the time to prove your worth.'

She gave a groan. It was going to be difficult pretending that she liked Professor Macaulay, but she was prepared to be pleasant for the sake of her father and the expedition. However, she wouldn't fawn over him the way his students did. Nor would she bow and scrape before him like that gillie person, Frazier, whom she liked no better than the professor. The man had the appearance of a villain and was not the kind of person she would want to come across down some dark alley.

Meredith drummed her fingers on the heavy oak dressing-table and wondered what she could do to induce a state of sleep. In the end she took out a leather-bound notebook and began to write a journal, which she hoped to keep going throughout the year. There was not much to report upon as yet and she found herself unconsciously drawing the face of Professor Macaulay. The likeness she achieved had a certain sinister element that she could not erase, so she snapped the book shut and slid into bed between cool, starched sheets.

Outside, the sounds of the city were fading, though there was still the odd clip-clop of shod horses ringing on the cobbles as late revellers made their way home. Floorboards creaked in the corridor, doors clicked open and shut. And just as she was falling into a light slumber a sharp cry jolted her senses. She lay on her back, listening intently, but only a thick silence from the sleeping hotel met her ears.

She must have fallen asleep eventually, for suddenly it was morning and a maid was knocking on her door informing her that breakfast was now being served in the dining room. The novelty of having a bathroom of her own with hot running water delayed her. By the time she arrived the others had already finished eating.

'I'm sorry for being late,' she apologized, 'but the bed was so comfortable and the water so hot....'

'Let it not be a habit, Miss Jolly,' Professor Macaulay said curtly, flashing her a disgruntled look from beneath lowered brows. He threw down his napkin and stalked off, mumbling to himself about the capricious nature of the female sex.

The two students looked uncomfortable. Johnny stared down at a plateful of untouched food and could barely manage a smile, while Peter glared at the professor's back as if he would like to stick a knife into it. Quite a drastic change from the day before when both young men seemed in awe of their illustrious tutor.

'Come and have some breakfast, Meredith.' Her father was on his feet, guiding her over to a large buffet set out with silver servers. 'I think you'll like this.'

'Well, I'm glad someone is in a good mood this morning,' Meredith said, eyeing with hungry eyes the platters of bacon, scrambled eggs and sausage.

'Hmm.' Dr Jolly contemplated the food and helped himself to more toast and marmalade. 'I get the feeling that the boys have had a right good roasting from our leader. I didn't ask, but the atmosphere was as thick as that porridge there by the time I got downstairs. Best just to ignore situations like that, I always think. Have you got time to eat all that?'

Meredith glanced at her full plate and gave a shrug.

'I'm famished!'

'That hearty appetite of yours, young lady, will one day burst your stays!'

'Father!' She blushed prettily and glanced around to see if any of the other diners had heard, but all were too busy with their own business of eating and talking.

'*Daughter*!' Her father tapped a finger under her chin the way he used to do when she was a child and being mischievous. 'You have half an hour before we leave. Don't keep the professor waiting, eh?'

'I wouldn't dream of it,' she told him, sitting down and tucking in to her breakfast with healthy relish.

'Next stop Glasgow,' Dr Jolly said. 'That's the last time we'll see what we know as civilization for a long time.'

The next two days went by in a blur as they transferred from place to place, a train here, a coach there, a steamship and even a dog-cart when they arrived on the island of Harris. They slept in coaching inns, which were a long way from the standard of the Waverley Hotel in Edinburgh, but adequate.

On Harris Professor Macaulay left them sitting in the harbour, breathing in the smell of salt air and seaweed. A fleet of fishing vessels bobbed in the water and seamen called to one another as they hauled in the rigging and mended the nets. A boat sidled in, its belly lying deep with a full cargo of fish caught in the night. Its crew immediately off-loaded on to the dockside and began gutting and selling the cod and herring to local fish merchants, to a raucous invasion of gulls, diving and swooping as they tried to obtain an easy meal.

After about an hour, the professor returned with the news that he had found their chartered vessel and that the captain was willing to take them and their supplies over to St Kilda immediately. The main bulk of their supplies had been sent on ahead and was in storage in a nearby warehouse, so there was no need to delay the trip. Frazier was dispatched to organize the transfer of the supplies to the dock and before long the expedition team was ready to embark.

The captain of the *Saucy Mary* was an old seadog with a brown leathery skin and an eye that defied gravity due to getting in the way of a knife during a street brawl. He was Irish rather than Scottish, and could turn on the charm as well as the blarney as required.

When his good eye caught sight of Meredith his face lit up and he presented himself before her with a deep bow, his wide grin showing a row of teeth as discoloured and uneven as ancient tombstones.

'Well now, would ye look at dis lovely lady,' he said, his fingers tapping his chin as he inspected her closely. 'You wouldn't by chance be goin' to St Kilda with these gentlemen, would you, miss?'

'I am,' Meredith told him, holding her head up high, ready to deal with any ribald remark he might make.

''Tis no place for a lady, miss.'

'I'm going anyway.'

'Ach, but ye'll nivvor manage the landing dressed like that in those *volumptious* skirts. We'll lose you to the waves and dat's the truth of it.'

'What do you suggest I do, Captain?'

''Tis not for me to say, lady. I might be accused of talkin' out of turn, see?' Then he winked at her, crooked a dirty finger and beckoned her to come closer while he whispered in her ear. 'Now, if you was to forget that you was a lady, you'd be able to step from the boat to the jetty as lively as those two young sprats over there.'

Meredith caught the meaning of what he was saying and gave him a grateful smile.

'That can certainly be arranged, Captain, and thank you for your valuable advice.'

'Anything for a pretty lady, miss.' The captain touched the peak of his cap and bowed again. 'Captain Patrick Riley at your service. Now, how's about getting this party on board, eh, Professor?'

He led the way and they followed him gingerly up the sagging gangplank of a decrepit old fishing boat. Its timbers were crumbling in places, its flag faded and in shreds. It also stank highly of fish, though there was a crew member swabbing the deck as they stepped on board.

'What was that all about?' Dr Jolly asked Meredith a few minutes later. 'You and the captain seemed to be deep in conversation.'

'Wait and see, Father,' she told him and moved forward to the bow so she could lean on the rail and feel the wind on her face and keep the smell of the fish behind her.

'The boat is a mite smaller than I expected,' Dr Jolly said, looking uneasy as they watched the boxes of supplies being loaded and piled up precariously around the deck. 'It's to be hoped it's watertight.'

'I'm sure the professor wouldn't hire it otherwise,' Meredith told him, but she shared her father's concern. The boat had indeed seen better days: its timbers were worn and creaking painfully.

'Apparently, Captain Riley was the only man willing to run to St Kilda this week,' the doctor said, stroking his beard and gazing out to the distant horizon where clouds were gathering like balls of cotton wool.

Meredith followed his gaze, thinking that they couldn't have had a better day for the crossing. The weather was perfect. The sky was blue and the sea reasonably calm, though further out she could see a swell as the Atlantic undulated, like a living, breathing creature in slumber.

The shout of 'cast off!' dragged everybody's attention on to the weighing of the anchor and the pulling in of the great hawser. The crew heaved and coiled the thick rope, sweat beading on their lean, muscular bodies. With the captain at the wheel shouting obscenities at the men, the *Saucy Mary* nosed her way tentatively out of the harbour, the sails billowing as they caught the stiff sea breeze.

'This is the most exciting thing I've ever done!' Meredith's words were whipped away from her as the boat headed out into the open sea.

'I think,' said the doctor through clenched teeth, 'I'll head for the cabin.'

'Oh, Father...!' She saw his face blanch white as he gave her a tight smile and staggered away from her on unsteady legs.

'Seasickness,' said a voice beside her and she turned to find Peter smiling and wiping the sea fret from his eyeglasses. 'It takes some people like that. Johnny already has his head in a bucket down below.'

'Oh, was that why he was looking so worried?' Meredith said and received a strange look from the student.

'Er ... perhaps. He's the nervous type.'

'But not you?'

'No, I'm made of sterner stuff. Look!' He pointed at the sky, his face more animated than she had so far seen it. 'Gannets!'

A stream of big white seabirds flew across the bows of the boat, so low that Meredith could pick out the golden heads and the pure white feathers gleaming silver in the morning sun.

'How beautiful!' she exclaimed. 'They're so much nicer than ordinary seagulls.'

'Wait till you see the puffins,' he said, enthusiasm lighting up his face even more. 'They're great little birds with the painted face of a clown.'

'They sound wonderful,' she told him, then caught sight of the professor sitting alone in the stern, his profile set like concrete as he concentrated on the foaming wake of the boat as it got up speed and left the dock behind. 'What's Professor Macaulay *really* like, Peter?'

Peter shrugged his shoulders and gnawed on his bottom lip for a moment before replying.

'He's all right, I suppose,' he said hesitantly. 'He's a great naturalist, of course, and he's known worldwide. It's a huge honour to be asked to accompany him on any of his expeditions.'

'But...?' Meredith raised her eyebrows and noticed a cloud of discomfort pass over Peter's face.

'Should there be a "but"?' he said.

'I thought ... something in your voice perhaps...?'

He gave a wan smile and turned from her, leaning over the boat's rail. 'You're imagining things. Everybody likes Professor Macaulay. He's something of a demigod in his own profession.' Then he was looking at her again and the cloud had gone. 'Did you know that he once met the great Mr Charles Darwin?'

'The evolutionist? How exciting.'

'And he's been on two trips to the Galapagos Islands.'

'Really? Ooh!' Meredith made a grab for the rail as the wind changed direction without warning and the boat reared and swerved, the sails dipping dangerously low towards the waves.

Peter put out an arm to steady her, but he too was hanging on grimly and the pair of them almost lost their footing. Captain Riley was shouting orders to his crew and the men were scampering about wildly, tugging on ropes and making them fast.

'Well, that was a bit unexpected.' Meredith laughed, brushing her hair out of her eyes.

A wave rose over the prow, soaking them both. Meredith felt the cold dampness sinking in and her skirts were clinging to her legs. She immediately appreciated how inappropriate a lady's apparel was for sailing on the open sea.

'Are you all right, Meredith?' Peter looked at her with genuine concern.

'I think perhaps I need a change of clothes.' As she spoke, another gust of wind knocked the fishing boat off course again and more seawater poured over them. 'I hope it's not going to be like this all the way to St Kilda!'

Slowly and carefully she made her way aft to the captain's cabin where their personal belongings had been stored, the rest of their supplies being on deck beneath waterproof tarpaulins. She found

Johnny and her father lying supine on two bunks, looking decidedly unhappy, their faces greyish green.

'Well, this is a fine thing and no mistake.' She laughed, despite her sympathy with their sickly state. 'We're not five minutes at sea and you're both ill already.'

Dr Jolly swung his legs off his bunk and sat with his head in his hands, groaning softly.

'Damn silly seasickness!'

'You'll get used to it, probably, after we've been sailing for a few hours, Father.'

'Thank you for that good news, daughter. Now, please just leave me to die in peace.'

'I will after I've got out of these wet clothes. Where's your valise?'

'What do you want that for? And why are you so wet?'

'A high wave got me.' Meredith was searching through the collection of hand baggage and pounced with a cry of satisfaction on her father's valise. 'Close your eyes, both of you, because this is the only place a lady can get changed.'

Johnny, whose eyes had not opened since she came down into the cabin, turned to face the wall and curled up with his knees pressed against his chest. Her father lay down again, covered his face with a coarse woollen blanket and told her to hurry, because the thing smelled as though it had been used by a horse.

It gave her a strange feeling to be donning her father's clothes, but the freedom the trousers and the loose shirt gave her was immediately evident and appreciated. Thank goodness, though, that her father wasn't too portly and there was a leather belt, so she could tighten the waist sufficiently to stop the trousers slipping to her knees. The shoes, however, would be a problem, for Dr Jolly had large feet. Johnny, on the other hand, had small extremities, so he was a better bet.

'Johnny, do you have a pair of shoes I can borrow?' she asked and received a pathetic groan for an answer.

She took the groan for a 'yes' and found his valise. There was a pair of light canvas shoes with rubber soles that she found ideal once she stuffed the toes with cotton wool from her toiletry bag.

'Can I look yet, Meredith?' Dr Jolly said in a muffled voice. 'I'm beginning to suffocate in here.'

'Yes, I'm respectable again.'

When he emerged from under the blanket he was so astonished that he momentarily forgot his sickness. She stood before him, hands on hips, legs apart, looking for all the world like a young man ready for anything. Except, that was, for her corn-coloured curls, which even now she was pushing out of sight beneath his best cap.

'Good God, Meredith! What are you thinking of?'

She gave him a lopsided smile and a smart salute, touching her fingers to her forelock. 'Captain Riley was perfectly right when he said that a lady's clothes were of no use on a boat. This is much more practical.'

'I dread to think what your Aunt Agnes would say if she were here now.'

'She would have a fit of the vapours and order more bombazine.'

Meredith was amazed when she mounted the companionway to return on deck, at how much lighter she felt without the multiple layers that she had discarded. The rough wool of the trousers irritated her fine skin slightly, but she could cope with that. It was worth it to be able to move about without the danger of getting tangled up in skirts.

The wind continued to gather strength and before they had covered four leagues it had turned into a gale, bringing with it monstrous black storm clouds. An hour later and lightning flashed, coming in forks from the west and the east, followed by great drum rolls of thunder.

The captain had dealt out sou'westers and yellow oilskin jackets, for which they were grateful, but before long it was the professor who took charge and ordered Meredith and Peter down into the cabin, where they found Dr Jolly and Johnny no better, though they no longer had anything in their stomachs to evacuate.

The claustrophobic effect of being in such an enclosed space soon began to tell on all of them, so it was with great relief that they noticed, some four hours later, that the sea had ceased to boil and was down to a gentle simmering. They chanced it up on deck and almost wished they hadn't, for the boards were still awash and the exhausted crew were bailing out with every implement to hand that would hold water.

'How far is it now, Captain?' Professor Macaulay shouted. The old Irishman pushed back his cap and leaned heavily over the wheel.

'About as far again and more, I'd say,' he said. 'We're drifting in the right direction.'

'Drifting!'

'Ay! The men need to rest. The good Lord knows they won't get any once the big storm breaks.'

'I thought we'd just had a big storm. Isn't it over?'

'That was just a little tiddler, I'm t'inking, compared with what's to come.' He lifted a heavy arm and pointed. 'Look over there. Dat's what we've got coming. You'll know when it's about to hit us. There'll be a God-almighty calm just before it breaks. That's when you have to batten down all the hatches or we'll be sunk good and proper.'

The small group of naturalists stood at the rail and stared at the horizon where the sea met the sky in an inky blue-black smudge. Outwardly they showed no fear, but Meredith felt sure that hers was not the only heart to turn over and beat erratically.

All around there were distant flashes of lightning, but no thunder. Even the gulls were silent, riding the oily swells like the paper boats that children sail on placid lakes and ponds. The only sound was the constant wash of the sea as it slapped the prow.

'The captain's a fool.' Macaulay, his jaw set firmly, ground out the words. 'He assured me that the weather was set fair for today. Tomorrow was doubtful, but today was supposed to be fine.'

'What do we do now, Professor?' Peter asked. 'Do we not need to turn back?'

'Turn back? Don't talk such rubbish, boy. These boats are made for rough seas.' The professor rubbed a hand over his face and it rasped against his unshaven chin. 'We'll go on. There's no choice.'

'I can't help thinking that we'd be better off heading back to Tarbert until—' Dr Jolly got no further, for the professor cut him short.

'I'm in charge of this expedition, Jolly, and I say we go on!'

'I think my father is right,' Meredith spoke in her father's defence.

'You are not here to think, girl,' Macaulay said savagely. He went to stand by the captain, where he looked big and fearsome; Meredith was more than ever convinced that she was right to be wary of him.

'Pay him no heed, my dear,' Dr Jolly said. 'He's just as worried as we are and it's making him irascible.'

'The professor is always right,' Johnny piped up, then lowered his voice until his words became almost inaudible, but Meredith heard them anyway. 'Even when he's wrong.'

CHAPTER 4

THE STORM BROKE just as Captain Riley had predicted. After they had passed two hours of calm drifting, bobbing gently up and down like a cork, the clouds closed in and it became as black as night. Fiery streaks of lightning ripped through the sky and everything vibrated with deafening bursts of thunder.

The boat was tossed this way and that and was in constant danger of turning over; it would have done so were it not for the expertise of the captain and the muscle power of his crew. The hatches were battened down and covered with sandbags, but still the seawater seeped through crevices and dripped on to the miserable passengers below decks.

At one point, there was a loud cry of 'man overboard' and the boat circled drunkenly, once, twice, three times, before continuing on its plotted course. Johnny cowered in a corner of his bunk, prayed and crossed himself several times. The gillie, Frazier, gave him a dirty look, but kept his thoughts to himself. Peter remained surprisingly calm, as did Dr Jolly, who held on tightly to Meredith's hand. He said nothing, but she found the contact comforting, though it did little to allay her fears that the boat would capsize and they would all be drowned. Fortunately it seemed that fear was a good cure for seasickness. Only Johnny kept a bucket close to hand, but even he had no further use for it.

Professor Macaulay appeared surprisingly unmoved by the experience, though his eyes were smouldering with anger as if he might take up the question of the storm with God. He sat apart from the others, staring into the gloom, avoiding all contact.

'Will it never stop?' Johnny sounded close to hysteria. He hung his head low towards his knees and clamped his hands over his ears.

'Hang on, Johnny,' Peter said, slapping his fellow student on the back in a friendly fashion. 'It can't go on for ever.'

They were suddenly plunged into darkness as the one small oil lamp spluttered and went out. Peter struck a match and tried to relight it, but he gave up with a shrug.

'The oil's all used up,' he said, feeling his way back to the bunk where Meredith and her father sat. He sat down on the other side of her. She was grateful for the feel of his shoulder pressed against hers.

For five more hours they weathered the raging storm, with no sign of its abating. The shouts of the crew were now few and far between as exhaustion overcame them once more. A noise above the passengers' heads made them look up. They saw the hatch open and the captain's face appeared, illuminated by lightning as water streamed from his nose and chin and poured down into the cabin.

'If anyone knows how to pray,' he said, 'I advise you to pray right now, for neither the boat nor the crew can take any more of this battering.'

The hatch slammed shut again. Meredith felt her father's fingers tighten on hers and Peter's hand grasp her wrist.

'Professor Macaulay,' the doctor said, 'I seem to remember that you were once a missionary for the Evangelist Church.'

'It's a long time since I saw eye to eye with God,' Macaulay replied sourly. 'If there's any praying to be done, you'd better do it, Jolly.'

'I'm not a pious man,' Dr Jolly said, his voice raw with emotion. 'However … God save our souls.'

There was a moment's silence punctuated by a childlike whimper from Johnny, and a small chorus of 'Amen'; then Meredith spoke out.

'Well, I'm not ready to die yet!' she said with fervour. 'Do you hear that, God? I refuse to give in!'

But the storm continued to roar in their ears like a monster from the deep. The boat creaked and gradually began to break apart.

The storm had passed over the isles of St Kilda before reaching its climax. Even so, there had been little warning and men were stranded on Boreray, where they had gone to shear the sheep. There they would remain until the island's one and only boat could lift them off the next day, weather permitting.

It was late in the evening when the shout went up that a vessel had been sighted far off, where the storm was still raging. The place became astir with excitement, for the last boat had not made it and supplies were low.

Lachlan MacGregor was crouched over his account books, his nose almost touching the page as he inked in the figures that he would present to the factor when he came to collect the rent. He heard the cry go up and heard feet slapping the ground by his cottage from the direction of Village Bay.

Knuckles rapped on his door and through the slats he heard Jamie Crawford calling his name.

'Mr MacGregor, sir! They say there's a boat foundering just off Dun. They've seen a light.'

Lachlan reached for his coat and his stout cane, without which he could no longer walk with ease, and went to join the people gathered on the jetty. Men, women and children were there, regardless of the cold wind that whipped around them and the rain that fell in great splotches on their heads.

'Where is this boat, then?' he shouted, squinting into the darkness and seeing nothing.

'It was Archie who saw the light!'

'Ay, Mr MacGregor,' Archie piped up. 'It was just a pinprick, but it was there all right. Up and down it went, up and down. Then it went out.'

'Is it the factor come for the rent, perhaps? He'll not be happy to be caught in the storm.'

''Tis not the factor's boat. He's too canny to set out in this weather.'

'No.' Lachlan moved to the edge of the waves that lapped the shore and continued to peer into the distance. 'If there's a boat at all it will be the one bringing the naturalists.'

'They'll all drown and that's a fact!'

'We'll see, we'll see.' Lachlan grabbed hold of the nearest boy. 'Laddie, will you be the one to go and fetch Logan?'

'He'll not be well pleased, Mr MacGregor.'

'Pleased or not, he needs to know, and better he knows now than after the bodies are washed ashore.'

The boy set off at a run and was back within the half-hour.

'Well, laddie?' Lachlan demanded.

'He's coming, Mr MacGregor, sir.'

Then the word spread down the line of people still waiting, torches flaming in every hand. 'Logan's coming!' could be heard repeated like a whispered echo the whole length of the bay. 'Logan's coming.'

The man whose name was on all their lips soon appeared in their midst. They parted to let him pass, pointing towards the distant light that was once more lit and clearly seen. He did not falter and was soon clambering over slippery rocks until he was at the highest point, and there he waited, a tall, lone sentinel, oblivious to the rain and the wind that tore at his clothing and his long dark hair.

'Prepare the boat,' Lachlan ordered. 'And bring the ropes.'

Professor Macaulay and Frazier forced the hatch open and climbed on to the deck, pulling the others up after them. After Meredith's courageous outburst, they had decided that they would rather take their chances above than go down with the boat like caged rats.

The boat was still tossing about aimlessly in the storm. Captain and crew, what was left of them for two more men had been lost overboard, were lying exhausted, their strength completely spent.

But all was not lost. Peter fought his way to the prow of the boat and started yelling excitedly.

'I can see land!' he cried. 'And lights.'

Captain Riley raised his head and crossed himself several times before saying in a hoarse voice, 'The Lord God be praised, we're saved.'

'Not yet we're not, man!' Professor Macaulay shouted, pointing to where a pale moon shone down through more threatening clouds as the eye of the storm moved westwards and the sea between the fishing boat and the bay of Hirta once more became turbulent.

'We've got to get closer,' Dr Jolly said. As he spoke the timbers of the old vessel creaked and moaned, there was a great snapping sound and the mast shattered and came down on top of them, sails and all.

It was a miracle that no one else was killed. One man was knocked unconscious as the boom swung out of control. Another suffered a broken arm. But the fact that they were so close to being safe sent a rush of adrenaline through what remained of the tired crew and they fought valiantly to steer the boat closer to the island.

'Look!' There was a touch of hysteria now in Peter's normally calm voice. 'They're coming to get us!'

'I don't believe it!' Dr Jolly peered through the lashing rain. 'They must be mad!'

'Or very brave,' said Meredith at his side.

A boat had been put into the water and they could just make out men at the oars and another at the helm. It was a Herculean task to row in such a boiling cauldron, but the men were making superhuman efforts. Slowly and painfully, the boat fought against the wishes of the sea and made progress, miraculously reducing the distance between the two vessels.

'They must think they can do it,' the captain said, 'or they wouldn't attempt it. They can't afford to lose the boat, since they only have the one.'

Little by little the two boats approached one another over an interminable period of time. Eventually, the captain announced that he dared not drift any further or they would run aground and be battered against the rocks.

'I'm dropping anchor,' he shouted, signalling to the crew. 'From here on we'll just have to trust in Providence. If the good Lord sees fit to save our souls ...' He shrugged his shoulders. 'Well, it's for him to decide.'

As if a heavenly hand had poured oil on the troubled waters around them, the sea suddenly became still. The boat from the island was only fifty yards away and Meredith could make out plainly the men hauling on the oars as if their very lives depended upon it.

'Ahoy there!' Captain Riley hailed them. A man on the boat gave a wave and a shout back, though it was in a strange language that bore no resemblance to English.

Within minutes the two boats were side by side, their timbers rubbing and grating together with the undulations of the sea. It was a large, sturdy boat that they had sent from the island, manned by eight oarsmen. Even so, it was immediately obvious that it would not take all the human life that was aboard the *Saucy Mary*.

However, the captain lowered the rope ladder and beckoned to the party of naturalists.

'Passengers first,' he said, wiping the rainwater from the end of his nose. 'I'll stay with me boat, and the crew.'

'Take my place, Captain,' said Dr Jolly. 'You're a brave man and you got us through the storm.'

'Father, no!' Meredith pulled at his arm, the fear of losing him showing in her eyes.

'Little lady,' the captain said, his voice gathering force, 'I will not be separated from the *Saucy Mary*, and my crew are too spent to shimmy down that ladder.'

'For God's sake, stop wasting time!' Professor Macaulay pushed past them and slung his leg over the side, not prepared to wait a moment longer.

Johnny followed, scrambling and scrabbling like a scared rabbit, but Peter hesitated.

'Go on, laddie,' the captain said. 'And be ready to catch the young lady here and give a helping hand to her father.'

'Captain …' the doctor started to argue, but was soon silenced by a quick and decisive wave of the captain's hand.

'No captain worth his salt ever deserts his vessel, Doctor. Go, and God bless ye all.'

Meredith clung frantically to the rough rope of the ladder as she put one tentative foot after the other. She knew she was at risk of falling into the waves every time there was a swell that could so easily loosen her grip. However, she found strength and courage from somewhere and soon she was being manhandled into the waiting boat.

'Over here, laddie!' one of the oarsmen shouted in English. Hands pulled her back and shoved her unceremoniously on to a wooden plank that served as a seat.

Happily, she thought, they had not noticed that she was a woman and she was glad, for she didn't want preferential treatment, or the embarrassment of being found dressed in man's clothing.

Her father was the last to board. With them all safely installed, the boat turned and headed back to the island. They were within hailing distance when the storm returned with renewed vigour. As fast as the men pulled on the oars, the waves dragged them back out to sea. Then there was a shout from the shore and men were forming a human chain from the island, roped together as they plunged into the sea and tried to reach them.

'They'll never make it,' Meredith heard her father say.

Within seconds a heavy rope snaked out over the boat. The first throw slid back into the water, but the second was caught by Peter and Johnny. They hauled it in until the helmsman grabbed it and made it fast. Then, as they were being pulled in to the bay, a sudden squall caught them off guard. The boat tipped, turning over in the heaving waves, emptying out its passengers among the jagged rocks.

Meredith had no time to scream. The icy water was over her head before she knew it and she, like the others, was floundering, legs and arms kicking, fighting to get to the surface and breathe. It looked as though all was lost, but hands gripped her and pushed her up on to the jagged rocks. All around her was chaos. Her eyes stung with the salt, her lungs were bursting as she fought to get a foothold.

A shout from above made her look up as she found a crevice to hang onto. Through a blur she could see a tall, dark silhouette. He was climbing down towards her, reaching out for her hand, but she dared not move.

'Let go, dammit!'

She almost fell back into the water. How could Professor Macaulay have got to land so quickly? And yet, there was a slight difference in the tone of the voice, and the bulk of the man was less.

She felt his grip on her wrist and finally gave herself into his keeping, praying that he was strong enough to haul her up the few feet over the jagged rocks to safety. She need not have worried. Even with her clothes weighed down with seawater he lifted her as if she were no heavier than a sack of feathers. He then slung her over his broad shoulders and carried her the few yards to the village street, where he deposited her unceremoniously on the stoney ground.

She had only a fleeting glimpse of his face in the torchlight before he was off to lend a hand to the rest of the party. It came as quite a shock to see his features, dark and rugged with eyes as black as the night that surrounded them. But it wasn't the professor. Just someone younger who resembled him.

As the men plunged again and again into the cold Atlantic waters, the women came forward with blankets and hot drinks. Impossible to see what was going on at the water's edge: Meredith could only sit and shiver, her teeth rattling in her head with the cold and the shock of the situation. She didn't dare wonder what had become of her poor father and the others.

'How many were you, lad?' The same deep voice sounded in her ear and a heavy hand shook her shoulder.

Meredith pulled off her father's cap, which had somehow stayed put on her head and her hair fell about her shoulders.

'There were six of us,' she said in a trembling voice and saw astonishment register on his face.

'The saints deliver us,' said a female voice from the crowd, ''tis a wee bit of a lassie you've got there, Logan!'

Astonished murmurings went through the onlookers. Meredith struggled to rise, but quickly discovered that her legs wouldn't support her. She found herself being lifted again as the man called Logan swept her up in his arms.

'The factor's house is nearest,' someone said. 'We've lit a fire in there. It'll do until the morning.'

'My father...!' Meredith murmured weakly. 'Have you saved my father?'

'Be still,' came the abrupt order and the man tightened his grip on her limp body. 'They are all safe.'

The next thing Meredith knew was her waking up to sunshine streaming through a tiny window. There was the smell of smoke from the embers of the fire from the previous evening. Someone, she hoped it was a woman, had undressed her, reclothed her in a rough tweed skirt and a thick woollen jumper, and covered her with heavy blankets. When she struggled to prop herself up on her elbows she found that she wasn't alone. Her father, the professor and the other three were also dressed like peasants and were beginning to stir.

'Father! Father, are you all right?'

Dr Jolly gave a groan, but he was smiling when he sat up and nodded to her across the small living space of the stone cottage.

'I think we're all present and correct, my dear.'

There was a rattle of stones outside. The door opened to admit two elderly women with weathered faces, who bore steaming pots of porridge. Meredith thought she had never seen anything so welcoming in all her life.

'You must eat,' one woman said, passing the porridge around. 'Then we will take you to your quarters and you will meet Mr MacGregor, who will advise you.'

'What about the men on the fishing boat?' Dr Jolly wanted to know.

'They're safe. Our men worked through the night to fetch them and the supplies you brought with you to the island. The storm blew itself out in the early hours. Today they will mend the boat and the fishermen can return to the mainland tomorrow.'

'That's good news indeed,' Dr Jolly said and the women nodded gravely as they ducked out of the cottage like shy, demure young girls.

For the next few minutes there was no sound in the room except the scraping of spoons on bowls as the naturalists ate their first breakfast on Hirta.

It was midday before someone came to conduct them to the quarters that had been prepared for their long stay on the island on the orders of the factor.

'You're to wait here for Mr MacGregor,' said the man, doffing his cap and backing out of the cottage.

'Lachlan MacGregor,' the professor said, tugging at his moustache. 'I didn't expect him still to be alive. He's the village elder and a force to be reckoned with, though he must be in his eighties by now.'

'That rescue last night,' Dr Jolly spoke up, 'I've never seen such bravery.'

'Or such strength,' Peter added. 'Yet they're not exactly the brawniest of individuals.'

'They're hardened by the life they live,' Professor Macaulay told them. 'Every day is a fight for survival.'

'The man who pulled me out of the water seemed different somehow,' Meredith said, recalling her rescuer. She gave a laugh. 'For a moment I thought it was you, Professor Macaulay!'

Macaulay lowered his brows and frowned darkly.

'Stupid girl!' he muttered, but he seemed a little disturbed by her words as he turned to his gillie. 'Frazier, go and see what's keeping MacGregor. The sooner we start work the better.'

Frazier nodded and headed for the door, but it opened before he got there and Lachlan MacGregor himself stepped inside. Meredith saw at once why he was the revered village leader. He had a noble bearing and despite his great age he still looked powerful, though there was not an ounce of spare fat on his body.

'Please …' he said, his voice soft and courteous. 'Sit you down. Might I ask who is in charge?'

'I am.' The professor spoke curtly. 'We've already met.'

'Indeed.' The old St Kildan fixed his penetrating gaze on Dr Jolly. 'But you, sir, have never been to our island. Would I be right in thinking that?'

'You would indeed, sir,' the doctor said.

Lachlan nodded slowly, his eyes drifting over the assembled group and coming to rest on Meredith.

'We did not make provision for a female,' he said. 'But the parliament discussed the situation this morning and there is a place for you in the cottage of Flora MacInnes, a single lady of our parish. But you must not let her influence you with her strange ways. They are not always acceptable to us here on St Kilda.'

'I'm not sure that I like the idea of my daughter keeping company with anyone who is considered "strange",' Dr Jolly said. 'Can she not be lodged with a family?'

'Our cottages are small,' Lachlan said. 'We have but one room, as you can see. Do not distress yourself over Mistress MacInnes. Your daughter will come to no harm under her roof. You have my word on it.'

'I need separate quarters for myself and my gillie,' the professor stated and received a contemptuous look from Lachlan.

'I know it is not ideal, but we have little accommodation to spare, unless your man will take his chances in one of the old cleats behind the village....'

'Och, no! Not one of those things!' Frazier, having already seen the round earthen dwellings, did not relish living in one for a whole year. The cottage they were in was primitive enough with no running water, only what was brought in buckets from the nearest fresh-water springs scattered about the island.

'There is the byre at the narrow end of the cottage here,' said Lachlan. 'It has room there for two, perhaps, if you are willing to manufacture a sleeping place there.'

'I expected private accommodation.' The professor was far from pleased with the arrangement and showed it. 'What about the factor's house?'

'No,' said Lachlan firmly. 'That would not do.'

'Oh, come now, Macaulay,' Dr Jolly spread his hands, pleading for reason. 'We didn't come here looking for comfort or luxury. Let the two boys take the byre and we three can bed down in the wall alcoves here. I can see no objection to that.'

'How will I find the cottage of Flora MacInnes, Mr MacGregor?' asked Meredith. She received a genial smile from the old man.

'She lives apart, up and over yon hillside,' he said. 'I have asked Logan to take you there.'

'Logan?' She frowned, and then remembered her rescuer of the night before. 'Ah, yes, the man I thought was Professor Macaulay. I must thank him for delivering me from a watery grave.'

The old man inclined his head.

'This person you call Logan,' Professor Macaulay said, 'who is he? Is he a St Kildan?'

Meredith saw concern in the professor's regard, saw how the gillie backed off into a shadowy corner of the cottage as if afraid.

'You will meet him soon enough. He lives the life of a hermit with no desire to be a part of our community, but there is no man stronger, and no man braver. He has saved lives on more than one occasion, so we accept him.'

'But who is he?' Professor Macaulay's face was beaded with perspiration and he nervously fingered his cravat as if it had become too tight around his neck.

The grating of a foot on the doorstep made them turn. A long shadow fell into the room as someone entered and Meredith recognized her dark-eyed saviour of the previous night.

'Ah, Logan.' Lachlan beckoned to the big man. 'We were just speaking of you.'

Meredith watched, transfixed, as Logan stepped into the room and the light fell upon his face. The professor staggered back with a choking gasp and Frazier pressed himself even further against the wall as though he wished it would swallow him up.

'Stuart!' The name was but a whisper and Professor Macaulay's face became ashen.

'Father!' said Logan. An uneasy silence fell over the group of people standing there.

The professor brushed a trembling hand over his disbelieving eyes, then stared again at the tall young man, who resembled him so strongly that there could be no doubt that they shared the same blood.

'It cannot be!' Professor Macaulay whipped around to face the gillie. 'You told me he was dead!'

'I – I saw him go over the side with my own eyes, Professor!' Frazier said, his words tumbling out of his slack mouth. 'I did! I swear it's true. He went into the water and never came back up.'

'Then what is this, man?' The professor shot a hand out in Logan's direction. 'His ghost, eh? He doesn't seem too dead to me!'

'On the contrary,' Logan spoke up, his ebony eyes flashing. 'I have been dead to you for five years and that is the way I would like it to stay.'

Lachlan MacGregor placed himself strategically between the two men, one hand flat against the younger one's broad chest.

'Here on Hirta we have learned to live with our grudges,' he said slowly and clearly. 'I beg of you both to keep the peace between you, for all our sakes.'

Meredith was happy to see that the storm clouds had departed and although there was a brisk wind that whipped this way and that over the hillside, the weather seemed settled at last. On her way up to her lodging place, following Logan's long strides as he marched ahead, she saw how the *Saucy Mary* no longer listed brokenly in the bay. And even as she looked, the island's boat set off with men on board in the vessel's direction.

'Are Captain Riley and his crew leaving us already?' she said to Logan's straight back. He came to a halt, which allowed her to catch him up.

'He must go while the weather holds good,' he said. 'His boat has been repaired and is again seaworthy. It is not worth lingering or he may find himself and his men stranded on Hirta for weeks, if not months. We are governed by the elements here.'

'It's a pity. I would have liked to say goodbye to the captain and give him my thanks. He was a good man.'

'He was a foolish one to bring you out here when he did.'

Logan flashed her a look, then took up his stride again. She had to hurry, breathlessly, to keep up with him, her baggage weighing heavily, but not nearly as heavily as her trunk, which he carried with such ease on his shoulder.

'Is it true, Mr Logan, that you are Professor Macaulay's son and that he thought you were lost in the sea?'

She caught sight of the twitch of a muscle in his cheek as his jaw set firm. She thought that he did not intend to answer her, but she was wrong. After a few moments' silence, he spoke in a low voice tinged with hate.

'I no longer acknowledge the name I was given at birth,' he said. 'Nor do I acknowledge my father. I adopted my uncle's name and his father's before him. Two better men never lived and so the name is good enough for me. The people here accept me simply as Logan.' He gave her another searching look. 'And that is what you must call me, too.'

As he led the way up the steep slope of Conachair behind the village, Meredith had her first real view of the island. It was very green, with not much in the way of flat land. There were no trees, only rocks dotted across the boggy, moorland. The sodden turf sucked hungrily at her feet, making loud slurping noises with every difficult step she took.

At one point she lost one of her boots completely, they having been donated to her by someone with larger feet, and she had to suffer the cold wet ooze of the earth between her toes while Logan retrieved it for her and replaced it on her foot.

While he struggled to fasten the boot more securely, Meredith was obliged to hold on to him for balance. She took the opportunity to look down over Village Bay with its straggling crescent of cottages and gardens and the oval stone enclosure that was the graveyard with its drunken scattering of primitive headstones and wooden crosses.

She winced as Logan pulled on the boot laces and tied them tightly around her ankles, but did not complain. It was the only way to keep the things from being sucked off again.

When he eventually straightened up, wiping his muddy hands down his trousers, he paused to make a long study of her face. His expression was heavily pensive and she could not make out whether he liked what he saw or not.

'Why would a young woman of genteel upbringing wish to come to such a desolate corner of the world?' he asked.

'Why would any man give up his life on the mainland to live here?' she countered with a question of her own.

'I have my reasons.'

'And I mine.' Meredith raised her head and jutted out her chin to show that she was not a weak female, but one of sturdy character and strong resolve.

'I can think of many places that are more hospitable than St Kilda.'

'But it was to St Kilda my father was invited by Professor Macaulay.'

His face remained as rigid as stone, then he heaved her trunk back on to his shoulder.

'We must press on. Flora is expecting us.'

'I can't see why I must be billeted so far away from the others,' she said, already panting as she fought to keep her footing on the slippery, moss-covered ground.

'It was the decision of the parliament.'

'But I'm part of the team of naturalists. I will have to be with them to carry out my part of the work.'

'The walk will put muscles on your skinny legs.'

She could only see the back of his head, but she felt sure that he was mocking her. No doubt he had got a good look at her legs when he fished her out of the sea.

'There's nothing wrong with my legs, thank you very much,' she said. 'And they are certainly not skinny!'

'No, I think I have to agree with you there.'

'They're very strong, actually,' she said, feeling her cheeks start to burn at his comment. 'I walk the Northumberland moors, where I live, every day, rain or shine.'

'Ah! You are to be commended. So, you are from Northumberland. Do you and your father know Professor Macaulay well?'

'Not at all.' She stopped to catch her breath and he turned, making a large silhouette against the afternoon sky. 'My father attended his lectures in the past, but that is all.'

'I see.' Logan looked to the horizon and she again saw his cheek muscles working. 'Come on. Not much further. Flora lives just over the next hill.'

The land dropped away into a soft hollow and there, nestling in the indentation, was the strangest construction of stone and turf. Unlike the more modern cottages of Village Bay, each of which had chimneys at both gable ends, this house had a central aperture from which tendrils of grey smoke rose and dispersed into the atmosphere. There were various enclosures around the cottage, containing livestock. In the midst of a small group of brown-and-white goats, a tiny, bent figure could be seen feeding them scraps from a bucket and speaking to them as if they were her children.

As they approached the old woman looked up, shading her eyes from the sun's glare. Even at a distance, Meredith could see that her hair was pure white and tied in a long tress behind. Her skin was like the coarse, dark bark of a mature tree and it was impossible to hazard a guess at her age. However, when she called out in Gaelic, Flora's voice was surprisingly deep and strong.

'You'll have to remember your English, Flora,' Logan called back to her, ushering Meredith ahead of him into the well-kept garden that seemed to flourish with vegetables and aromatic herbs.

'So, child,' Flora said, inspecting Meredith closely. 'You are to be my houseguest.'

'I'm afraid so, Mistress MacInnis,' Meredith said.

'Have they told you I'm a witch?' The old woman's eyes twinkled mischievously as Meredith shook her head. 'Don't you believe them. Simple people they are, with simple minds for the most part. All except Lachlan MacGregor, who is a wise man, *most* of the time. And this one, here,' she added, inclining her head in Logan's direction.

'How are you today, Flora?' Logan asked, lowering Meredith's trunk and flexing his muscles.

'The same as ever. I won't see another spring. My days on this earth are dwindling. No doubt the people will have something to celebrate soon.'

When Logan turned to Meredith an affectionate smile played about his mouth, so attractive it set him far apart from his sneering father.

'I've been listening to this talk from her in all the years I've been here. She's indestructible and she knows it.'

'Get away with ye, laddie. Now, bring the young lady inside and we'll take soup together.'

'All right, Flora. Is it to be your famous nettle soup, then?'

'Aye, and especially for you I've left in the sting of the plant!' Flora's mouth twisted into a mischievous smile and she gave a wink. 'Come you inside, lassie. It's a long time since I've welcomed a visitor. Come and tell me all about yourself.'

Meredith felt the warmth of the old lady's welcome. She thought she might like it here after all.

CHAPTER 5

THE NETTLE SOUP that Flora served up with chunks of coarse grain bread had not looked particularly appetizing, but was surprisingly good. It had taken a while before Meredith stopped gazing around the old woman's abode, for it was more than just a little archaic with its beaten earth floor, central fire and recesses all around the rough stone walls which served as open cupboards.

Although sparsely furnished, it lacked none of the essentials and even went to the extreme luxury of having a proper bed, though this was worrying in itself, as there was only one. Logan, who seemed perfectly at home in Flora's living room, saw her eyes lingering on the bed and read her thoughts.

'Don't worry, Miss Jolly,' he said. 'The bed is for you. It was brought here especially from the factor's house. Flora prefers to sleep the way she has done all her life, in the wall recess over there.'

At the far side of the room, where the light from the oil lamp didn't reach, she could just make out the long alcove filled with pillows and blankets. She gave a sigh of relief and thanked God that she wouldn't have to share the narrow cot with her hostess.

'I'm very grateful for all the trouble you've gone to, Mistress MacInnis,' she said.

'Och, nobody calls me that,' the old lady said, showing her bare gums in a broad grin. 'It makes me feel old. My name is Flora, and that is what you must call me.'

'And I am Meredith.' Meredith received a pleased nod.

'A pretty name, don't you think, Logan?' Flora said, but Logan made no comment one way or the other.

'I'll be on my way,' he said, rising, his head bowed beneath the low rafters. 'There's peat to be cut and stacked.' He glanced over at Meredith. 'I will call for you tomorrow after breakfast and walk with you down to the village.'

'Please don't trouble yourself, Logan,' Meredith said quickly. 'I can find my own way, I'm sure.'

'Perhaps, but I have to come anyway, since I am expected to be your guide, at least for a short while.'

She was surprised to hear this and said so.

'Logan knows these islands better than any man born here,' Flora said, nodding wisely. 'It is well that he will lead you and your party.'

'It is not my choice,' Logan said, a cloud passing over his countenance. 'It was Lachlan's decision. There is no other man to spare. Last year was poor for all our harvests, so we must work extra hard if we are to survive this coming winter.'

'I'm sorry,' Meredith said. 'We seem to have caused some difficulties for you in coming here.'

'Not you, not your father or the two young men you brought with you,' he said.

'Professor Macaulay and his gillie?'

'Yes.' It was a curt sound, snapped out through tightened jaws.

With a nod to the two women he took his leave.

'What is the trouble between Logan and his father, Flora?' Meredith asked and the old woman held up a misshapen finger.

'Best you do not know, child. There is some knowledge that we are better off without. Here on the island we do not speak of such things, nor do we ask questions. Now, let us talk. I will tell you the history of Hirta.'

'I would like that very much.'

Meredith smiled warmly and thought that she would enjoy having the old lady for company after all. It was certainly preferable to sharing the same accommodation with a group of men whom she hardly knew.

Josiah Jolly had gone down to Village Bay to say his goodbyes to Captain Riley and his crew, commiserating on the loss of the two men, and congratulating the roguish Irishman on his brave handling of the fishing boat.

'Och, 'tis all in a day's work, Doctor.' Patrick Riley grinned broadly and scratched at his stubbly chin. 'In these waters we all know the risks and know that we take our life in our hands every time we set sail.'

Dr Jolly clasped him by the upper arms, gripping hard. 'Nevertheless, you did a grand job, Captain.'

'Yon Professor Macaulay doesn't seem to think so,' Riley said, his face curling with dislike. 'You'd best be on your mettle with that one, Doctor. He's a bad lot.'

'Oh, he's a bit difficult, I'll grant you that, but I don't think he's that bad, really.'

'I swear to you, sir,' the captain licked his thumb and wiped it down his lapel, 'I've come across his type before. He's no gentleman like yourself. You watch over that nice lassie o' yourn, you hear?'

'Meredith? Why, you can't think that...?'

'I do think that,' Riley said cunningly. 'And I'm not after being wrong. He's got the evil eye, has yon professor fellow.'

'Well, let's hope that, on this one occasion, you are wrong, eh?'

Captain Riley's response was no more than a rumble in his throat, then there was a cry from the jetty that the boat was ready and he went off at the gallop.

Josiah Jolly watched the island's boat go alongside the *Saucy Mary* and stood there until the captain and his reduced crew clambered aboard and pulled up anchor. Then, as the larger vessel nosed its way out of the bay, heading back for Harris, he forgot that he was not a pious man and offered up a prayer for their safe delivery back to the mainland.

When he returned to the naturalists' quarters, he met Frazier coming out of the cottage, laden down with his personal affairs. The man gave him a sour grimace.

'What's up with you, then, Mr Frazier?' Dr Jolly asked.

'The professor doesn't think it's fitting for his gillie to share his accommodation,' the gillie replied glumly. 'I'm to bed down in the cleat at the back of the cottage. That's where they usually keep the animals, isn't it, eh?'

'Not to worry.' The doctor tried to make the best of things. 'It could turn out for the best. At least you'll have your own quarters and you'll be able to make of them as you wish.'

'Aye, you could say,' Frazier said and walked on with heavy feet.

Inside the cottage the atmosphere could have been cut with a knife. Professor Macaulay was fuming and the two boys looked like remorseful children after a good scolding.

'So!' Dr Jolly said, as brightly as he could. 'I see we are all settling in well!'

The following morning, the doctor was more than pleased to see his daughter striding down the hillside at the side of Logan. There was a bright, enthusiastic smile on her face, and she showed every sign of having spent a restful night, which was more than he could say for himself during his first night on Hirta.

'Reporting for duty, Father,' she said, kissing his cheek.

'And I'm glad to report that your typewriting machine survived the journey and is awaiting you in the cottage.'

'What about my sketchpads and pencils?' Meredith asked anxiously.

'All safe and sound.'

'Hallelujah!' she cried, giving him a tight hug, aware of Logan's eyes on her all the while and wishing he would look elsewhere. It was hard being her natural self under such close scrutiny.

'Good heavens, girl,' her father cried. 'I hardly recognize you in those dreadful clothes!'

Meredith laughed, looking down at the hand-woven skirt and knitted jumper and shawl she was wearing. 'They are not exactly the height of fashion,' she said, 'but they are surprisingly warm and comfortable. Flora gave them to me. Father, she is the most amazing person and already I've learned so much about these islands.'

There was an uncomfortable moment when Professor Macaulay appeared. Meredith noticed how he and Logan avoided looking each other in the eye and her curiosity about the relationship between the two men grew.

'Are you ready, gentlemen?' Logan asked in an impartial voice, then went on without waiting for an answer. 'Today we must put the cattle to pasture. There is turf to cut for fuel, fishing and curing. I'm told that you are here to study all aspects of life on these islands.'

'Why have *you* been chosen to guide us?' Professor Macaulay demanded harshly. 'You are not a St Kildan!'

'No, but I am the only man they can spare. Without me your expedition will be worth nothing.'

'This is preposterous!'

'Take it or leave it.'

Professor Macaulay seemed lost for words. Dr Jolly came forward and patted Logan's shoulder.

'We'll be glad of your help, laddie,' he said kindly. 'What do we do first?'

One day merged into another as the naturalists settled in, slowly witnessing the harsh existence on the archipelago and the island of Hirta in particular, which was the only island in the group that supported human life. In between helping with the chores they took time out to study the flora and the fauna on the islands. Meredith transcribed their scribbled notes on her machine, and when there was time to spare she wandered off with her sketchbook and made neat little drawings of everything she saw. Back at the cottage she turned the drawings into watercolours, storing them safely in linen and oilskin bags to preserve them.

Sometimes she would accompany her father, who was eagerly taking photographs and developing the plates in an outbuilding alongside stacks of drying peat. And when her back and her wrists ached from sketching or pounding the keys of her machine she would go down to the bay and wander barefoot along the shore where the sea-washed shingle was smoother.

It was here that Peter found her on a day in July. She was sitting on a rock with the wind blowing through her hair and sea-fret glistening on her clothes. It had rained again through the night, but there was a promise today of blue skies and sunshine, which always lightened the mood, even if the wind did constantly buffet the island and put foamy white crests on the waves.

'I wish I could see what it is that's making you smile, Meredith.'

'Hello, Peter. Was I smiling?'

'You're always smiling. I don't know how you do it, given that we're marooned on a desert island in the most primitive conditions.'

She laughed and patted the rock beside her, inviting him to sit.

'It's not so bad, really.'

'Not for you, perhaps,' Peter said with a wry smile. 'You only share your accommodation with the old lady.'

'Yes, I must say I don't envy you your accommodation. It must be cramped in the cottage and I know my father snores most dreadfully.'

Peter nodded grimly. 'And Johnny has bad dreams and calls out in his sleep. As for the professor, he never sleeps, but paces the floor, muttering to himself hour after hour, and then he's like a bear with a sore head in the morning.'

'It must have been quite a shock for him finding his son alive, after thinking him dead for so long,' Meredith said.

'He didn't exactly seem to be overjoyed, did he?'

'When you go out with them, foraging, do they speak?'

'No. Mainly they ignore one another. This morning Logan took us in the boat to the cliffs of Oiseval near The Gap. The men of the village had been there yesterday catching young fulmars, so there wasn't much left. Logan demonstrated how they do it, climbing up sheer rock faces like a steeplejack, taking the birds, roping them together and lowering them back to the boat. I tried, but I have no head for heights and I couldn't even get a foothold.' Peter gave a sudden winsome grin. 'Logan's more mountain goat than man. Quite an amazing fellow really.'

Something made Meredith glance over her shoulder with a shiver. A sixth sense, perhaps, that made the hairs on the back of her neck prickle. Where the rocks rose behind the shingle beach the lone figure of Logan stood. Even at that distance she felt she could see the brooding expression on his rugged face.

'There he is now,' she said. 'He's such a mysterious individual, don't you think?'

'Like father like son, perhaps,' Peter said with a grimace.

'I hope not,' Meredith said, finding the idea totally abhorrent.

Although she had little upon which to base her judgement of Professor Macaulay, she continued to experience feelings of dislike towards him. Except when the group ate together for the frugal midday meal, she saw little of him. Her father appeared to get on reasonably well with their leader, but then he got on well with everyone. Josiah Jolly was the soul of tact and knew well how to handle difficult people with kid gloves. It was a talent Meredith felt she had not inherited, which was unfortunate. She had a tendency to speak her mind, sometimes regretting her bluntness later on.

'They say that food is very scarce at the moment,' Peter said, hurling a flat stone into the sea and making it skim the waves. 'We had boiled sorrel and seaweed for supper again last night.'

The food supplies they had brought with them had mostly gone overboard during the storm and what was left had lasted only three weeks, so they were obliged to rely on the villagers to provide what they could spare. It turned out to be precious little, the only meat being small portions of fulmar, a little dried pollack and crab.

Meredith again looked to where Logan was standing, as still as a monument. As she watched, there was a sound that caused Logan to turn. A small child ran over the rocks towards him, calling out his name. Logan scooped the child up in his arms and began walking back to the village with the little girl perched high on his shoulders, squealing with delight.

'Is Logan married, Peter?' she asked.

Peter shrugged. 'He won't be drawn on his private life, but I have seen him with a little girl of about four years. She called him 'Dada'.'

Meredith looked back again, but Logan had gone, probably into one of the cottages with the child. She made a mental note to quiz him the next time they walked together from Flora's house. It was no good asking Flora. She would not discuss anything but the history of the islands and her love affair with her animals and the herbal remedies she made up from the plants she grew in her garden. People treated everything she did with open disdain, but secretly used her medicinal potions when all else failed. By then, Flora complained, it was often too late to help them.

Flora had been so angry when a newborn baby had died of an

infection because the woman they called the nurse had placed a poultice of cow dung on the child's umbilicus.

'If they had brought the wee bairn to me,' she cried, 'I could have saved him.'

Meredith had no doubt that the old woman's remedies worked. She had produced a healing salve when Meredith scalded a finger, and a tea made from sage and wild thyme had settled her stomach after eating something that disagreed with her.

'Well, I'd better go,' Peter said, though he showed a reluctance to get up from their shared rock. 'Johnny and I have volunteered to help cut turf up on Connachair. It's a good job the weather's milder this month. There's hardly any dry peat left to burn and what there is will be needed for cooking.'

'You're beginning to sound like an islander, Peter.'

Meredith smiled affectionately at him. She liked Peter a lot. He was a quiet, inoffensive young man and reminded her very much of her father. He went about his business without complaint, meeting the challenges and not getting despondent when he failed or depressed when the weather was miserable, which it was frequently.

'It's all right being on these islands for a short time,' he said, brushing sand off his trousers. 'Mind you, I don't think I'd want to spend the rest of my life here. I like my comforts too well.'

Meredith hung on a few minutes longer after Peter had left her. She couldn't help dwelling on the subject of Logan and Professor Macaulay, wondering what had passed between them on that first expedition five years ago. The subject was forever surfacing in her inquisitive mind. It must have been something serious, for there was no love lost between father and son. In fact, she had only seen hate in their eyes every time they were together.

She worked later than usual that day because all the men were out and it was easier to concentrate with just the faint swish of the tide on the beach and the more distant crash of waves on the rocks to disturb her. Because the summer light stretched into the night it was easy to lose track of the time and it was seven o'clock before she knew it.

Meredith quickly packed away her notes, wondering what was keeping the men. Peter had gone with the boat, fishing around the island of Dun and hoped to return with a fish or two for supper. It was a task usually carried out in the evening, so they would be late back. Her father and the professor had strolled off, after lunch, in opposite directions, hoping to find different varieties of wild plants to record. Dr Jolly had been weighed down by his camera equipment, the professor with his flower-presses and specimen boxes. Johnny had followed behind, like a nervous dog coming to heel. They should have been back an hour ago and would have been, no doubt, had Logan been with them. On this occasion, however, Logan had been obliged to help a party of crofters execute some urgent roof repairs on two of the older cottages that were used to store hay and turf.

When Meredith came to the door of the cottage she saw immediately why there was such a strange, enveloping silence, for all around the island was blanketed in a thick fog. Somewhere a dog barked and a seagull screamed. The sounds echoed eerily across Village Bay. Even though The Street was only yards away, she could see absolutely nothing beyond a faint shadow that was the end wall of the first house.

Wrapping a shawl tightly about her, she set out in what she believed was the general direction of Flora's cottage. The old lady would be wondering what had kept her. It didn't take long for Meredith to realize her mistake. In such a thick fog all landmarks were obliterated and it became impossible to know in which direction she was going.

Turning round, she tried to retrace her steps, but that too proved to be a mistake, for she ended up in a place she did not know, feet slipping and slithering on mossy rocks as the ground fell away beneath her on a steep descent to the sea.

She turned again, tentatively putting one foot forward and met thin air. Feeling herself fall, she twisted her body and her fingers found purchase on the cliff face, enough to haul herself up until she was lying, breathless, her heart pumping with sheer panic inside her chest.

As she lay on the damp grass her ears picked up the sound of heavy breathing so close she felt as if she could reach out and touch whoever was out there.

'Hello!' she called out, but there was no answer, just the sound of someone in a panic rushing past a few feet away.

She saw the silhouette, heard his sharp, choking intake of breath and knew it was Johnny. But what was he doing here on his own, floundering about like a startled rabbit? And where was the professor?

'Johnny!' she cried, but he had gone, leaving only the fading sound of his feet plodding heavily on the sodden earth.

When all was silent once again, Meredith crawled forward on all fours until she was sure that no dangerous drop yawned before her, waiting to swallow her up. If necessary, she would lie here, she thought, until the fog had cleared. And then, like the fool she was, she would head back to base, to Flora's earthen hut or the Naturalists' stone cottage in Village Bay. Whichever was the nearest.

Five, ten minutes passed before she heard the next human sound and heaved a sigh of relief.

'Hello!' she called again, as loud as she could. 'Over here!'

The footsteps slowed, halted, then approached and she saw the smoky shadow turn into the solid man.

'What the blazes are you doing out here in this fog?'

She looked up the long, muscular length of Logan's legs as he towered over her, but was too relieved to feel embarrassment. It was when he hooked his hands under her arms and dragged her roughly to her feet that she wanted to run and hide from those deeply penetrating eyes that seemed to pierce right through to her very soul.

'Thank you,' she said, a little ungraciously. 'I was caught unawares by the fog.'

'Obviously. Flora was concerned when you didn't appear at your usual time. What on earth possessed you to wander about in this?' He was scolding her and she didn't like it.

'I'm not a child, Logan, so don't treat me like one.'

'Then don't behave like one. Give me your hand.'

She kept her hands tightly clamped to her sides, but he grabbed one and started walking, pulling her after him.

'Let me go, will you!'

'You'll be telling me next that you weren't lost.'

'I wasn't!' Meredith gave a gulp, and then decided it was best to come clean; she had never been a good liar. 'Well, all right, I was lost, but I would have found my way, eventually, once the fog lifted.'

'The fog here can last for days,' Logan told her. 'You might have been killed wandering blindly about like that. Or died from exposure.'

'I wasn't the only one. Johnny is out here somewhere. I heard him go by me and shouted, but he must have been too scared to hear me.'

'Johnny?'

'Yes, he went off with Professor Macaulay just after lunch.'

'Did he, now?'

'Yes, he did, and my father hasn't come back either and I'm worried about him. And what about Peter?'

'Peter will be fine. He's with the men. The St Kildans can find their way around blindfold, whether they're on land or on sea.'

By the time they reached The Street the fog was drifting away to the north, disappearing as fast as it had come. A light flickered in the Naturalists' cottage, so at least one of them was back and Meredith hoped it was her father.

Dr Jolly was, indeed, safely returned. They found him bent over a pan of boiling water in the process of making a welcome pot of tea. Johnny was slumped on his bunk in the corner, his face streaked with dirt and tracks where tears had coursed down to his chin. The doctor indicated, with a jerk of his head, that they should ignore the boy.

'He's a little emotional,' he whispered. 'Best let him come out of it himself.'

Johnny's mouth worked, but no sound came out at first, then he cleared his throat and they saw his Adam's apple move up and down as he tried to swallow with difficulty.

'He ... we ... the professor and I got separated ... the fog ... it was so thick....'

Logan picked up the single oil lamp and held it over Johnny's bunk.

'What's that on your face, lad?' he asked as the light picked up an angry bruise on Johnny's cheekbone. 'How did you get it?'

Johnny fingered the bruise tentatively and shook his head.

'I ... I must have fallen ... knocked myself ...' He gulped audibly. 'It's nothing.'

Logan stepped forward hovering over the distressed boy like an eagle over a lamb.

'You were with Professor Macaulay,' he said. 'What happened?'

Johnny gave a vigorous shake of his head and his eyes bulged fear-fully. He gave the impression, Meredith thought, of being horribly guilty. But of what?

'Nothing! Nothing happened! We … we got separated in the fog.'

Logan looked doubtful, but his next words were cut short by Professor Macaulay himself stumbling through the doorway. He was dishevelled and his eyes had a red-rimmed wildness about them. There were scratches on his face and blood on his shirt collar. When he saw Logan he stiffened visibly.

'My dear professor,' said Dr Jolly. 'Whatever has happened to you?'

'Damned fog!' The professor pushed his way through them to his bunk and threw himself down on it.

'You're bleeding,' Meredith said. 'Let me dress those scratches before they become infected.'

'Leave me alone, girl.' He flapped her away.

'What really happened?' Logan demanded harshly.

'Nothing, I tell you.'

'What did you do to the boy?'

The professor gave a sneer and looked across at Johnny, who shrank even further into his dark corner.

'What makes you think I did anything? Johnny is like a son to me. Is that old jealousy of yours making you imagine things again, Stuart?'

'Don't call me that. I disowned the name Stuart Macaulay the day you left me here to die.'

As a hush descended, with nobody daring to speak, there was a hue and cry from The Street and a rattle of stones as someone ran in the direction of their cottage. The steps halted outside, followed by a fierce banging on the door. It burst open. The young man who fell into the room was covered in grime and so breathless he could hardly speak.

'Logan!' He bent double in an attempt to regain his breath.

'Jamie Campbell, what is it man? What's happened?' Logan took the lad by the shoulders, gripping him hard.

'An accident, Logan! Yon stranger has fallen and hurt hisself real bad.'

'Does he mean Peter?' Meredith asked, her face blanching with concern for her friend.

'They're bringing him,' the young man said and seconds later a group of islanders entered the cottage, carrying the injured man between them in a plaid.

'Clear the table,' Logan instructed.

As Meredith whipped away cloth and dishes from the table she was relieved to see that it was not Peter who had had the accident, but the gillie, Frazier. He lay, grey-faced and moaning with pain; blood seeped through his trouser leg.

'A pillow for his head,' Logan said. 'I'll need scissors and dressings.'

When the cloth was cut away from the wound it was plain for all to see that the leg was broken.

'He needs a surgeon!' Meredith said.

'He has one,' Logan replied and there was a sarcastic laugh from Professor Macaulay.

'Is this another patient you're planning to kill with your ineptitude, son?' his father said in a loud voice.

Logan ignored him and looked at Dr Jolly. 'He'll need something for the pain,' he said. 'And you'll have to hold him down.'

Josiah Jolly nodded and unearthed a bottle of brandy from his bag. He uncorked it and held the bottle to the injured gillie's mouth.

'Here, Frazier,' he said. 'Drink as much of this as you can. It'll deaden the pain.'

Frazier gulped down the brandy, coughing and spluttering as he did so. Meanwhile, Meredith had unearthed their first-aid kit and sorted out some dressings and bandages.

'What can I do to help?' she asked Logan.

'Manufacture some kind of gag that he can bite on to so he won't bite through his tongue,' he told her. 'Then, if you, Doctor, and Jamie, can hold on to him while I put the bone back in place ...' He hesitated and looked over his shoulder at Johnny, who was staring with wide, shocked eyes. 'You, lad, go to Lachlan's cottage and ask him for wood that we can turn into leg splints.'

Johnny nodded and shot out of the door, grateful that he was not to witness the operation on Frazier's leg.

The brandy was beginning to take effect for Frazier was rambling and his speech was slurred and muffled through the gag that Meredith had placed between his teeth. 'Dinna worry, Professor, sir … I'll tell no one … ye hear … no one. I'll finish the job, honest to God I will … I'll—'

The words ended in a scream as Logan gripped the gillie's ankle and pulled on it for all he was worth. The two ends of the bone miraculously slipped back into place. Meredith felt faint at the sight, but recovered when Logan gripped her shoulder.

'No fainting on me now, woman,' he said brusquely. 'Have you any more of that brandy, Dr Jolly?'

The doctor handed over the bottle. Logan went to the roughly built dresser and poured an inch of brandy into six cups, handing them around.

'I never drink spirits,' Meredith said, her nose curling at the smell of the stuff.

'It's medicinal,' Logan told her. 'Drink it.'

Meredith started to argue, but her father, having already knocked back his tot, put his finger under her cup and pushed it towards her mouth.

'Do as he says, my dear. Doctor's orders.' Then he turned to Logan. 'That was good work, Logan. Are you a qualified surgeon?'

'I was, once.' Logan said. 'In a former life.'

In the background, a derisive laugh could be heard from Professor Macaulay.

CHAPTER 6

THERE HAD BEEN a good catch of fish that night, so the people of Hirta rejoiced. They came out into The Street and sang songs of praise to God. The sound could be heard up and down the hillsides.

'Flora will think it's her birthday,' Logan said, putting a large codfish in his bag, together with a lobster and two eels, and slinging it over his shoulder.

'Does that mean she'll forgive me for being late back for supper?' Meredith asked with a dimpled smile.

'Flora does not hold grudges.'

'She's a very special person,' Meredith said and he gave a slow nod of agreement. 'Logan, do you mind if I walk back with you this evening?'

He shrugged. It was a gesture of indifference and she would have preferred it had he shown pleasure in having her company. Perhaps she was expecting too much of a man who chose to live the life of a hermit.

She bade the others goodnight, extracting a promise from her father that he would keep an eye on Frazier in case he became feverish. Logan waited for her outside and began striding out the minute she appeared. The mist had dispersed, for which she was thankful, and the night was clear.

'Do slow down, Logan,' she said, running after him, trying to place her feet carefully on solid ground rather than the spongy marsh that was everywhere. 'With your long legs I find it difficult to keep up.'

He turned and looked down at her. For once his regard was neither cold nor hateful.

'You did well back there with the gillie,' he said. 'Some women would have lacked the courage.'

She fixed him with a challenging stare and asked: 'Is it true that you were a surgeon back on the mainland?'

His head lifted sharply and his eyes drifted away from her.

'Yes,' he said, starting to walk again, though at a slower pace.

'Then why on earth did you not continue? It's such a worthy profession.'

At first she thought he was not going to answer her. When he did eventually speak his voice was low and guarded.

'I operated on a young woman. It was nothing more complicated than a tonsillectomy. The scalpel ... my hand was jolted ... my elbow bumped by someone behind. The scalpel slipped and ... she died.'

'Oh! Oh, how tragic, but ...' Impulsively she reached out and caught his arm. 'It was an accident ... surely...?'

'They said it was carelessness ... that I was not worthy of my chosen profession.'

'Oh, but...!'

'I don't wish to discuss it,' he said, once more striding out so that she had no choice but to walk several paces behind him.

When they reached Flora's hut the old lady threw up her hands, smiling widely at the sight of the food with which Logan presented her.

'You will stay and eat with us, Logan,' she said, but Logan had no desire to linger.

'I have no appetite, Flora,' he said. 'I will repair the breach in the cleit wall so that your goats don't wander, then I'll go.'

'He has the head of a mule when the fancy takes him,' Flora said a few minutes later as Meredith watched the old woman skilfully scale and gut the cod.

'I found out today that he's a surgeon,' Meredith said. 'One of our party fractured his leg and Logan reset it without blinking an eyelid.'

'It is his skill as a surgeon, as well as his strength, that make the St Kildans accept him. There was a time, child, when they were ready to throw him back to the mercies of the sea.'

'Why was that?' Meredith asked, anxious to learn more about Logan and his mysterious past.

'We do not speak of the business of others,' Flora reminded her, gathering up the fish bones and the head of the cod and placing them in a cauldron. 'There, that will make a good soup for tomorrow. Tonight we will eat fresh fish. There is too much for one meal, so I will salt the rest and it will keep.'

She wrapped the fish steaks in sorrel leaves, seasoned with sprigs of thyme and poached them in goat's milk. It was delicious, served with boiled potatoes and seaweed bread. Meredith hoped that her father and the others had eaten as well as she, but doubted it. Mr Frazier, much as he was an unlikeable sort of fellow, had turned out to be a fair cook. However, with him out of commission because of his injury, it would fall to someone else to prepare the food. She couldn't see the professor offering to do it and her father, she knew from experience, was a disaster in the kitchen. She hoped that Peter or Johnny would save the day.

The meal over and the plates cleared, Flora presented Meredith with the task of some urgent mending, claiming that her old eyes could no longer see well enough and her fingers were not so nimble as they were when she was a younger woman of eighty. Among the items for repair were two men's shirts, needing buttons replacing and collars turning. Flora saw Meredith frowning at them and chuckled gleefully.

'No, I do not have a man secreted away, young woman,' she said. 'Those shirts belong to Logan.'

'But doesn't he have a wife to do his mending, Flora?' Meredith asked, remembering the child that called him 'Dada'.

'The girl he took for his wife is long dead,' Flora said, then looked annoyed at herself for speaking of things that did not concern her. 'No more questions, child. I am now going to sing you some old songs that were forbidden by the minister, for he saw them as pagan worship.'

'And now?'

'He is no longer with us, so we can discard his strict preachings. Listen well, now, for they tell of our history.'

And off she set in a clear voice with just the hint of a warble on the high notes. Although Meredith could understand not a word, the songs being in the ancient language of St Kilda and Gaelic, it was a pleasing sound and she wished there was a piano so that she could learn the music to them.

*

At the beginning of August there had been no school for a whole week while every man, woman and child were occupied in killing and salting the seabirds for the winter. It often seemed to Meredith that schooling on the islands took a lowly place on the list of essentials. The children were more often working than learning and the excuses for the school being closed seemed to outnumber the reasons for keeping it open.

There were times, though, when there was no question of priorities. Like the day when excitement rippled through the island as the boat, which had gone to Dun for the fishing, towed in behind it a thirty-foot whale that had been caught up in a cast-off fishing net. For once the islanders were not going to worry about shortage of food or oil or even rent to the island's landlord, for some time to come.

It had been a busy month with all hands helping to harvest the crops. The men had made several trips around the islands to pick up fulmars and kittiwakes, and Logan had gone with them. Meredith had bravely accompanied them once and saw how they scrambled over the high, vertical rocks like human crabs, snaring the birds and lowering them to the waiting boat. It filled her with admiration.

The only day the St Kildans did not work was the sabbath, on which day the party of Naturalists were treated to an additional sermon in English especially for them. It was a long and tiring business and Dr Jolly invariably fell asleep and had to be kept awake by a sharp jab from his daughter's elbow.

On the third sabbath of the month Meredith, having seen Logan several times with the child, plucked up enough courage to question him on the matter.

'Logan, who is the child I've seen you with?' she said. 'A pretty little girl with dark curls like your own.'

Meredith got the immediate impression that the question bothered him. His stony silence made her regret that she had spoken, but then he gave a long, indrawn breath and directed his response to the ground between them.

'She is called Fiona,' he said. 'Her mother died at her birth.'

'Is she your daughter? Flora said that your wife had died.'

His glance nearly cut her in half.

'Flora knows better than to gossip about my affairs.'

'I'm sorry,' Meredith said, feeling a humiliating flush creep up her neck into her cheeks. 'I didn't mean to interfere. It was just curiosity on my part.'

'There isn't anything about me that you need to know,' said Logan, lengthening his stride so that she was again obliged to trail behind in his shadow.

When they reached The Street the whole village seemed to be standing there looking out across the bay to the distant sea. The air was electric with expectation. Children played and laughed hysterically while the adults, their faces glowing with hope, spoke together in lowered voices.

Logan grabbed hold of the first lad he came across.

'Jamie, what is it? What's happening here?'

Jamie Campbell's eyes shone out of a rosy face. He pointed beyond the bay.

'Look you there, Logan!' he said, his voice high with emotion. 'There's a boat. A boat is coming!'

Meredith shaded her eyes and looked towards the hazy horizon. At first she could see nothing, but then she made out a smudgy shape that was soon recognizable as a steamship coming from the direction of Harris.

As the boat drew nearer there was great activity in the village. People scurried in and out of their houses and the cleits and soon the Street was lined with makeshift stalls displaying skeins of wool and woven goods, dried and salted birds and fish and gannet eggs by the score. It was as if the whole place had transformed itself into a market.

'What are they doing?' she asked Logan as they continued on to the Naturalists' cottage.

'The boat will be carrying tourists,' Logan said. 'They buy souvenirs and some of the items can be exchanged for things we need. Shoes for the children, school books, pieces of jewellery for the women, though not many of them have occasion to wear baubles.'

'They're so quiet,' Meredith said, 'and yet I can feel their excitement.'

'It's only the second boat to arrive at St Kilda this year,' he told her. 'You would be excited too if you spent your life here. There'll be some mail, too, no doubt. Families will learn who has died and who has been born and who has done what in the last few months. There will be dancing tonight and Lachlan will play his fiddle.'

'Oh, that's wonderful. And the people – the tourists? Will they stay on the island?'

'No, they will come and stare and pass comment as if the people here are freaks and cannot understand their language, but nobody pays them any mind. What they spend, what they bring to us, makes the living easier. Their ignorance is soon forgiven.'

As they approached the cottage, they could see that the gillie, Frazier, was sitting outside, taking the air, his splinted leg stretched out before him. Even in repose, for he seemed to be sleeping, he retained his sour expression.

'How is Frazier's leg faring?' Logan asked.

'I check it regularly,' Meredith told him. 'It looks fine and he is beginning to move about with the help of a crutch that Peter made for him out of driftwood.'

Frazier, when he had sobered up after the operation that saved his leg, had refused to have anything more to do with Logan. He spent most of his time hiding away in his windowless cleit that smelled of sheep and cow dung. It was only when he started to burn up with fever from an infection that he had allowed Meredith to come in and treat the wound with a healing potion made up by Flora.

'No more infection, then?'

'No. It's healing well. You did a good job on him, Logan. I don't understand why he isn't grateful. You could have left him to suffer and he would have lost the leg, but you didn't. What is there between you that makes him behave so appallingly?'

'For the answer to that question, Meredith, you must ask Frazier or the professor, but I suggest you would not be wise to do so.'

It was the first time Logan had called her by her given name and it pleased her. It had taken weeks, but at last he was beginning to mellow and seemed less and less like Professor Macaulay, which could only be a favourable sign. She had yet to see a real smile from him and hoped that she might see it before the year on the islands had run its course.

The door to the cottage opened as they reached it and Dr Jolly came out, stooping beneath the low lintel. He stopped to light his pipe, and then bade Meredith and Logan a good morning.

'Have you seen the boat arriving, Father?' Meredith asked. The doctor peered out to sea through the grey-blue tobacco smoke that drifted up before his eyes.

'Ay, lass. It looks as if it's causing great excitement in the village.'

'Logan says it will be bringing mail, among other things.'

'Well, that's good.' Dr Jolly sucked reflectively on his pipe, his eyes twinkling merrily at her. 'I've been wondering how your Aunt Agnes is getting along without us. No doubt there'll be a word or two from her, telling us how she's filled the house with bolts of new bombazine. I hate to think how much it will be costing me!'

Meredith laughed and explained to Logan, who was looking from one to the other of them curiously.

'My aunt, Logan, lives all her days in mourning. And, since she is a lady of style, it must always be the best bombazine material that she has her dresses made out of.'

Logan inclined his head and she thought she saw the shadow of a smile and a sparkle in his eyes, and was quite perturbed at the way it made her heart leap.

'Perhaps you should have brought the lady with you,' he said. 'A few months on St Kilda would have cured her of that habit.'

'On the contrary, Logan,' Dr Jolly said between satisfying puffs, 'my sister-in-law would have all the females on the islands dressed in the dreaded stuff. Agnes is a force to be reckoned with and no mistake.'

And then Logan forgot himself and gave a spontaneous laugh. It was, Meredith thought, such a pleasant sound and it transformed his face so much that she could not take her eyes from him. His father must once have looked just like that. What, she asked herself, could possibly have happened to change the man into the very different human being he now was?

'We have called a holiday today, Meredith,' her father told her.

'With the boat arriving and all chaos breaking out, it seems fitting that we make it a day of rest. After all, we've not had a proper day off since we arrived. Don't you agree, Logan? I'm sure you will appreciate some time off too.'

An hour later Meredith stood, arm in arm with her father at the water's edge to watch the first boatload of passengers disembark from the ss *Dunara*. Peter and Johnny were there too, but Professor Macaulay had chosen to go off by himself to the top of Conachair looking at the heathers and the rarer grasses such as Wavy Hair and Purple Moor grass. Both he and the doctor had been pleasantly surprised by the amount of flora on an island that seemed, at first glance, to be so desolate.

'Thank heavens the sea is reasonably calm today,' Dr Jolly said as they watched elegantly clad ladies clambering from the boat with little cries of indignation as they were carried bodily by the seamen in order to get them to dry land without getting their dainty feet wet.

'They look rather royal, Father,' Meredith said. 'Just look at the way they are inspecting the inhabitants. They might as well be at the zoo.'

'It's quite possible that there are one or two royals among them, my dear. I've heard that St Kilda is a favourite stopping-off place for members of the royal family.'

'Goodness!' Meredith scanned the column of passengers making their way slowly up The Street, hoping to recognize someone important.

'Isn't that Logan down there on the beach?' Dr Jolly pointed to a small group of men deep in conversation at the water's edge where a boat full of supplies had been dragged on to the sand.

Logan was easily recognizable by the fact that he stood head and shoulders above all the others. As she watched, the men shook hands and Logan came away, his muscles bulging with the weight of the boxes he carried. He was heading towards them when the uppermost box tumbled and emptied its contents at his feet.

He turned his head this way and that, looking for someone to help, but all the young men were busy with the tourists. Meredith picked up her heavy skirts and darted forward over the shingle. Logan saw her coming and his face relaxed into a rare smile that was mirrored in his eyes.

'You look as if you need help,' she said, coming to a halt at his side.

'What makes you think that?' he asked and the laugh-lines around his eyes deepened.

Meredith regarded the scattering of objects all around them. 'I hope nothing is broken,' she said, carefully replacing bottles and jars and tubes in the tumbled box.

'It's to be hoped not,' Logan said, watching her every movement. 'They're medicines from the mainland. Two of the passengers are doctors. It was lucky that I got to them before the nurse, or she might have thrown them back in the sea.'

'Doesn't she hold with modern medicines, then?' Meredith had come across the dour-faced woman on occasion and knew how formidable she could be.

'She is steeped in the old ways and refuses to budge from her beliefs. Between her and the preachers they send us it's a wonder the islands didn't die long ago.' Logan adjusted his hold on the boxes he was carrying and nodded to the now full box that Meredith held in her arms. 'Can you manage that?'

'Yes, of course,' she said. 'I'm not a weak wee lassie any more, as Lachlan used to call me.'

'No, I'll give you that. You've grown thinner with island living, but it suits you well enough.'

She would have preferred it if he had said she had grown bonnier, but she would have to settle for what he did say. Coming from Logan, it was a compliment.

They had just set out walking with their burdens when they were hailed from behind. They turned to see young Jamie Campbell waving his arms above his head. Where Logan was Jamie was never far away, it seemed. Like a lot of the younger boys on the islands, Logan had become the object of hero-worship.

As they watched, the boy ran forward, splashing through the foamy surf as he came running towards them still waving and shouting.

'What is it, lad?' Logan asked as the boy, breathing hard, sank to his knees before them.

'Logan, 'tis a letter.'

'A letter?' Logan frowned. 'For me? It's not possible. Who knows I'm—'

He stopped speaking abruptly and looked at the letter in Jamie's hand through half-closed eyes.

'No, not for you, Logan,' Jamie told him. ''Tis for Professor Macaulay, but it's all eaten into by the sea water, for the postbag was dropped and some of the letters were lost. See how the ink has smudged and the seal has come undone.'

Logan took the letter the lad held out to him and his fingers shook discernibly. He stared at his father's name, then turned it over carefully in his hands and stared even harder, his facial muscles going into spasm, his nostrils flaring.

'What is it, Logan?' Meredith touched his arm and he flinched as though her fingers had burned him. 'What's wrong?'

'This letter ...' he said, his voice a croak in his restricted throat, 'it's from my mother.'

''Tis for the professor,' Jamie repeated, looking with anxious eyes from Logan to Meredith and back again.

'Aye, Jamie. Thank you for bringing it to me.'

'You'll give it to Professor Macauley?'

Logan did not reply. Jamie nodded as if he had, then walked back towards The Street and the bustling crowds. He walked slowly, turning to look over his shoulder now and then, puzzled at Logan's attitude.

'I can give it to the professor, Logan, if you would rather not speak to him,' Meredith held out her hand, but Logan ignored it and slipped the letter into his pocket, his hand lingering over it before he once more took up his parcels and continued towards the Naturalists' cottage.

'I will deal with it,' he said over his shoulder, avoiding her questioning gaze.

'Professor Macaulay has gone up Connachair,' she told him. 'I imagine he will be there for the rest of the day, though he has asked Johnny to join him later. He could take the letter for you.'

'I'll deal with it, I tell you!' The good humour had disappeared and his face was once more tight with anger.

'I'm sorry, Logan,' Meredith apologized. 'I'm just trying to help.'

'It's not your business,' he said and she saw his back muscles flex as he pulled himself stiffly upright. 'Don't get involved.'

The sudden rebuff came as a heavy blow to Meredith's midriff. She had hoped that they were on their way to being friends, but it seemed that she was wrong. Logan was a man on the edge of something she did not understand. He obviously did not like anybody getting too close to him. He was a man of secrets and she couldn't help but wonder just how terrible those secrets were.

'Dr Jolly, will you take charge of these supplies for me,' Logan said, laying the boxes on the rough table in the middle of the cottage. 'My house is too far away to store all these medical supplies. I will take some to store for safety, but the rest must be close to the people who may have need of them.'

Dr Jolly changed his pipe from one side of his mouth to the other and contemplated the pile of boxes with interest.

'That will be no trouble, Logan,' he said. 'There's a small cleit at the back, next to the one used by Frazier. It's good and dry and not used for anything, though you have to go through the back of the house to get to it, so it's quite safe.'

Logan nodded and sorted through the boxes, transferring various items into a smaller box that was more practical for him to carry across the island to where he lived. He tied a piece of rope around it, fastening it securely, then slung it over his shoulder and made to leave.

Meredith looked up from the cauldron of fish broth she was stirring. 'Will you not eat with us before you go, Logan?'

'Thank you, no,' he said, regarding her with her sleeves rolled up to her elbows and a spoon in her hand.

Her cheeks were rosy from the sea air and the steam from the cauldron. A damp tendril of corn-coloured hair fell over her forehead. He wanted to go to her and push the hair out of her eyes, and maybe touch her velvety skin, tracing her fine features down to the hollow at the base of her throat.

Logan was so taken by the unexpected surge of desire that coursed through him that the earth seemed to tilt on its axis. He grabbed at the doorjamb to steady himself. He wanted to speak, but his tongue felt thick and paralysed in his dry mouth.

Meredith put the spoon down and came towards him, wiping perspiration from her brow with the back of her hand. He had never noticed how blue her eyes were, and in this dim light they were as navy as the midnight sky in winter that was lit by moon and stars.

'Logan, I'm sorry I annoyed you earlier,' she said, tucking back the very tendril of hair that he had longed to touch. 'My father always tells me that I am too curious for my own good.'

He gave a small shake of his head before he could reply to her and when he did force out the words he barely recognized his own voice, it was so ragged.

'You have no need to apologize, Meredith,' he said. 'It is I who should apologize. I should not have spoken to you in the way that I did.'

'It's already forgotten.'

Her smile warmed him. It was almost too much to bear. For five years he had lived on this island without so much as a thought for the girl he had left behind him in Edinburgh, or of the child bride he had felt obliged to marry out of compassion and duty. This gentle, unassuming English girl was awakening something in him that he had thought beyond recall. For this reason he had been cold towards her. However, it was becoming more and more difficult to retain a wall of indifference between them. Especially when she looked at him the way she was doing just now, with her heart in her eyes.

'Thank you,' he murmured, stepping back. He made a clumsy departure, nodding briefly to Dr Jolly as he went.

Outside, he came to an abrupt halt when he almost bowled Frazier over. The gillie had been trying to negotiate the uneven paving with his one good leg and the makeshift crutch.

'Och, will ye look where ye're goin', man!' Frazier bellowed, but pulled up short when he saw that it was Logan.

'How's the leg, Frazier?' Logan asked. 'You shouldn't be putting any weight on it yet. It's too soon for it to be properly healed.'

'A man could die of boredom while he's waiting,' Frazier said sulkily, then a change came over him. He lost the belligerence and his head hung down low. 'The leg's fine, Logan, thanks to you.'

'I didn't expect your thanks.'

'No, I daresay you didn't, not after ...' He twisted his head to the side and spat into the wind. 'I fair expected you to let me die. Others would have done in your situation.'

'We don't all have the killer instinct, Frazier. I swore the Hippocratic Oath when I became a surgeon. I still believe in it and save lives where I can. Even your miserable hide.'

The gillie gave a growl and Logan thought he was about to leave him without a further word; but no, the man swung towards him and hooked his thick pugilist's fingers into the front of his pullover. Logan prepared to defend himself from a blow, but instead the gillie put his face close to his, breathing out his foetid breath.

'I owe ye, Stuart Logan Macaulay,' the man said in a hoarse whisper. 'I owe ye a muckle. Because of that I'll tell ye that your father doesn't intend for ye to leave this island or for it to be known on the mainland that you're still alive. And if he has his way, you'll be dead before the twelvemonth is up.'

'So, he still has plans for my demise, eh?'

'As far as he's concerned, I never said a word. He has me trapped good and proper. I could go to the gallows for what I done in the past. He saved me then, but at a great price. You could say he owns me. I'm obliged to carry out his orders to the letter. I'm telling ye this so ye can be warned, that's all.'

'Don't think I haven't already worked that out, Frazier,' Logan said. 'But my father will find that I'm not so easy to get rid of, as you know, having tried to do just that five years ago.'

The gillie released his hold on Logan. His eyes had become cruel slits.

'Next time,' he growled through tightened lips, 'you might not be so lucky.'

CHAPTER 7

THE LETTER BURNED a hole in Logan's pocket with every step he took. He had considered going up Connachair to deliver it personally to the professor, but that was no more than a passing thought produced by the remnants of a conscience he had discarded long ago.

After only a few yards, he changed direction and headed towards The Gap, bypassing Flora's cottage. He could see the old woman in the distance, tending her goats. She looked up, waved, called his name, but he took no notice and marched on over the next rise, not stopping until he came to the house of stone and driftwood that he had built with his own hands near to the famed Callum Mor's ruined abode.

Even then he did not stop, but went on until he reached the top of the cliff that overlooked Glen Bay, where all he could hear was the breathy swish of the waves washing the beach and the cries of the seabirds in aerial display against a pale-blue sky. He sat down on a flat boulder and let the sounds engulf him. He remained like that for nearly an hour until he could stand it no more. He took out the letter and held it so tightly that his fingers cramped with the effort.

He knew it was wrong, but he could not stop himself extracting the sheet of paper he found inside the damaged envelope. It smelt vaguely of Devon Violets and a hazy vision of his mother in her favourite lilac dress with its frothy cream-lace collar floated before his eyes. He slowly unfolded the paper, dreading the reaction he would have as he read his mother's words directed to her husband, a man whose cruelty she had withstood and hidden from the world. Her pride and fear had even driven her to forbid each of her three children to speak of it for

in her eyes it would cause the family too much shame if the truth came
out.

His vision blurred as he tried to read Anne Macaulay's neat script
and he had to scrub at his eyes before he could focus. His mother's
handwriting was no longer as regular as he remembered it, and it
seemed that the letter had been written by a hand made unsteady by
the inner turmoil she was obviously suffering.

Dear husband, the letter began,
*It is with the greatest sadness that I must inform you of the death
of our daughter, Janet.* Logan's throat constricted and he threw
back his head with a groan of despair, reading on with difficulty.
*The asylum into whose care you delivered her informed me of
the tragedy this morning. The child she bore was born deformed
and did not survive beyond twenty-four hours. Janet, apparently,
took her own life while the balance of her mind was greatly
disturbed. They send their condolences and, if I could, I would
send you my broken heart, but all I can do is send, with this
letter, the tears that fall on it as I write.
God forgive us both.
Your obedient wife,
Anne.*

A gust of wind from the sea whipped across the cliff top and the
letter was almost wrenched from Logan's hand as if by divine inter-
vention. He held on fast to the page, crumpling it into a ball and went
to throw it from him, but stopped short and thrust it, instead, back
into his pocket. His very being was filled with an insupportable rage.
He would, after all, deliver the letter and watch the professor's face as
he read his wife's tragic words.

For a few moments he continued to sit, shoulders slumped, head in
hands as he murmured his sister's name over and over.

'Janet, oh my poor Janet! That it should come to this!'

The raucous cry of a raven from the direction of Connachair
pierced his grief and he turned to see the big black bird soar off into
the distance. In his mind he saw it as the evil spirit of the man he had

once called Father, and it seemed to be laughing, mocking him even. Fergus Macaulay, Logan thought, did not deserve to be on this earth. He was the Devil incarnate and he had to be stopped.

There was no one with more right to do the job than Logan and if it meant swinging for it at the end of the day, so be it.

Professor Fergus Macaulay was sitting on a mossy mound, his big frame perched on an artist's stool that looked far too small to accommodate his weight. He was surrounded by his notebooks and had spent some time scribbling notes and rough drawings on the pages, but he could not keep hold of his concentration. His mind wandered constantly. Yesterday a man from The Street had spat at him. He thought it was possibly the father of the girl over whom there had been trouble on his previous visit, though no words were exchanged and the girl herself no longer seemed to be present.

It was a blessing, therefore, that he had seen fit to bring Johnny, though the lad wasn't proving easy. He kept running away like a prepubescent schoolgirl. Idiot boy, did he not know on which side his bread was buttered? There was Peter, of course, but the professor had no fancy for him and had not even tried him out. No, it was Johnny who would give him the ultimate pleasure, once he got over his damned 'nerves'. A snivelling youth drowning in tears and mucous killed the joy and deadened the desire.

On the other hand, there was the Jolly girl, but that fool Stuart, or Logan as he now liked to be known, kept a close eye on her. He was probably saving her for himself, though he would have no shortage of pleasures among the simple island folk, male or female. Meredith Jolly would not be easy. She had an intelligence and a character that belied her female gender. A tough nut to crack, that one. He wasn't sure that Logan was man enough for her. Whereas he … A licentious smile spread over his face at the challenge he saw lying before him.

A rattle of stones made the professor look up sharply, to see Johnny climbing the hill with slow, hesitant steps. The boy was red in the face and his forehead glistened with perspiration, though the day had become cool and overcast. Macaulay could hear his laboured breathing and the choking gulp the lad took as their eyes met.

'So, you came, laddie!' A broad smile split Macaulay's face in two, but his eyes remained coldly calculating.

'Y-yes, s-sir,' Johnny stuttered as he drew to a halt, his knees sagging. 'Thank you, sir.'

'Bravo! Well, don't stand a mile off, Johnny. Come here and sit by me.'

Johnny's eyes went wild for a moment and he seemed unable to move. Then, slowly, he stepped forward, mopping his forehead with his handkerchief. He lowered himself to the mossy earth and sat cross-legged at the professor's feet.

'That's it, Johnny. Nothing to be afraid of.' Macaulay stroked the boy's hot face, brushed his fair hair out of his eyes. 'There now, that's better. I've been waiting for you. What kept you from me, eh?'

Johnny's jaws locked and he began to shake his head, then he remembered the one piece of news that he knew the professor would be glad to get.

'Pr ... Professor ... there were letters from the m-mainland ...'

Macaulay frowned, but looked vaguely interested. 'Is that so, Johnny?'

'Y-yes, sir and ... there was one for you.' The nervous quiver was still evident in Johnny's voice. 'But Jamie Campbell took it....'

'He did, did he?' The frown deepened. 'And what, pray, did Jamie Campbell do with this letter that was meant for me?'

Johnny gulped again and fingered his shirt collar that had become too tight for his turkey-red neck.

'I-I'm not sure, sir, but I think ...' he swallowed with difficulty, the words sticking in his throat, 'I think he gave it to Logan.'

As soon as he finished speaking he knew he should have kept his own counsel.

The professor's face became suffused with rage. He lunged at Johnny, taking a fistful of shirt front in his steely fingers.

'You *think*?'

'Yes, sir ... I mean, no, sir ...'

'Did he give it to Logan or not? Speak up, boy, if you value your hide.'

'Yes ... yes, he did, sir.' Johnny's fear mounted as the professor heaved him to his feet and gave him a violent shake that made his teeth rattle. 'Yes, sir, I'm sure he did, and Logan went off with it.'

'Hell and damnation!' Macaulay threw the boy to the ground and turned away, muttering to himself. 'I should have made sure that he could never be resurrected. That fool Frazier is a worthless imbecile. There'll be no mistake the next time. I'll see to that!'

'Sir!'

'What is it?' Macaulay followed the boy's gaze across the moorland where a tall figure was approaching with fast, businesslike strides. He shaded his eyes and squinted short-sightedly into the light.

'It … it's Logan, Professor, sir!' There was a tremor in Johnny's voice, for he sensed trouble. He knew also that Logan's presence had given him a reprieve from the professor's lascivious attentions and he silently thanked God for that. 'Perhaps he's bringing your letter, sir.'

Johnny's legs were threatening to give way. He sank to the ground and the professor stepped over him. His whole body was quivering with an unnamed fear as he watched father and son come face to face.

'I hear you have a letter for me … *Logan*!' Macaulay held out his hand, which Logan ignored.

'Johnny,' Logan said. 'Leave us. Go on, lad. Get back to the village.'

'I … I …' Johnny looked from Logan to the professor.

'Do as he says, boy,' Macaulay said in a low, menacing voice and the boy took off at an unsteady gallop. 'Where is this letter, then?'

Logan slowly retrieved the crumpled sheet of paper from his pocket, but did not immediately hand it over.

'It's from my mother,' he said. 'She speaks of my sister.'

'And what does she say of dear Marion?'

'Not Marion. Janet. What did you do to her, *Father*? Why did you put her into an asylum?'

'Ah, that! You know yourself that she was always … shall we say … nervous, to say the least.'

'Ay!' Logan's hands clenched into tight fists. 'It was because of you. You destroyed all our lives, starting with my mother.'

'There isn't a person in this world who would believe you, Logan. You put a stain on your own name when you killed that young woman.'

'I killed no-one and you know it. If the truth be known, you were behind the person who jostled my elbow during that operation.'

'They never found anyone who could corroborate your story.'

'You must have paid them well.'

Macaulay gave a sardonic smile. 'I was miles away at the time, converting heathens to Christianity. Besides, it was still your hand that held the scalpel.' He held out his hand again. 'Now, give me that letter.'

'Read it and burn in hell!' Logan said, throwing the scrap of paper into his father's face.

It fell at the professor's feet. Logan remained planted on the spot as his father stooped to retrieve it, smoothing it out in order to read his wife's words. The only change to his expression was a small twitch of his thick black brows.

'Dear me,' he said. 'Such a pity, but then she never was strong, either in mind or in body. Too much like your dear mother, I fear.'

The back of Logan's hand crashed into the side of the professor's face, sending him staggering backward. The blow caught the older man by surprise and he registered the shock like a man who had done nothing to deserve punishment.

'You didn't wield any weapon,' Logan said through gritted teeth, 'but you are responsible for Janet's death, just as I'm sure you were responsible for her state of health.'

'You're deranged, like your sisters. Perhaps I should have put all of you in the asylum. Long before I left home to come on this expedition, your sister, Marion, was showing signs of vegetation. There was no reasoning with her—'

'There wouldn't be! Not after you had abused her, like you abused Janet. Like you abused the girl I was forced to marry here on the island to save her from the shame of being an unwed mother. Did you know you have another daughter, eh? Fiona is four years old and I'd kill any man who touches her the way you touched her mother.'

'How is little ... what *was* her name again?'

This time Logan launched himself across the space between them and knocked the professor flying, landing on top of him with fists and legs flailing. The two men rolled over and over while Macaulay tried in vain to extricate himself, but Logan was younger and fitter. He fought blindly, punching without restraint. There was no way he was going to let Fergus Macaulay walk away.

Jamie Campell had delivered a second letter, this time a tale of woe from Aunt Agnes addressed to: *Dr Josiah Jolly and Miss Meredith Jolly.*

'Did the professor get his letter?' Jamie asked. 'I gave it to Logan this morning.'

'Father?' Meredith's eyebrows rose enquiringly and Dr Jolly sucked on his pipe reflectively before answering.

'Hmm,' he said, between puffing out blue smoke. 'Logan was last seen marching off with murderous intent in those devilish eyes of his. I would hate to get on the wrong side of that young fellow.'

'Where was he going, do you know?' she asked. 'To Connachair?'

'No. Towards The Gap. He has a house over there, as you must know.'

'Yes, but I've never been there, Father, as *you* must know.'

'I'm glad to hear it, daughter.'

Meredith had an uneasy feeling that she could not explain even to herself. She wrapped a shawl about her shoulders and set off, telling her father that she was going back up the hill. And it was to Flora's cottage that she headed first.

'What is it, child?' Flora had been on her knees tidying around her aromatic herbs, planting new ones, her hands thick with moist black soil.

'Have you seen Logan, Flora?' Meredith asked from the gate.

'Ay. He passed by here not too long ago on his way home, and in a foul mood he was too, by the way he walked. Might have had a poker up his rear end, so stiff was he. I called out but he never looked the side I was on, not even when he doubled back a few minutes later.'

'Which way did he go? Quickly, Flora. I have an awful feeling that Logan might do something drastic.'

Flora struggled to her feet and peered short-sightedly at Meredith.

'What kind of thing, child?'

Meredith tried to contain her impatience. Flora was not one to be hurried.

'There was a letter,' she said, 'brought from the mainland by the boat that put into the bay this morning. It was addressed to Professor Macaulay, but Logan took it. We know that there is already bad feeling between the two. I'm afraid Logan might do something he'll regret.'

'And what do you propose to do about it, child?'

'I don't know, Flora, but ...' Meredith cast around, hoping to see Logan somewhere on the hillside, but there was nothing but the wind riffling through the clumps of grass and a group of cormorants passing over, flying low.

'But you feel you must do something to save Logan from whatever is in his heart at this moment?'

A pregnant silence fell between the two women and Meredith felt tears prick behind her eyelids.

'Yes,' she admitted.

'Then go to him.' Flora's skinny arm snaked out. 'He went towards Connachair.'

'Thank you, Flora!'

'Child! Whatever they say about Logan, he is not a bad person, but I fear that what happened to him before he came to these islands poisoned his mind. It will take more than your good heart to mend him.'

Meredith was already running in the direction of Connachair. 'I know that, Flora,' she called out over her shoulder. 'But I have to try.'

'God go with you, child!'

With a stiff wind behind her, Meredith felt that her feet hardly touched the ground, and yet her flight to Connachair seemed to take for ever. Then suddenly she could see them. Two silhouettes on the high ridge. There was no doubt in her mind that they were Logan and the professor. And they were fighting. As she drew closer she could hear the blows and the guttural gasps accompanying each one as they found their target.

Meredith stopped and sucked air into her straining lungs. She shouted, waved her arms above her head, but the men were too embroiled in their battle to notice. After a few moments' rest, she pushed herself forward again, still calling out Logan's name.

He must have heard her, or seen her out of the corner of his eye, because he hesitated and that was when the professor threw a lucky punch at him, knocking him clean off his feet. The force behind the blow made Logan roll as he hit the ground. He rolled once, twice and Meredith's mouth dried, her tongue becoming paralysed as she saw him disappear from sight over the cliff edge.

'No! Oh, Logan, no!' she cried out as Fergus Macaulay stepped to the edge. She saw his foot lash out, then stamp the ground where Logan's fingers were clinging on precariously.

The professor, at last aware of her presence, whipped around, his face full of hatred as his hands reached out towards her. Meredith felt his fingers dig deep as he latched on to the front of her frock, bruising the flesh beneath, then she was flying backwards, arms spiralling ineffectually.

She hit the ground and felt every bone in her body jolt with the shock of the impact, but it was nothing compared with the shock of knowing that Logan was moments away from certain death. The cliff was high and sheer and below there were only jagged rocks and the cruel, raging sea.

Struggling back to her feet, she saw that the professor had returned to the cliff edge and was yet again trying to dislodge Logan's fingers where they clung desperately to the edge of the cliff. This was not a difference of opinion between father and son. It was going to be out-and-out murder, unless Meredith could put a stop to it.

'Stop!' she yelled at the top of her voice, then launched herself at the professor with all her might, not even thinking that they might all go over and be dashed to pieces on the rocks below.

Once again the professor fought her off so viciously that she was winded as she hit the ground. Everything went black for a brief second, then she was aware of hands pulling her back to her feet and Logan's voice in her ear.

'Little fool! Are you trying to kill yourself?'

How he had managed to climb to safety she didn't know and didn't much care. He was there, alive and clasping her in his arms as if he would never let her go. She was paralysed with fear and he had to lift her bodily, removing her to a place of safety. Behind them Professor

Macaulay stood, swaying, perilously near the sheer drop over which he had tried to send Logan to his death.

'Don't think you can go back,' he shouted raucously, his face purple with rage. 'You think you can ruin me and everything I stand for. Well, let me tell you, laddie, nobody would listen to you. They all believe that you are responsible for—'

Two things happened simultaneously. The professor choked on his words and clutched at his chest. And the ground beneath his feet gave way. As they watched, he gave a strangled cry and disappeared from sight. But like Logan, he was left hanging by his fingers to a crumbling ledge that seemed to disintegrate in his grip.

Meredith could imagine the turmoil that must be going through Logan's mind at that dreadful moment. A few short seconds ago his father had actually tried to murder him. Now, the tables had turned and it was Fergus Macaulay who was on the brink of death, but happily not at Logan's hands. Poetic justice was about to deal a final blow.

Logan muttered a curse and suddenly he was leaping forward, flattening himself on the ground and reaching desperately for his father's hands. Meredith let out a cry of alarm, thinking that the end had surely come for both men. There was a long moment when it looked impossible, then slowly and straining with every ounce of strength he had left, Logan pulled his father up and over the edge until he was clear of the drop, and safe.

Logan sat back on his heels, his breath rattling in his throat, his whole body trembling with the strain of his actions. He stared down at his prostrate father and his face was expressionless. Any hate or resentment that had been there previously, had vanished.

Meredith knelt down beside him and placed her hand on his shoulder.

'Oh, Logan!' she said, a sob in her voice. 'I thought you were going to kill him.'

He turned towards her and gave a wry smile. 'So did I,' he said; then every bone in his body appeared to sink inside his flesh and he wiped a shaking hand over his face. 'I've been dreaming of his death for five years. Longer if the truth be known. I always thought I'd be the one to kill him. When it came to the point I couldn't do it.'

'You don't owe him anything,' Meredith said. 'Not any more.'

She took hold of his shoulders and turned him to face her more fully, but he kept his head lowered until she leaned forward and placed a gentle kiss on his cheek.

'Why did you do that?' he asked hoarsely, fingering the spot her lips had touched. 'Am I to be rewarded for being a coward?'

'You're no coward, Logan,' she told him. 'You're a hero. You could have let him die, but instead you saved his life. You could never be like him. As Flora says, you are a good man.'

'Flora said that, did she?' He grimaced and wiped perspiration from his forehead with the back of his hand. 'What else did she say about me?'

Meredith shook her head. 'Nothing. You know how discreet Flora is.'

A groan from the professor, who was beginning to stir, made them look around sharply. He was mumbling incoherently and scrabbling about on the tussocks of stiff grasses and the pink sea thrift, but his limbs lacked coordination.

'What are we going to do with him, Logan?' Meredith asked as they both got to their feet.

Logan's arm came out and barred her from stepping any closer to the floundering professor.

'Keep your distance,' he ordered, 'I don't trust him. He wouldn't think twice about killing both of us.'

'Stu ... art!' The name fell from the professor's lips as if he was spewing out cotton wool. 'Help me!'

'Don't call me that name!' Logan said sharply then he went to stand over his father, legs wide, his body firmly balanced. 'Get up! Stop grovelling.'

'C-can't ...' The older man's face twisted horribly and a stream of saliva ran freely down his chin.

'If you're expecting sympathy from me, forget it, *Father.*' Logan bent forward and hooked a hand beneath the professor's armpit, in an attempt to drag him to his feet, but it was useless. 'Get up, damn you!'

But Professor Fergus Macaulay was incapable of standing. He sank back to the ground in a helpless heap and whimpered like a beaten dog.

'Logan, I think ...' Meredith dared to take a step forward and tugged at Logan's sleeve. 'I think he's had a stroke. Look at him.'

Logan took in the professor's twisted features and dribbling saliva for the first time.

'You're right,' he said, throwing his head back with a groan. 'Oh, dear God, I used to be a good doctor ... a good surgeon! I can't even recognize a cerebral accident any more when it happens right under my nose.'

'Don't blame yourself, Logan,' Meredith said. 'In the circumstances it's understandable. Now, let's see about getting him back to the village.'

'Flora has a donkey and a cart. We'd never make it otherwise.'

'All right. You fetch the cart. I'll stay with him.'

'No, Meredith, it's not safe. I can't leave you here.'

'Look at him!' Meredith indicated the professor, sprawled pathetically on the ground, burbling nonsensically and trying to focus without success. One eye seemed almost to have been dragged down from its socket over his cheekbone. 'He's helpless. Go on. I'll be all right.'

He hesitated, and then gave a nod. 'I can see now why your father is so proud of you,' he said.

'I'm lucky to have him as my father,' she told him with a warm smile. 'Bring a blanket back with you for the professor. It's turning chilly and I'm afraid he's in a very bad way.'

'You would do a kindness, even to a murderous scoundrel like him?'

'I wouldn't begrudge a humane act to a rabid dog,' she said. 'Besides, I feel that the stroke may be punishment enough for the professor's crimes, whatever they might be.'

'I'm not sure I agree there, but then you don't know him as I have known him.'

'Hurry, Logan. Fetch the cart.' Meredith took off her shawl and draped it over the semi-conscious professor. 'Go now!'

She had no idea how much time elapsed. The ground upon which she sat became hard and damp, so she got up and marched to and fro, stopping constantly to listen for Logan's return. She counted the seabirds that passed overhead until she became giddy. Now and then she edged forward and peered at the professor. He was still breathing, but it was impossible to tell the extent to which the stroke had affected him.

Meredith was shivering uncontrollably with the cold when she eventually heard the clip-clop of the donkey's hoofs as it plodded up the steep hill of Connachair. Between them, Meredith and Logan lifted the limp body of the professor on to the small dogcart and covered him with a heavy plaid. Logan was silent as they made their way carefully down to the village.

'Is he really such a bad man?' Meredith asked as The Street came into sight.

There was a long pause, then Logan flexed his shoulders and urged the donkey on. 'If you really knew him you wouldn't have to ask that,' he said. 'The world sees him as a great and talented man who can do no wrong. They do not see him in the confines of his own home, with his own family. All that happens in private is brushed under the carpet. My mother, my two sisters, they have kept their silence rather than suffer the shame of his sins being made public.'

'He was a cruel father?' At last Meredith felt able to pose some questions.

'More than just cruel.' Logan passed a hand over his troubled eyes as memories floated by inside his head. 'He abused and violated his wife and children … in more ways than one.' He gave her a quick glance. 'I had my suspicions, but my sisters would never speak of it to me. My mother had taught them the rule of silence too well.'

Meredith stifled a gasp of horror, realizing what truth lay behind his words. She could think of nothing more heinous than a father who used his daughters in such a way. 'Dear God!' she breathed from behind her hand. 'And you…?'

'I was more fortunate than my sisters,' he said, his voice fading into a guarded whisper. 'By the time I was growing up, he was travelling around the world, so I didn't see much of him. Oh, he wasn't averse to taking a stick to me when he was home. Marion, my elder sister, did her best to protect me … to her own cost, I fear.'

'And when you were older?'

'I left home to go and live with my grandfather. A better man never lived. He took me under his wing and was much more of a father to me than the professor ever was.'

He urged the donkey on even more with a touch of a stick on its grey flanks. By his side, Meredith fell silent, taking her cue from his grim expression.

How sad, she thought over and over again. Any other man would have broken under the same circumstances. But not Logan. He had the strength and the perseverance of a survivor. It was a characteristic that she could not but admire.

CHAPTER 8

CONTRARY TO ALL expectations, Professor Fergus Macaulay did not die. His collapse caused much talk and even more speculation among the St Kildans as well as his own group. One day followed another and everyone waited for his inevitable demise, but he kept on going against all the odds.

For the first two weeks after the stroke the professor lay abed, the village nurse and the gillie in attendance. During the third week his condition began to improve. They propped him up in a chair, where he sat limp of body, head lolling, mouth falling slackly open and dribbling. Whether he had any speech was debatable, for he ignored questions as if he were deaf and made no effort whatsoever to communicate.

'The poor devil just sits there like a vegetable,' Dr Jolly said and drew heavily on his pipe.

Meredith's fingers stopped tapping the keys of her writing machine and hovered in suspended animation. She could hardly believe what she was hearing.

'Poor devil, indeed!' she said acidly. 'I find it hard to be sympathetic towards such a horrid man.'

'And yet you yourself refused to leave him on the hillside to die.' Dr Jolly patted his daughter on the shoulder. 'Come now, girl. It's not like you to sit in judgement.'

'I know what he did to his family ... and to Logan.'

'We only have Logan's word on the matter.'

'Well, I believe him.'

'There are those in the village who think that he is no better than his father.' Dr Jolly's eyes narrowed.

'No! I can't believe that. Logan wouldn't … he *couldn't* be like that vile man!'

Meredith pulled out the paper from her machine with such force that it tore, which made her contrite. 'I'm sorry, Father, but I'm not in the mood for this work today.'

'Leave it and come back to it fresh tomorrow,' he told her. 'And Meredith, my dear, I do hope you are not sweet on Logan, eh? He's a man with too many secrets. It won't do you any good to become too close to him.'

Meredith dropped her head in her hands and massaged her forehead where a migraine was threatening to develop.

'Of course not, Father,' she told him without conviction, for she was already far too fond of the big, brusque Scot with the stormy eyes and a history that might not bear looking into. 'He hardly pays me any attention. When we're together I might as well be one of the men.'

There was a soft chuckle from Dr Jolly. 'I never thought I'd be glad to hear you say that! Peter now, he never stops paying you attention. The poor lad's properly smitten and you don't even notice. You could do worse you know, than set your sights on that young man. He comes from a very respectable family. His father is one of the richest men in the county of Durham.'

Meredith blinked up at him, rosy cheeked, feeling her headache getting steadily worse.

'Peter!' She hadn't even considered him as a prospective suitor, any more than his rather effeminate friend, Johnny. 'He's far too unworldly. I like him well enough, Father, but that's all. I'm sorry if I've been giving him any cause to think otherwise. Quite honestly, the last thing I want just now is a romantic attachment. I'm far too interested in what we're doing here.'

'Is that so? Well, I'm relieved to hear it.'

'Oh, yes! The islands are endlessly interesting.' Meredith was doing her best to change the course of their conversation. 'The other day the men let me go out with them in the boat and I watched them clambering all over the rock face of Boreray. They only caught twenty-five fulmars and a few Solan geese, but it was wonderful to watch them work. They move about like spiders. Logan is as surefooted as they are and …'

Her cheeks flushed crimson as she realized she had already steered the conversation back to the subject from which she was trying to escape. Her father smiled wistfully and placed a finger beneath her chin, turning her face up so he could see her eyes.

'Hmm,' he said thoughtfully. 'Something tells me that I'm a little too late with my paternal advice. Take care, my dear. On the islands he may cut a romantic figure, but back on the mainland it's a whole different world. You're feeling vulnerable at the moment, I fear. A new experience for you. Don't get hurt, eh?'

'I have no intention of getting hurt, Father,' Meredith said, hurriedly tidying up the papers that were strewn about the table and shuffling them in some semblance of order. 'I'm blessed with your good sense.'

'Ay, indeed.' He sighed. 'And your mother's lovely face and sensitivity. Let's hope that it's the good sense part of you that prevails.'

The days were still long, even at the end of August, but the weather had turned stormy, putting a stop to much of the work on the islands. The group of Naturalists often found themselves either lending a hand to the fowlers and crofters in between storms, or confined to the house when the gales were wild enough to lift the roof, and sometimes did.

On the first day of September the seas calmed, the sun shone and everyone got back to work with renewed vigour. Turf had to be cut for winter fuel, so school was not held that day. Lessons were few and far between at this time of year, it seemed, for one reason or another. There had been two outbreaks of influenza, necessitating the closing down of the schoolroom for three weeks on each occasion. And when work was heavy or fuel low the children were expected to do their share of the toil. It was a miracle that the young St Kildans received any education at all. It was a rare child indeed who left school being able to read and write.

On the few days each month that school was held, the pious teacher – for they were usually students of divinity taking a year off from their studies – would concentrate mainly on religious instruction, laying down the rules and regulations of the Church rather than the reading, writing and arithmetic in which the islanders were so lacking.

It was no wonder then, that on that brisk but lovely autumn morning, Meredith found a queue of villagers waiting for her as she reached the cottage. At the head of the queue was Jamie Campbell, more cheerful than she had ever seen him, as were the rest of the men and women who turned hopeful eyes on her as she opened the door.

'Good morning!' She smiled and nodded to each of them in turn.

There was a clearing of the throat and there was Jamie, pink-cheeked and cap in hand, looking eager to speak to her.

The lad was nudged forward by the two women standing behind him. He whipped off his cap, then cleared his throat noisily, but still he did not speak.

'What can I do for you, Jamie?' Meredith asked, feeling the welcome rush of heat from the interior of the house and the smell of burning peat mingling with the kitchen aromas of soup and baked fish.

'Did you see the boat, Miss Jolly?' he said, excitement making his voice sound younger than his twenty-one years.

Meredith frowned and shook her head. She had come down the hill from Flora's cottage with a mind too occupied to notice anything other than the sharp bite in the still air, and thinking how rare it was not to be blown and blustered about by the wind.

''Tis there on the horizon,' Jamie assured her and there were grunts of agreement from the islanders behind him. 'Only, you see, it won't be staying long and we wondered if you … well …'

He stopped, his embarrassment overflowing, and twirled his cap round and round in his calloused hands. There were murmurs of encouragement and people nudged one another, winking and grinning nervously.

'What is it, Jamie?' Meredith prompted.

'Och, I dinna ken. You're probably too busy to bother wi' us folk, but—'

'But it would be very nice if you *would* bother with us, Miss Jolly,' another, bolder crofter spoke out and heads nodded up and down the queue.

'I see,' Meredith said, slowly, not seeing at all, but not wishing to upset them. 'But what is it you want me to do for you?'

'We have relations, miss,' said a woman big with child and three little ones clinging to her skirts. 'In Australia ...'

'We have some in America!' said another.

'Ay, and in Tobermory and other places on the mainland,' announced a third.

Soon, they were all talking one on top of the other and Meredith had to hold her hands up to stop them.

'Please,' she told them, 'one at a time or the boat will have been and gone before I know what it is you want. Now, Jamie, you be spokesman.'

'Ay, thank ye, Miss Jolly,' Jamie said, expanding his chest proudly now that his embarrassment was leaving him. 'We've heard ye clacking away on that there writing machine of yours and we wondered if ... well, they say that it's better and quicker than hand-writing and most of us here can't write anyway, so ...'

'You want me to type some letters for you? Is that it?'

There was a unified 'yes'.

'Will ye do it, miss?' the older crofter asked. 'Will ye?'

'Of course I will,' Meredith agreed, happy that she could do something to help these good-natured people who had so little in their lives and expected less. 'Just give me a minute to set myself up inside.'

They entered, one by one, none of them wishing to intrude on the privacy of others. Not that there was much of a private or secret nature in the words they dictated. Most of the letters were short, lacking in real news, but it was important to them all that they were able to send word of their doings to their friends and relatives, even if it took months between letters.

'... sorry to tell you that your auntie died after I wrote to you two years ago. She was the one with a green eye and a wart called Jessie, married to your Uncle James who took a young girl for his wife, moved to Skye and we haven't heard of them since, though by the state of her when they left, you're probably an uncle yourself by now, twice removed....'

Meredith's fingers were tapping furiously as she tried to keep up with the old woman who was the last in the queue. It was almost lunchtime and everybody who wasn't out cutting barley and oats, making hay or storing feathers, was gathered down on the beach to welcome the passengers of the SS *Albatross*, now at anchor in Village Bay.

'... and your brother Finlay is wanting to get himself wed to one of the Macintosh girls from Harris. He doesn't mind which one and it'll be a good thing when he's married, for it might cure him of his boils....'

There were some cheers from the beach as the boat passengers disembarked.

'Right!' old Mrs McQueen reached forward and pulled the paper out of Meredith's machine, unable to wait any longer. She picked up a pencil and put a large X at the bottom of the letter. 'He'll know who it's from all right. Thank you kindly, Miss Jolly. I'm off now to sell my wool and my cloth to the tourists, for 'tis the best on Hirta, even though that Mrs MacDonald thinks differently.'

Meredith flexed her shoulders to ease her aching back. She was relieved that her session at the typewriter was over for now and planned to ask her father if she could have the rest of the day off. Too many days had passed when she had not had sufficient air or exercise.

'Time off, eh, daughter?' Dr Jolly looked at her sternly, but there was a half-suppressed twinkle in his eyes as he rocked on the balls of his feet, regarding her closely.

'I'll work doubly hard tomorrow, Father,' she promised him. 'It's such a lovely day. I thought I might take a picnic lunch up to Ruaival and do a little sketching.'

'They say that great minds think alike.' Josiah Jolly beamed at her. 'Take enough for two. Young Peter went off this morning in that direction and left his lunch behind.'

'That's not like Peter,' Meredith said. 'He's usually so well organized.'

'Aye, but he's been a little distracted of late.'

'Oh, I wonder why that is?' Meredith hadn't noticed anything untoward, though she had to admit that Peter was so quiet and distant that his presence was far from remarkable.

Her father gave her a strange look as if he could not comprehend her. He picked up his pipe and signalled to her to accompany him outside so that they could speak in private, away from the others.

'Now, girl,' he said when they were alone and the door was closed behind them. 'Something tells me that you've been working too hard.'

'I'm fine, Father,' she said with a laugh. 'I'm really enjoying the work and I'm getting used to the harsh conditions. Flora is quite a character and although she can be a little mysterious and brusque, she looks after me well and keeps me amused with all her folk tales about the islands.'

'Well that's good and I hope you are writing everything down that she tells you. Since the professor's stroke it looks as though the book we'll produce from the expedition will be largely produced by you and me.'

'Is he any better, do you think?' After the fight on the cliff top Meredith had kept her distance from Professor Macaulay. She found it difficult to feel sorry for the man after he had tried to murder his only son, and who would probably have murdered her too, if he had had the opportunity.

'He's improving slowly,' Dr Jolly said, 'but this is about you, Meredith. You know, my dear, there is a life beyond our work with the flora and fauna and it's time you—'

'Settled down? Marriage do you mean? But I'm happy as I am.'

'You can enjoy the best of both worlds, if only you open your eyes and see what's happening around you. Haven't you noticed that Peter is head over heels in love with you? I do believe I've hinted at it before.'

Meredith's lips puckered as she grimaced at her father.

'Oh, Father, really!'

'Yes, really. He has already spoken to me and I have given him my blessing, but told him that he will have to win you over. Something tells me that he's got his work cut out.'

'He has indeed! I like Peter immensely, but ...' Meredith drew in a breath and held it before letting it out again slowly. 'I don't see him at all as a prospective husband. A friend, yes, but that's all. Besides, I think he is rather too close to Johnny for my liking.'

'Ah, Johnny! Yes, there's a young man with problems, but I think Peter is just being supportive. Actually, Johnny seems to be a bit more settled now.'

'Yes. Strangely enough, he's looked much happier since Professor Macaulay had his stroke. I do believe he was afraid of that man.'

Dr Jolly frowned and sucked meditatively on his pipe, sending clouds of smoke up into the atmosphere. Father and daughter exchanged glances.

'Anyway,' he squeezed Meredith's hand, 'take the rest of the day off. Go and find Peter and ... well, it's up to you, of course, but be gentle with him. He hides his feelings like many of us men, but I think his heart is vulnerable where you are concerned.'

'Don't worry, Father. I'll be kind ...' she gave him a coy look '... but firm. He's not the man for me, of that I'm sure.'

The doctor gave a shrug that said he wasn't convinced. She knew exactly what he was thinking. He wanted to steer her away from any kind of involvement with Logan and he was probably right. The trouble was, her mind and her dreams were full of Logan and she was having the greatest difficulty keeping him out of her heart.

Ruaival was the old Norse name for 'red hill'. Meredith saw no red in the hill that she climbed, but it was the best place to sketch the Dun Passage and the tiny island of Dun itself. It was also very historic, for it was here that was found the Mistress Stone and this was what Meredith searched.

She had so far filled two sketchpads with drawings of plants and one with studies of the few mammals on the islands, such as the St Kildan fieldmouse, which was known as the Viking mouse; the very special primitive Soay sheep and rams with their dark coats and sweet faces and, of course, the birds: gannets, fulmars, puffins and so many more that inhabited the islands and were an important food and oil source for the inhabitants.

Now, it was the turn of the geology of the islands and, on hearing so much of the Mistress Stone, Meredith was anxious to make it the subject of her first sketch in a new pad. According to local legend, when a man proposed to a woman the whole village gathered around the Mistress Stone, where he had to demonstrate his manhood and climbing skill by placing one foot in front of the other, toe to heel, and then, balancing only on one heel, bending forward, he must place his clenched fists in front of his feet on the rock. After a successful and fearless performance he was 'accounted worthy of the finest Mistress in the World'.

Such a romantic notion, thought Meredith, as she chose her best vantage point and assembled her painting tools in order to best capture the characteristics of this symbolic rock. The day was perfect, the air was clear and there wasn't too much wind, though she still had to weigh down the blanket she was sitting on with large stones to stop it from taking flight. She was glad that she had taken to wearing her hair in a long plait. Some short tendrils escaped and blew across her eyes, but if she turned her face more into the wind she could cope with that.

As always, at the moment before her pencil or brush touched the virgin paper Meredith felt an excited lift beneath her ribcage. She loved sketching and painting more than anything else, except perhaps marching briskly over the fells and moorlands, whether she was in Northumberland or here in St Kilda.

Her preliminary drawing of the Mistress Stone was finished in minutes. It was a huge slab of rock, high against the skyline, which had been laid across two pillars like a lintel stone. She could well imagine how dangerous it would be to perch on the top of it, but Flora assured her that the bravest young men on Hirta still did this to prove their love for the lady of their choice.

'Once a man does that,' Flora had told her, 'risked his life for the one he loves, she is obliged to say yes.'

'Did any man do that for you, Flora?' Meredith had asked and saw a dark cloud pass over the old woman's countenance.

'Aye, there was a man, once,' Flora said, her eyes staring into the middle distance as she remembered. 'He was a good man, too, and I had turned my back on him for many a year, since we were wee bairns together. But he was determined to have me, so he climbed the Mistress Stone for me and the whole village turned out to see him do it.'

'How wonderful! And did you marry him?'

'I married no one, child.' Flora picked up the edge of her apron and dabbed at her moist eyes. 'We watched him climb, and then we all saw him fall. Right from the top, he fell, like a gannet diving into the sea. Only he landed on the rocks below and was dead before I could even say I would marry him.'

Meredith sorely regretted asking the question. She had assumed that a woman as old and as wise as Flora must have been married at some stage in her life. The title of Mistress MacInnes accorded to her was obviously out of respect for her great age and nothing to do with her marital status.

With a sigh, Meredith dipped her paintbrush in a jar of water and held it poised over her palette of colours. In this light, with the sun behind it, the stone looked almost blue. She touched the fine squirrel-hair brush to a square of indigo and started carefully working in the shadows, looking up constantly so that she would record the contours correctly.

The work on the stone was almost finished when she looked up one last time, thinking that the hour was late and she should stop to eat something before continuing. That was when she saw something moving just below the stone where the rocks were almost vertical. It was difficult to be sure, because there were no bright colours, but she was almost certain that there was a man up there.

Meredith got to her feet, moving forward, shading her eyes and squinting into the distance. It wasn't so very far, but the light was blinding. Curiosity got the better of her and she started out towards the base of the stone, thinking that to see this spectacular, historic event was something of a bonus. She even thought to carry her sketch-book with her, for this was something her father would want to include in their study of the islands.

'Hey, there! Meredith!'

She spun around at the sound of thudding feet coming up behind her and saw Johnny, red-faced and arms flailing as he tried to catch her attention. It didn't take him long to reach her, but he was so out of breath he could hardly speak.

'Johnny, what on earth is wrong?'

Johnny bent almost double, drawing in raucous gasps of breath and coughing each time he tried to speak.

'Peter!' he managed to get out at last. 'That's Peter up there ... on the Mistress Stone.'

Meredith looked back at the stone and could now clearly see a figure clinging on to the vertical face of the rock supporting the perilous stone perch at the top.

'What? Is he mad?' she said. 'Why is he doing it? Is he possessed or something? He'll kill himself!'

Johnny gulped and nodded, perspiration dripping from his nose. His narrow chest wheezed as he desperately sucked air in to his lungs.

'It's you, Meredith,' he croaked out. 'He's doing it for you.'

The stunned silence that fell on Meredith's ears was broken by the harsh cry of a fulmar passing overhead. For a moment she thought it was Peter crying out as he fell, but no, she could still see him clinging to the rock face like a limpet.

'He's a fool!' Meredith immediately felt guilty, because Peter wasn't a fool and she knew it. He was a very nice, gentle young man and he didn't deserve to die because of her.

'He's in love,' Johnny said morosely. 'If he's a fool, then he's a damned lucky fool and I wish ...'

Perhaps it was the wind, which had risen considerably in the last few minutes, but his eyes seemed full of water.

'He's not moving,' Meredith said, holding her breath, for Peter had not moved an inch while they were talking. 'He must be in trouble.'

They moved forward until they were close enough to call out to the rigid figure on the rock. Meredith held back, not wishing to cause him embarrassment lest it make him fall. It was Johnny who went closer and spoke to his friend. Peter looked so small and vulnerable up there, and even at that distance, Meredith could tell that he was afraid.

Johnny came running back, after having shouted up to Peter several times without response.

'He's frozen,' he said. 'He can't move a muscle by the look of it. He's too scared even to speak. What do we do now?'

Meredith didn't take very long to reflect on the question. She cast about her for a few seconds, then gripped Johnny's shoulder.

'Johnny, go and get help. I saw men cutting turf on my way here. They'll know what to do.'

Johnny nodded and set off at a run. Meredith edged as close to Peter as she dared. The rocks under foot were like knives. One slip and it could injure her for life. As for Peter, if he fell now it was almost certain death and she would not want that. Not for all the world.

Dear God, but he looked petrified. He mustn't let go, he mustn't fall. She would never forgive herself if he got killed in an attempt to gain her favour. What a waste that would be.

'Hold on, Peter!' she shouted. 'Help is coming.'

At the sound of her voice Peter's head jerked, the movement making his position even more dangerous. A shower of stones came down as his foot slipped, then he searched to find purchase again.

'Meredith!' Her name was caught and whipped away from his lips by the wind. 'I'm sorry. I just ...'

'Don't say anything! When we get you down from there we'll talk, Peter. I promise you, we'll talk.'

The minutes stretched out and Meredith's neck became stiff from dividing her time between watching Peter and looking for the help that must surely come soon. It was perhaps only a few minutes since Johnny had rushed off, but it seemed much longer than that. She did not know how much longer Peter could hold on. Between the cries and constant aerial manoeuvres of the seabirds she heard him groan occasionally. Any moment now he could come plunging down and she would regret not paying him more heed. How could she have been so cruel as to ignore him?

'I can't hold on much longer, Meredith!' His voice was no more than a desperate croaking whisper on the wind. 'My fingers are numb. I can't feel my feet.'

'You must hold on! For God's sake, hold on!'

She was about to jump forward, her mind in turmoil, but a pair of strong hands grabbed her and swung her off her feet.

'Stay back, little fool!' Logan put her down and steadied her before turning back to Peter. 'What's the idiot boy doing up there? No, don't waste time telling me. Jamie! The rope.'

Jamie Campbell threw a coil of stout rope. Logan caught it and slung it around his shoulder, then, without further words, he started the ascent towards the Mistress Stone. Meredith looked away, unable to watch, fearing that the worst would surely happen before Logan got to Peter. Johnny had returned and was down on his knees beside her, panting heavily. She gripped his shoulder.

'Thank you, Johnny. I just hope we aren't too late.'

'If anybody can get him down from there it's Logan,' Johnny said between exhausted gasps. 'It was lucky he was with the turf-cutting party.'

'Yes,' Meredith murmured. 'Very lucky.'

Logan was climbing the rocks, finding handholds where there appeared to be none. All the while he was speaking to Peter in a low, encouraging voice. At a certain level, he could go no higher and had to work his way horizontally around the rock until he was directly beneath Peter.

'If Peter falls now he'll take Logan with him,' Johnny said in a fearful whisper.

'Oh, don't!' Meredith clasped a hand over her mouth to stop the scream that was getting ready to escape if she saw either of the men lose their hold. 'Dear God, don't let him die! Please don't let him die!'

She realized with horrified shock that the life she was begging God to save was not, in fact, Peter's, but Logan's. Silently, she added a remorseful: *I don't want either of them to die!*

Slowly and with what seemed like superhuman strength, Logan was hauling himself up beside Peter until he was almost on top of him and hanging from the highest point with one hand, while reaching out to Peter with the other.

And that was when Peter let go. There were gasps all around as he started to fall.

'Oh no!' Meredith shouted, now clamping both hands over her mouth.

It looked impossible, but Logan's free hand had shot out and grabbed the younger man's jacket. Peter was hanging like a limp rag doll for a brief few seconds, then Logan was pushing him up to the flat surface of the Mistress Stone with all the strength he could muster.

Once Peter was securely on the top, Logan pulled himself up beside him and gave the spectators down below a brief wave.

'Och, he's a fine man, yon Logan,' Jamie said, then he, too, was scaling the rock to the midway point.

Logan tied the rope around Peter and began lowering him down. It was a bumpy ride because Peter seemed unable to help himself and Meredith cringed at the thought of the bruises he was going to have to show for his crazy escapade.

Halfway down Jamie took charge of Peter, together with one of the crofters who had come with them. Then it was Logan's turn to descend, which he did amazingly quickly as though it was nothing more than a moorland hillock.

Peter's legs were trembling visibly when he walked the few yards to where Meredith and Johnny stood waiting. He gave them a weak smile and Meredith surprised him by throwing her arms around him and hugging him tightly.

'Oh, Peter, I thought we'd lost you!' she exclaimed and, over his shoulder she saw the glowering face of Logan as he coiled the rope.

'I hardly think that it was an act that deserves reward,' he said gruffly, then walked away, followed by Jamie and the crofters, their excitement for the day over, happily without mishap.

CHAPTER 9

'WELL, WASN'T THAT fun?' Meredith said teasingly, trying to make light of what had just passed, though her own heart was still palpitating at the thought of what might have happened.

'Oh, lor', she calls it fun!' Johnny laughed weakly and mopped his brow with his handkerchief. 'I thought he was gone for sure.'

Peter sat on the ground, his arms hanging limply over his knees, his head drooping low between them. He was still shaking like a leaf and it would be a while before he got any strength back in his legs. Meredith didn't care, as long as he was safe.

'I'm sorry,' he kept whispering to the ground, over and over again. 'I'm so sorry!'

'You frightened the wits out of us, my friend,' Johnny said. 'What on earth were you thinking of? There aren't any gannets up on the Mistress Stone. Anyway, it's not the right stone to climb if you want to prove your worth as a provider.'

'What?' Peter's head shot up.

'No. You have to perch on the tip of the Lovers' Stone and that's a lot more dangerous that this old beauty here.'

'Don't even think of it, Peter,' Meredith said quickly, sitting down beside Peter and indicating to Johnny to join them. 'One flirtation with death is one too many. Next time you might not be so lucky. Here, let's eat something before we head back.'

She delved into her bag for the food she still had and shared it out between them. Peter, however, declared that he wasn't hungry and gave his share to Johnny, who seemed to have refound his appetite these days. For her part, Meredith suddenly felt ravenous and enjoyed the coarse-grain bread with a slab of Flora's ripe goat's cheese and some crisp, peat roasted puffin.

'I still can't get used to eating these seabirds,' Johnny said, inspecting the flattened carcass in his hand and wrinkling his nose, 'but sometimes they're awfully good.'

'I have to admit,' said Meredith, 'that the puffins are my favourite bird. They're so sweet and comical. Served up as food they rather resemble kippers.'

'Taste like them, too,' Johnny said, eyeing a second piece greedily. 'Anybody mind if I help myself to the last bit?'

'You're not frightened of being an old maid, then, Johnny?' Peter said, reviving and getting some of his normal colour back.

Johnny's cheeks flushed crimson and he stared off into the distance, ignoring his friend's remark and nibbling reflectively on his puffin. Then, quite out of the blue, he stood up, wiped his fingers and marched off.

'I don't think I'll ever get married,' they heard him say, the words muffled.

Meredith watched him as he slowly plodded down the hill towards Village Bay, gradually disappearing from sight. She couldn't help thinking that he was a particularly sad young man with troubles that she hardly dared guess at. Peter, on the other hand, although shy and quiet, was far more level-headed, despite this last foolish escapade. She turned to him now and found him watching her.

'A penny for your thoughts, Peter,' she said with a cheery smile. His face crumpled into a frown.

'I was just ... well, you must think I'm some kind of idiot to do what I did just now,' he said hesitantly.

'Yes, but a very nice idiot, really,' Meredith said and saw the look of relief he gave her. 'Now, what was that all about?'

He heaved a great sigh and scrubbed a hand over his face, smearing the dirt that was already there.

'I was practising,' he said. 'The thing is, I have a fear of heights.'

'In that case it's a good job you chose the Mistress Stone', she said, 'instead of the Lovers' Stone. You might not have lived to tell the tale.'

'I wanted to prove something ... to you, Meredith.' He cast his eyes down to the ground and she had to hold back because he looked so pitiful sitting there that her natural instinct was to give him a big, sisterly hug.

'You have absolutely nothing to prove to me, Peter,' she told him. 'I already like you and think you are ... well, you are so *nice*.'

'Only nice? I mean ...' He was floundering and his face grew pink with embarrassment. 'I did hope that you could ... well, that we could ...'

'Peter, please don't misunderstand,' Meredith said, placing a hand on his lean shoulder, thinking that he could do with some fattening up. 'I want us to be friends. Good friends.'

'Is that's all?'

'Yes ... no! Oh, I don't know!' She broke away from him and paced up and down. 'I'm a little confused inside at the moment, Peter.'

'It's Logan, isn't it? I've noticed that you never look at me the way you look at him.'

Meredith stamped her foot impatiently, raising a cloud of dust. 'I wasn't aware, Peter, that I was looking at anybody in any particular way. I came here to help my father and, quite honestly, all I'm interested in is my work.'

'Are you sure?'

'Yes, of course!'

'Then why do I feel that I have to compete for your hand?'

'That, Peter, is something you must decide for yourself.' Meredith closed her eyes as her face puckered into an expression of self-loathing. 'Oh, I'm sorry! Don't let us fall out over this. Come on. Let's get back to the house. There are still one or two hours of daylight left and I can type up my father's notes.'

Meredith set off at a brisk pace, leaving Peter to follow behind. He did so, slowly, showing no desire to catch up with her. He was probably still suffering from the shock of his perilous adventure. And the chagrin of having failed before her eyes.

As the house came into view, she turned and waited for him. He was marching along, head lolling from side to side, eyes fixed on the ground. As she watched, he muttered something under his breath and kicked out viciously at a stone. The stone bounced a couple of times, then rolled a few yards before bouncing off Meredith's foot, making her jump.

Hearing her gasp, Peter looked up in horror.

'I'm sorry! Ah, God, Meredith, I can't seem to do anything right when I'm with you.'

'Maybe you're trying too hard,' she said with a sympathetic smile.

'Your father thinks I'm not trying hard enough,' he grumbled, his mouth downturned at the corners.

Meredith sighed, not knowing quite what to do with him at this moment. He seemed to think he had to compete with Logan for her affections. If he had not mentioned it she might not be thinking as she was just now. The fact that she blushed every time she mentioned Logan's name was disturbing. Just the very mention of him stirred up a fire inside her, yet when she was with him she kept telling herself that he was the last man on earth she should be attracted to. If, indeed, attraction was the emotion she was experiencing. He was, after all, the son of Professor Macaulay, and he must have inherited some of his father's bad traits.

'You're wrong, Peter,' she said with an authority she did not quite feel. 'My father's wrong too. And more than that, Logan is wrong, if he thinks ...' Her words tailed off and she shrugged her shoulders. 'Oh, never mind.'

Then they were walking together side by side and when Meredith's foot slipped on a mossy stone Peter grabbed her hand to steady her. He didn't let go of her until they reached the house. Strangely enough, she found the contact more pleasing than she would have expected.

'Tell me what you want me to do, Professor!'

Frazier stalked around the slumped figure of his master like a prowling leopard weighing up his prey. The professor's one good eye followed him. The slack mouth moved, struggling to form words, but it was too much. Frazier had no doubt that Macaulay understood everything that was said to him, but he was unable, or unwilling, to make any reply.

A small gurgling sound escaped from the professor's throat, but it was unintelligible. Frazier was frustrated. He did not possess a brain that enabled him to work things out for himself. Tell him what to do and he would carry out the instruction to the letter. Thinking and planning were not his greatest strengths.

The one important item exercising his mind at the moment was whether the professor was still able to guarantee his safety. If not, Frazier could very well end up in prison or on the scaffold. As long as they were here on this island he was out of danger, but their time on Hirta was perhaps beginning to run out. The doctor was already talking about cutting their stay short if a boat was by chance to come into the bay earlier than their scheduled departure date.

'Don't do this to me, sir!' Frazier rounded sharply on the sick man with a glint of desperation in his eyes.

He took the professor by the shoulders and started shaking him vigorously. Fergus Macaulay looked like a rather oversized rag doll. His good eye closed, but the other stayed wide open, fixed that way by the stroke. Globules of saliva escaped from his slack mouth and splashed the face of his gillie.

At that precise moment, Meredith happened to stroll around the corner of the house and was horrified at what she saw.

'Mr Frazier! Good heavens, what are you doing? The professor is paralysed.'

'He can speak, I know he can!' Frazier looked at her over his shoulder with a madness in his expression she had not seen before; it unnerved her.

'I don't think so,' she told him firmly, but her voice shook. 'Now please stop doing that. It's to no avail … and it's cruel!'

Frazier stared at her, his eyes bulbous like shiny glass marbles, then he let go of the professor. The man fell back in his chair with a breathy grunt and lay there like a dead man. Meredith looked at Fergus Macaulay's waxy skin with traces of purplish-red veins and felt a sudden rush of sympathy for him.

A second later, the sympathy dissipated when the professor's good eye shot open and fixed upon her, dark and malevolent. He grunted again and it ended in a moist expiration of air from his struggling lungs. One hand shook discernibly as he struggled to raise it, but all he could manage to raise was the long, bony forefinger. And it was pointing at her.

'What's he trying to say?' Frazier asked, sounding near to hysteria. 'Tell me, woman! What does it mean?'

Meredith shook her head and took a step back, her stomach lurching with unrecognizable fear. How could this man, this pathetic half-dead human being, fill her with so much terror and loathing.

'I don't know, Frazier,' she whispered hoarsely.

Frazier's eyes widened as he looked beyond her, then she felt the warm presence of someone standing close behind, so close that as she stumbled an inch or two back she collided with a hard ribcage. Hands gripped her upper arms, steadying her.

Even when Logan released her she could still feel the impression of his steely fingers bruising her flesh.

'Stay away from him,' he said in a low voice full of serious warning. 'Stay away from both of them, Meredith, if you value your safety.'

'Your father can do no more harm to anyone,' she said, rubbing furiously at her arms. 'Look at him. He's helpless.'

'Don't waste your pity on him. He's the Devil's advocate and the Devil always looks after his own. Isn't that true, Frazier?'

The gillie had straightened and backed off, but now that Logan was speaking to him he sank down inside his skin like a cowering animal expecting a beating. He scrubbed around his bristly face with a rough, dirt-ingrained hand, but refrained from any response. Unable to meet Logan's piercing gaze, his eyes wavered from left to right, then returned to the professor as if seeking some instant solution. No solution was forthcoming. Frazier turned on his heel with a snarl and marched off.

Meredith felt a streak of cold rain fall on her hand, then more drops, pattering all around. She could see the rain bank coming in from the sea like a great grey pall and a freshening wind was tugging at the skirts around her ankles.

'We must get the professor into the house,' she said, stepping forward hesitantly, knowing she could not do it alone, for although he had become a shadow of his former self since the stroke, he was still a big, heavy man and, unable to move himself, he was a dead weight.

She looked at Logan, but he had already turned and was striding away from her.

'Logan, please…! He'll catch pneumonia and die!'

'Let him!' was Logan's reply and he quickened his pace, head and shoulders hunched against the driving rain.

She could not believe that he could be so callous, no matter what his father had done. Then she remembered the little he had told her about what he and his family had suffered at the hands of this cruel, amoral man.

'He's right,' she thought. 'It would be a blessing for all concerned if the professor died here and now.'

Meredith looked at the sick man and Fergus Macaulay looked back at her, his glistening head wobbling uncontrollably. It was impossible to distinguish the rain from the saliva running down his face. Rain diamonds glistened on his woollen shawl. He seemed oblivious of his sodden state. The pathetic sight of him made her heart contract with unbidden pity.

She considered the situation and wondered whether she could manage to drag him to his feet. It was just possible that he could walk the few steps to the house with her support. However, when she approached him, some unseen force took hold of her body and she could not lay her hands on him. Not while that one evil eye was upon her.

'Need a hand there?'

She spun round with a gasp, then let out a sigh of great relief when she saw Peter and Johnny hurrying from the beach hauling full collection bags between them. They had been out searching for shells and pebbles and one of the bags would undoubtedly contain seaweed and other plants that grew along the shores of the island.

'Bless you!' she smiled radiantly. 'I couldn't be better pleased to see the pair of you. Can you carry the professor back into the house? I'm afraid he's already soaked through.'

'So are you, by the look of it. Here, Johnny, grab the other side of the chair and try not to topple him out.'

She saw Johnny hesitate, but then he put down the collection bags and helped Peter lift the professor in his chair and put him back inside, where it was warm and dry.

'Why do you worry about him so much?' Johnny said later. All three of them were steaming in front of the peat fire as the rain came down the chimney and hissed in the flames. 'I mean, he's never going to recover, is he?'

'Oh, Johnny, I don't know ...' Meredith stared into the fire and drew in a deep breath.

'He won't, will he? Recover?' The boy looked fearful as he voiced the question and it wasn't until Meredith silently shook her head that he relaxed. 'Thank God!'

'Johnny, what is it? I thought you liked Professor Macaulay. He said you were like a son to him. What has happened between you two?'

Emotion struggled visibly beneath the surface as Johnny looked at her, his eyes turning moist.

'You shouldn't ask,' he said thickly. 'You wouldn't understand.'

'I'm sure that ...' But she got no further, for Johnny left the fire and threw himself into the shadowy alcove that served as his bed. 'Johnny?'

Peter touched her hand and shook his head. 'Let him be, Meredith.'

'Can't you tell me, Peter, what it is that trouble him?'

Peter gave a wry smile and again shook his head after a glance at the professor, sitting on the other side of the fireplace. Fergus Macaulay appeared to be asleep, his head thrown back and his hands lying limply in his lap which was piled with thick blankets.

'There are some things, Meredith, that are better not talked about.'

'I think perhaps I know what you mean,' Meredith said with a shudder. 'My father has spoken of them. Men who like the favours of boys. I wouldn't have taken the professor to be that way inclined. Not after the way he has leered at me on occasion.'

'He makes no distinction between the sexes, Meredith, as long as they're young and pretty. He's the worst kind of pervert.'

'And yet you still came with him to these islands? Knowing all that?'

Peter passed a hand over his face with a deep sigh. He chewed on his lips and Meredith could see that he was struggling to decide whether or not to respond to her questioning.

'I know it must seem ludicrous,' he said eventually, 'but I was greedy for the kudos the expedition would give me. It was important for my career to have my name linked to one of the most revered naturalists in the world.'

'And has it been worth it, Peter?' She could not prevent a little coldness creeping into her voice.

Peter smiled. He took his eyeglasses off and gave them a good polish with his handkerchief.

'Don't worry, Meredith,' he said. 'He hasn't laid a finger on me. I'm not his type, you see, thank God. He prefers Johnny's pretty face.'

'Dear Lord! So that was why Johnny has been acting so strangely. Poor boy.'

'As you say...poor boy. But he's not the only one. There have been many before him.'

'Why haven't they thrown the man into prison before now?'

'Nobody has had the courage to speak out against him. He's too important, too careful, and too dangerous to cross.' Peter's gaze slid across to the professor. 'At least, he was. Now, perhaps, he's paying the price for his unsavoury past.'

A sudden chill descended on Meredith and she huddled closer to the fire. She didn't want to think about the professor and his iniquitous activities. She fought to keep her head empty of Logan and Peter, too, but in many ways that was more difficult. For some time now she had tried to replace her unaccountable feelings for Logan by counting the virtues of Peter.

They both jumped when the door swung open, banging against the wall as the wind played with it and the rain entered the room. And with it, Dr Jolly, his wet clothes clinging to his body as if glued there, rain droplets jewelling his head and shoulders.

'Dear me! What weather! At least the people here are never short of fresh water.'

'My goodness, Father!' Meredith jumped up and pulled her father to the fire while Peter fought to close the door. 'Just look at you. Get those wet clothes off at once!'

'Don't fuss, child! I'll change my clothes when I'm good and ready,'

Dr Jolly said, opening his haversack and taking out a bulging specimen bag.

'What have you found, Dr Jolly?' Peter asked eagerly. 'Is it something rare? I do hope so.'

Dr Jolly emptied the contents of the bag on to the table with a mischievous chuckle. 'Well,' he said, 'after living on seabirds and fish and even more unpalatable things for the last few months, I think this is a rare delicacy indeed!'

'Fungi!' exclaimed Peter, his eyebrows shooting up.

'Mushrooms,' said Meredith with a bright smile and she clapped her hands in delight.

'*Agaricus campestris*,' Dr Jolly announced as if he were announcing something of regal importance. 'Or, if you prefer, the common field mushroom.'

'Johnny! Look what we've got for lunch!' Peter backed up his shout with a tug at Johnny's sleeve and the unhappy boy showed a reluctant interest in what was going on.

'I'll make some soup,' Meredith decided. She rushed to get out a pan and as many other ingredients as she could find in the larder. "And some mushroom flatbread to eat with it and … oh, Father, will there be enough, do you think, for me to take some to Flora?'

With a further chuckle, the good doctor produced yet another bag of mushrooms that filled the room with their pungent, earthy aroma.

'Enough for a banquet, daughter!'

'How wonderful!'

It wasn't long before Meredith had worked her culinary magic and the whole group, including a slightly sulky Frazier, sat down at the table to a variety of dishes containing mushrooms, but all tasting delicious after the limited fare they had become accustomed to. The rich goat's milk provided by Flora gave the soup a creamy texture, the bread cakes were crusty and full of healthy grains with a nutty flavour, and Meredith even managed to make mushroom-and-goat's-cheese omelettes with gannets' eggs on a bed of bright-green kelp. It was, indeed, a banquet and she wished there had been something special to celebrate.

Beside her, leaning heavily to one side in his cushion-padded chair, Professor Macaulay made an impatient sound. She forked some omelette into his mouth and saw that he was eating it with relish, even if some of it escaped down his chin. He had swallowed a few spoonfuls of soup and, had he been anyone but the professor, she would have been happy to see such progress, for the man would soon be on the brink of death if he did not eat.

She broke off small pieces of the bread and fed them to him as she would have fed a baby newly weaned. He took them eagerly, one after the other, grunting his appreciation. At last, he seemed to have had sufficient and leaned back in his chair with a sigh of satisfaction.

'Well, Fergus,' said Dr Jolly, 'you certainly ate well today, eh?'

All eyes were riveted, not on Macaulay's face, but on the forefinger of his right hand, which rose and fell twice in short succession.

'Did you see that?' Peter gasped. 'Is he trying to signal something do you think?'

'Ah!' Professor Jolly was in the process of lighting his pipe; he sucked on it furiously to get it going. 'I have heard of people having strokes and being able to communicate in just such a way.'

'What was it you said to him, Father?' Meredith couldn't take her eyes from the professor's hands.

'I suggested that he had eaten well,' the doctor reminded her.

'And he raised his finger twice,' Peter said.

'Ask him something else,' Meredith suggested.

'All right.' Dr Jolly fixed his attention on Fergus's face and thought about what he should ask his colleague next. He sucked a few times on his pipe, then nodded. 'Hmm, yes, that's it. Fergus, have you been to St Kilda before?'

The finger rose, once, twice.

'Fine, fine! Is this your second visit to the islands?'

A slight hesitation, followed by the finger again rising twice.

'Very good, Fergus. Now—'

'Let me ask him something, Doctor,' Johnny intervened hastily, and Meredith noticed that the professor's good eye narrowed considerably as if anticipating a difficult question.

'All right, then, laddie, go ahead.'

There was silence as everyone waited to hear Johnny's question. He seemed to have difficulty forming the words that were fighting to be out through his trembling lips. At last he stepped up to the professor and, standing rigidly before his mentor with his chin tucked well in, he blurted out: 'Professor, is it finished between you and me?'

Fergus Macaulay gave no sign that he had heard or understood the question. Johnny remained there, unmoving for a minute or two, then his fists clenched at his sides and he repeated what he had just said, only with more emphasis. Still the professor did not respond.

'Perhaps we were mistaken,' Dr Jolly suggested. 'It was possibly nothing more than a coincidence. Leave it, my boy.'

But Johnny was not prepared to give up. For a third time the same question rang out, sharp and clear. 'Come on, you bastard! I know you can hear me. Give me your answer.'

Meredith put a hand on his arm, but he shook it off and stood his ground. At last the professor's good eye blinked and his face went into spasm as he struggled to speak, but it was hopeless. Nothing but a choking, guttural sound emerged and his chest heaved as he fought for breath.

'Answer me!' Johnny cried out desperately. 'Tell me it's over or I'll ...'

He raised a fist and took a step closer to the professor, whose whole body jerked as if shot through with electricity. Peter and Dr Jolly gripped Johnny's arms and forced him away.

'Come on, lad,' Dr Jolly said soothingly. 'No need for that now.'

Johnny looked back, his face twisting in mental agony. 'I need to know!' he whispered hoarsely.

There was a long growl from the professor, starting low and deep in his throat and eventually bursting out of him like the roar of some maniacal beast of the jungle. His right hand gripped the arm of his chair while his left hand hung powerlessly by his side. It was obvious to all that he was trying to raise himself, but it was too much for him. He sank back against the cushions, but they all saw the index finger of his right hand rise.

'That's just once,' Johnny gasped. 'He has to raise his finger twice for yes, isn't that so?'

'Johnny, keep calm,' Dr Jolly placed himself between the student and the professor, his hands held up, palms towards Johnny. 'I doubt he knows what he's doing.'

Meredith moved closer to the men. She had seen the professor's face and suddenly felt cold and shivery as if a ghostly hand had traced a slow path down her spine.

'I think he knows well enough, Father,' she whispered and the others then saw what she had seen. There was a crooked, lecherous smile on the professor's face and he was slowly shaking his head as he looked pointedly at Johnny.

Dr Jolly went to the back of the house and called out for the gillie to come and make the professor comfortable for the night. By the time he came back, Johnny had collapsed on a chair and was sobbing like a young girl. Peter was bending over his friend with great concern.

'I wish I knew what to do,' Meredith told her father as he drew her to one side for a confidential word.

'I'd say he was having a break-down,' he said, stroking his beard, plucking at it reflectively. 'I've seen it coming.'

'But he seemed so much better lately,' she said.

'He has a depressive personality. It's one of the most difficult conditions of the mental state to deal with.'

Meredith bit down on her lip and heaved a sigh. 'We're a happy little band, are we not, Father?'

Dr Jolly gave a short laugh and patted her cheek. 'Thank God for you, my dear, and young Peter there.'

'And you.' She smiled affectionately at him and gave him a kiss, then turned her attention back to the two students.

'It's a great pity that there is no communication between Hirta and the mainland,' Dr Jolly said, sucking on his dry pipe as he gazed out of a rain-streaked window. 'I would be asking for a boat to come and lift us off as soon as possible. As it is, we're probably destined to stick it out for another few months at least.'

Meredith felt an ominous stirring beneath her ribcage. She had misgivings about being on the island after all that had taken place, but the thought of leaving weighed her down like a heavy stone sinking inside her. However, it was not Hirta or its people she wanted to stay for, though she liked them well enough. They were naive but good-hearted people. However, it was Logan who was pulling at her heartstrings, wrong though she thought it was to be drawn to such a man as he was.

I believed I knew what love was, she thought, *but having met Logan, I realize just how innocent I have been up to now. If what I feel for this man is truly love, then it is a terrible thing and I would rather be without it.*

Almost as though her father had heard her thoughts, he said: 'What about Logan? Will he not come to escort you back to Flora's cottage? There's a storm brewing and it's already dusk out there.'

'No,' she said, remembering Logan's mood when he left them earlier. 'I don't think he will come for me this evening. Don't worry, Father. I know the way blindfold by now. I'll be all right.'

'You have a basket full of provisions for the old woman,' he said, noticing how full the basket was and how heavy it must weigh. 'Peter will go with you.'

'Really, Father, there's no need—'

'Nonsense, girl. Peter? Take my stubborn daughter back to her billet, will you. Don't worry about Johnny. I'll see to him.'

Peter seemed happy enough to be relieved of his watch over Johnny, whose tears had dried up, but he still sat, slumped and dejected, in the middle of the room, the dying firelight flickering over him like dancing demons.

Outside the rain had stopped, despite the oppresive clouds and the distant rumbles of thunder. Meredith felt guilty at leaving her father in sole charge, but was nevertheless glad to get away from the cloying, unhealthy atmosphere of the cottage. Peter insisted on carrying her basket and when he slipped his arm through hers she did not object, gaining a measure of comfort from it.

He left her at Flora's door, planting a tender, self-conscious kiss on her forehead, then hurried away back down the hill to Village Bay and the oddly assorted group of men with whom he shared a roof.

Meredith spent a long moment watching his silhouette grow fainter as he disappeared into the growing darkness. She fingered the spot where his lips had touched her cool skin and tried to imagine that she was in love with him. He would, she was sure, be a good and caring husband. What more could any woman ask?

And yet....

CHAPTER 10

FLORA WAS NOT alone, as Meredith found when she entered the cottage. Logan was sitting at the table with the old lady, resting on his elbows. They were deep in conversation, but they stopped talking abruptly as the door opened. Logan got self-consciously to his feet and with a brief nod to Flora and an even briefer glance at Meredith, he left without a further word.

'I'm sorry,' Meredith said. 'I seem to have disturbed you.'

''Tis not me you've disturbed, lassie,' Flora told her with a wry smile. She looked at her house guest from beneath lowered lids. ''Tis yon wee man you're disturbing, but I canna say that I'm surprised.'

Meredith was taken aback by the old lady's words and hesitated a few seconds before putting her bag of food on the table. Normally, she would have found the expression 'yon wee man' amusing when used to allude to a man as big as Logan, but instead of smiling, she frowned deeply at Flora's words.

'If Logan is disturbed, it's nothing that I've done, Flora,' she said bluntly.

'Och, lassie, you have big blue eyes, a winsome smile and the nature of an angel. What man wouldn't be attracted, I ask you that?' Flora pushed herself up stiffly from the table and bent to throw more peat on to the fire. 'And there's that Logan living the life of a hermit for too long. He tries to deny that he's a man of normal flesh and blood. He succeeded for a while. Until you came to Hirta, that is.'

'Oh, Flora.' Meredith's hands went up to her face. 'The things you do say! I have done nothing ... *nothing* to encourage Logan ... not in the way you mean.'

'You may blush like the virgin you are and deny everything, but I feel it in my old bones that you have more than just casual feelings for the man.' Flora held her with a hypnotic stare and Meredith felt sure that those wise eyes, ancient as they were, could read her like an open book. 'Well, I can see you're not going to say anything else on the matter, so I'll let it pass for now. Show me what you have in that bag.'

Meredith gave herself a mental shake and turned her attention fully on the contents of the bag, drawing them out one by one and placing them before Flora like offerings to a deity. Wheat cakes, goose eggs and the precious mushrooms.

The old lady clapped her hands in delight and claimed that she was doubly blessed that day, even though she had had occasion to scold God in his heaven for not answering her prayers.

'Oh dear, Flora,' Meredith laughed, the tension between them dissipating. 'What did you pray for?'

'I'll not be telling you. You might not like what I asked for out of the goodness of my heart, even though I could have asked for something different out of selfishness.'

'That makes me even more curious,' Meredith said, taking the mushrooms to the sink to wash and dry so they could be made into the soup that the men had found so delicious earlier in the day.

'Well, you just swallow that curiosity of yours, for I shan't be telling you, so there! Now, then, I have a bit of salted lamb in the larder, and with those potatoes we can make a good hearty stew fit for the laird of St Kilda if he were to drop in for supper. Please God that he won't see fit to visit until it's all eaten!'

Everyone agreed that it was a miracle that Professor Macaulay had not only survived the stroke, but was slowly making progress back towards surprising, though limited, mobility. This was put down, in large part, to the ministrations of the gillie, Frazier, who spent hours rubbing in oils and liniments from Flora's medicine cupboard. Every day he massaged the professor from top to bottom, back and front, until his fingers cramped and his arms and back ached.

No one had credited the gillie with so much loyalty, but for the last few weeks his absolute diligence could not be faulted. And by the time that the autumn winds had yielded their chill to the even more cutting winds of winter Fergus Macaulay was walking short distances, albeit moving as though there was lead in his veins. Only his right arm refused to respond to treatment, which frustrated him to a state of blustery anger. He would throw things, anything within reach, and lash out at the gillie with his good arm.

Speech was a bigger challenge, but he found that he could enunciate some words, though they were punctuated with animal grunts and snuffles while thick saliva ran from his slack mouth like a glycerine river.

Because Frazier needed to be close to his master at all times, he now occupied Johnny's bunk and Johnny was more than a little happy to have the gillie's cleit in exchange.

'Look at him, the poor wretch,' said Dr Jolly, one morning, indicating the professor struggling to eat his porridge: most of it spilled down his chin.

Meredith, sitting at her writing machine, stared out of the small window that looked on to the sweep of the bay.

'Why do we feel sorry for him, Father? He has done nothing to deserve our pity.'

'Perhaps not, but it's difficult not to feel for him, regardless of what he's done.'

'I'd like to think that this is his punishment,' Meredith said, tapping furiously at the keys of her machine, trying to block out the sound of the professor's groaning and pathetic attempts at expletives.

'You could be right, my dear, but I wouldn't wish that on my worst enemy. Death would certainly have been kinder.'

Meredith stopped typing and looked up at her father, careful to avoid the sight of the professor's semi-naked body. She had never heard her father speak like that before. He had always looked for the good in people, and usually found it, but it seemed there was no good in the professor, even in Josiah Jolly's kindly old eyes.

'I'm going out, daughter!' The words erupted from him as if it was a decision that had been made on the instant. Dr Jolly was already struggling into his top coat and reaching for a long, woollen muffler to keep out the icy November weather.

'Where are you going?'

'To see Lachlan. There are matters to be discussed.'

'Shall I go for you, Father? You have a head cold and should stay indoors on a day like this.'

'Thank you, but no.' Dr Jolly waved a hand at her as he pulled open the door and leaned into the howling wind that forced its way into the room. 'I won't be long.'

Lachlan welcomed Dr Jolly as he would an old friend. The two men often sat together, discussing life and anything else that came to mind. They came from different worlds, yet there was between them a rapport so profound they might have known one another all their lives. Some evenings they would sit together long into the night, staring into the glowing fire embers, then Josiah would regard his cold pipe, slap his thighs and announce that it was time he went. The old man would give a grunt and half a nod, neither pleased nor disappointed to lose the doctor's company. The doctor would trudge back to the naturalists' cottage feeling that he had spent an enjoyable time in good company. Lachlan would continue to stare into the flames as they turned from red to orange to yellow, then the embers would glow like charred flesh, finally dying, black and cold.

'This is not a social visit, Dr Jolly,' Lachlan said now, peering at the doctor from beneath his bushy white eyebrows. 'I can tell by the look in your eyes.'

'Lachlan, you're too wise for your own good sometimes,' Josiah said with a forced smile, for he had hoped to spend a few amicable minutes with the man before getting down to business.

'Can that be so? I think not. Now, what is it that is troubling you, my friend? Get it over with and then enjoy a wee dram with me.'

Lachlan was already rising and going to a cupboard to take out his famous gallon keg of whisky that his grandfather had made on the day of Lachlan's birth. He claimed that he would die when it was empty, but there were those who said that it must have been emptied many times over – or that Lachlan had died and been reborn with every last drop decanted into the thick glass bottle he used for special occasions.

'Is it not a little early in the day to be drinking whisky?' Josiah asked.

'Not if you are going to tell me something I won't like,' Lachlan said, his sharp old eyes twinkling. 'Besides, I had a drop with my porridge this morning as there's a chill in the air and my chest is crackling with the bronchitis.'

With hands as steady as a surgeon's, he poured out two tots in to thimble glasses and put them down on the table between them.

'We must try to get in touch with the mainland,' Josiah said without preamble. 'We need a boat to take us back.'

'Your work here is finished?'

'No, not entirely, though we've done well. It's Professor Macaulay. If we don't get him back soon he could die.'

'Ah, the professor!' There was something in Lachlan's expression that said he did not approve of the illustrious Fergus Macaulay. 'Aye, we gave thanks to God for not taking him before his time, but I fear there were a lot of hypocrites in the church that day, and may God forgive me for saying such a dreadful, heathen thing.'

'I'm not a pious man, Lachlan,' Josiah told him, 'but isn't it said somewhere: *To thine own self be true*? I'm sure you'll be forgiven.'

Lachlan stared down at the tots of whisky and licked his lips thirstily. 'So,' he said. 'You want to send a message, is that it? Well, drink up, laddie, and let's get the job done.'

'But …' Josiah looked around him, wondering just how they were going to achieve what seemed an impossible task, but his mind came up empty. 'How?'

'Never you mind how just at this minute. I have a mind to do some serious drinking before we venture out.'

Meredith was taking a short break from the difficult business of skinning and cutting up a sheep. Two men from the village had brought it in and not a better sight had they seen in a long time, though the poor animal was elderly and would probably cook tough. However, even tough mutton would be a welcome dish on the table in the place of salted gannet and dried puffin, all of which were oily and tasted of fish.

The sight which made her open her eyes wide and gasp for breath as the icy November wind struck her, was her father staggering along the beach on his way back from seeing Lachlan MacKenzie. At first, she thought that his unsteady gait was due to the wind which had sprinkled a covering of snow on the tops of the hills and was razor sharp when it came in contact with any exposed flesh. But no. When he was within a few yards of her she knew that he had more alcohol in him than was good for any soul.

'Hey, daughter!' He hailed her, his arms thrust up in the air, his legs bowing and wobbling over the stony path to the cottage. 'You will not believe what I have just been doing!'

'You've been drinking with Mr MacKenzie and you'll regret it in the morning when we have to sit through a baptism and one of the pastor's sermons.' She stepped forward and took his arm. 'Father! What on earth possessed you?'

'I think I'm a little tipsy, Meredith.' His words were slurred and were punctuated by one or two vigorous hiccups. 'Oh, dear! I do beg your pardon, my dear.'

'You're more than tipsy, Father. You're quite drunk. I've never seen you so ... so—'

'Now, now, Meredith. Don't scold. You sound just like your Aunt Agnes and that ... that's ...' He gulped in some air and steadied himself by leaning heavily on the door jamb. 'It's not good ... don't like it....'

Meredith gave a deep sigh and gripped his arm with both hands. 'Come inside before you fall down and break something, then where will we be?'

He tried to argue with her, but his mouth was too confused, so he just gave her a sheepish smile and allowed her to pull, push and lead him into the cottage.

'Oh, we have visitors!'

Peter and Johnny looked at one another, then burst out laughing, while Frazier, wielding a blood-soaked butcher's chopper, looked over his shoulder to see whom Dr Jolly meant.

Dr Jolly braced his legs, arranged his features and tapped the side of his nose. 'Sorry, no, we don't have visitors, but I do seem to be seeing two of everything and ...' He staggered to a chair and sat down heavily, staring in disbelief at the carcass on the table. 'Is that a sheep on the table, or am I imagining it?'

'Never mind the sheep, Father,' Meredith took a strong stand and wasn't prepared for any nonsense. 'Why are you drunk?'

'It's all Lachlan's fault. He wanted to send a message ... to the mainland.'

'But there are no telephones or telegraphs and it's too far for a beacon to be seen.' Meredith was hoping that her father was not making the sending of a message a fictitious excuse for being the worse for drink.

'I'll tell you all about it ...' he managed to rise from the chair and stagger perilously to his bunk, on which he fell with a belch and a sigh. '... later, daughter.'

And with that, he was asleep and snoring loudly until they turned him on his side and wedged a shoe in the small of his back. Meredith then made some thick broth with some of the mutton and oats and barley. When her father awoke he would need something substantial on his stomach – and something from Flora to cure the pain he would undoubtedly have in his head.

The following morning, when Dr Jolly had regained his senses, Meredith listened to what he had to say about his meeting with Lachlan.

'And you believed him!' Meredith was incredulous. 'Father, just how drunk were you when you supposedly sent this message?'

Josiah Jolly took a deep breath, wincing at the headache that was searing him with pain from his left eye to his temple and then forming an iron band around his head.

'I tell you, it worked when they sent it out in 1876, when a writer called John Sands was stranded here. That was the first St Kilda mail boat and they've used it on occasion ever since. Mind you, it doesn't always get the message through. That depends on the weather and the tides.'

The doctor was encouraged to go through the story yet again, for his small party of naturalists had sceptical minds and more than one among them believed it to be nothing more than a bit of leg-pulling on the part of Lachlan MacKenzie.

The two companions had dutifully emptied Lachlan's famous bottle of ancient whisky, Lachlan claiming that it was the only bottle on the island that would do the trick and assuring Josiah that he was not at all 'afeared' of death waiting for him round the corner.

'We've been companions for many a year, Death and I,' Lachlan had said.

When the last tot had been poured and drunk, a lifebuoy was found lurking in a nearby cleit. A sail was manufactured out of an old linen shirt and the bottle firmly sealed and attached with a message inside to the mainland requesting a boat as soon as it was possible to ride the seas that raged between the two pieces of land. They then took the makeshift 'mail boat' down to the bay and set it afloat, with Lachlan murmuring a Gaelic prayer until it drifted out of sight.

'And in seventy-six a boat arrived?' Peter raised doubting eyebrows and pulled reflectively on his ear lobe.

'Yes. Within three weeks the writer was taken from the island. So, you see, it's not so crazy after all.'

The doctor looked from one doubting face to another and shrugged his shoulders. The proof that he had not been fooled by the old St Kildan elder would undoubtedly come in the shape of a boat showing itself on the horizon. He, for one, would be more than glad to leave the place. He could think of nothing he would like more than to take his dear daughter back to the safety and comfort of her home, though he would miss the company of Lachlan MacKenzie.

As for the boys, he believed they were of his mind. Frazier's thoughts were hard to guess at, since he said little and it was impossible, most of the time, to read his belligerent expression. The professor, he was sure, would welcome the chance to receive proper medical care, and to be reunited with his family.

Josiah turned to look at Fergus Macaulay, wondering how much he had been able to take in of their conversation. He was sitting very still and had been silent all the while, a dark scowl on his face, though any other expression was difficult for him because of the way the stroke had disfigured him.

Behind him, the door opened, letting in a cutting draught of salty air. Josiah turned and found that Meredith was stepping outside, pulling a heavy shawl about her, obvious haste in her movements.

'Where are you going, Meredith?' he asked.

'I'm going to tell Logan,' she said, her face a serious study of light and shade, her eyes laden with anxiety.

He started to speak, but before he could utter a further sound, she was gone. Josiah felt a wave of darkness pass through him, weighing him down. He wasn't sure how to interpret it. His daughter had a strong will of her own. Once she had made up her mind, there was no turning her. One might more easily turn the tide. In fact, the girl had a spirit in her that raged, and was just as formidable as the sea that now kept them prisoner.

CHAPTER 11

MEREDITH STRUGGLED TO keep her balance as she climbed over the ridge, the wind buffeting at her skirts and dragging her this way and that, like hands pulling at her, trying to dissuade her from making her journey. Men and boys were busy everywhere gathering grass for the winter feed, which would later be divided fairly between the families that had livestock. They took little notice of her passing by, for they were too busy trying to stop the dry grass bundles being swept away by placing heavy stones on top to weigh them down.

Logan was not among them. Earlier in the day he had been helping to repair the church roof, damaged during the last storm. The hole in it had prevented the children attending school because of the danger of falling slates. But she had not found him there either and the work was finished, much to the disappointment of the children, who would be obliged to return to their lessons on the morrow.

Meredith had seen from a distance that Logan was not visiting Flora, for the old woman could be seen gathering herbs in her garden, chickens all around her feet, their feathers fluttering like frilled petticoats. The sound of their clucking rose and fell in volume as the wind caught it and tossed it about.

As Logan's hut came into view, Meredith saw wind-whirled wisps of smoke come from the central hole in the roof that served as a chimney. It was only a thin blue plume, which meant that the fire was almost out, so it was likely that Logan wasn't in there either. She bent forward, hands on hips, catching her breath, thinking that her journey had been in vain.

Then a movement, seen out of the corner of her watering eyes, caught her attention. Someone was working up on the next rise, cutting peat. It was Logan. There was no mistaking his large, muscular frame and the power he put behind the slashing, lifting and shifting of the turf squares. Meredith sighed with relief and started out towards him.

Logan did not know that she was there until she was almost on top of him. Her shadow, falling over his knife hand, made him turn abruptly, like a man caught out in evil doings or wicked thoughts. For a long moment they stared at one another, the wind singing a high-pitched lament that filled the silence and sent shivers down the spine.

'Logan...!' Meredith brushed away the moisture from her eyes.

'Meredith? What is it? What's wrong?' Logan threw aside his turfing knife and stepped up to her, his hands gripping her arms, his eyes searching hers. 'Has something happened? Tell me!'

She shook her head and gulped from the breathlessness that made her chest heave uncomfortably, rendering speech impossible for the moment. Logan gave her a little shake and demanded again that she tell him what he supposed was bad news.

'It's all right, Logan,' she was able to say at last, forcing a smile, though she felt her lips trembling as if she might cry sooner than laugh. 'It's just ... my father has asked Lachlan to send a message to the mainland to ask for a boat to take us off the island.'

Logan released her and stooped to retrieve his knife, then moved a few paces away. He went back to hacking at the turf with even greater fervour.

'What makes you think the message will get through?'

The wind was howling so loudly she could hardly hear him.

'Lachlan says—'

'Lachlan is an old man. He still believes in ancient means and measures.'

'But he says it's succeeded before ... the message in the bottle with the sail and—'

'Ay, once! Maybe twice, if Lachlan is to be believed, but ...' Logan looked at her over his shoulder, his face creasing into a wry smile.

'Och, he's like an old woman, is Lachlan. He believes in Gaelic magic and miracles that he swears are possible. Who's to say that it's not just his fanciful brain making up stories that people want to hear ?'

'My father isn't a fanciful man and he believes it could work.' Meredith blinked away more wind tears and sniffed, sure that there must be an icy droplet on the end of her frozen nose.

'Why are you crying?' Logan was again giving her his full attention.

'I'm not crying! It's the wind and I came all the way up here to tell you, because ...'

'Tell me what? Something I already know ... that you'll be leaving Hirta, sooner or later.' Now he was the one with eyes glassy with tears like shimmering stars in a black sky. 'Yes, of course you'll leave ... and I can do nothing about it. *Nothing*!'

His sudden outcry had been full of passion.

'No, Logan, you can do nothing to stop us leaving,' Meredith said. She hesitated nervously before finishing her sentence, 'but you can come with us.'

If her ears had not been deafened by the roaring wind and the crashing of distant waves on the rocky shore, she was sure she would have heard Logan's sharp intake of breath. He was looking at her in disbelief as if she had stated the impossible.

'You would have me share a boat with the professor and his henchman?'

She shook her head in frustration. 'Your father is too ill and too weak to do anybody any harm any more,' she said with a certainty in which she did not wholly believe.

'Evil accompanies that man wherever he goes. That devil Frazier would stop at nothing to please his master. It was his hand that tried to send me to a watery grave, but he did it on my father's order.'

'Oh, Logan, the professor is not the same man he was five years ago – and neither are you.'

Logan gave her a quick look, then concentrated on putting the cut squares of peat in a large hessian sack, which he then secured and heaved on to his shoulder.

'Promise me one thing, Meredith,' he said as he drew abreast of her. 'Don't trust the professor. Not even on his deathbed. And don't trust

Frazier. He'll kill you as soon as look at you if he thinks it will please my father. He's done it before, more than once, I'm sure.'

Meredith stuck out her chin. Her eyes, dry now that she had turned her back to the wind, searched Logan's face boldly.

'Come back to the mainland with us, Logan,' she said in a firm voice. 'Come back home. You can have a better life, take up your profession again. The world needs good surgeons.'

'I can't.'

Logan started to walk away from her, but after a few strides he stopped and lowered the sack of peat as if he had suddenly become weary. Meredith went to him and gazed questioningly at his distraught face.

'Why can't you?' she demanded, fearing the answer, but determined to have the truth out of him.

'I'm not wanted there,' he stated simply as he stared into the far distance.

'Yes you are!' She pulled him round to face her, hooking her fingers into the material of his jacket, holding on fast. 'You *are*! *I* want you … and I think … no, I'm certain that … *you* want *me*.'

He started to pull away from her, but she hung on determinedly, her feet slipping and slithering on a patch of frozen ground, then going from under her. Logan felt her go and grabbed her up into his arms so tightly it bruised her ribcage, but she didn't care. She saw something happening in his eyes, saw the tightening of the muscles in his cheeks before they relaxed and his head came down, his mouth seeking hers.

The kiss was long and hard and hungry. Meredith felt her head lift and her senses reel. It was the first time in her life she had been kissed by a real man. The boyish pecks and fondlings she had so far received were nothing compared to this. Her body was gripped in a surge of passion that made her tingle as it exploded through her and she knew Logan felt the same.

But it was Logan who stemmed the heated flow of what might have been; Logan who pushed her away and held her rigidly at arm's length.

'Oh, Meredith, my sweet girl …' His voice was ragged and he threw his head back, eyes tightly closed and gave a heartfelt groan. 'Forgive me. I promised myself I would keep my distance, no matter how I felt. I should never have … Dear God, you have no idea how difficult it's been keeping my hands off you!'

'I wish you hadn't, Logan … kept your hands off me, I mean.'

Meredith flushed scarlet at her own words. What would her father say if he heard his very proper daughter speaking in such terms and without an ounce of shame? Aunt Agnes would be mortified and be reaching for the tiny bottle of smelling salts that was her constant companion.

'I'm sorry,' she said with a gulp, seeing Logan's apparent horror at her words. 'I should not have said that … I am not normally a flirtatious person. Please … you must forget that I ever—'

'Flirtatious? Is that what you call it, Meredith?' His eyes were blazing, his chest rising and falling like the boiling ocean. 'If it's a mild flirtation you're wanting, you've come to the wrong man. I'm sure that Peter will oblige, or indeed any one of your many admirers on the mainland. You would be better off with any of them, rather than with me, I assure you.'

'It's not like that at all!' Meredith clenched her fists and gritted her teeth. How could he mistake her intentions in such a way? 'There are no admirers except Peter and he is nothing more than an infatuated boy.'

'Marry him, Meredith.' Logan avoided her eyes and gazed out to sea with a faraway expression. 'Forget about me. I'm not worthy of any decent woman.'

Meredith caught hold of his arm, her fingers holding on desperately to the coarse material of his jacket.

'I thought I knew where my future lay,' she said in a tremulous voice. 'I truly believed that all I wanted was my work and to follow in my father's footsteps. Then you came into my life and everything changed. Is it Fate that has brought us together, Logan? Fate, serendipity … whatever. I only know that we belong together. I feel it, right here, deep inside my heart.'

She saw his Adam's apple bob up and down as he swallowed, still avoiding her gaze. Meredith reached up and took his face in both her hands, tilting his head so that he had to look directly at her. He closed his eyes and gave a great sigh.

'Don't do this to me, Meredith, I beg of you,' he said, his voice cracked and raw and only just audible above the crash and hiss of the sea.

'Come back with us, Logan. You know where your destiny lies and it is not here in this desolate, God-forsaken place.'

He gave a dry laugh. 'I think God had forsaken me long before I came to St Kilda. Here, at least, I am left alone to my own devices and not judged for what I am supposed to have done in the past.'

'But you did nothing! All the blame and the guilt rest on your father's shoulders. You must go back and tell the authorities what really happened.' Meredith slid her arms about his waist and hugged herself to him tightly. 'Oh, Logan, you are worth more than these barren islands where the people have such strange ways.'

'The people here saved my life and took me in. I owe them so much. Would you have me turn my back on them now?'

'Of course not, but—'

'Then stop this charade, Meredith. It is as ridiculous as my asking you to stay here with me … which I would never do.' He pulled away from her and scrubbed a hand over his distraught face. 'Enough of this fanciful nonsense. The sooner a boat does come to take you off the island the better – better for both of us.'

'Logan!'

'Go, I tell you, and stay out of my sight.'

'Oh, Logan!' Meredith murmured, sinking inside herself, so heavy was she with the bitter weight of rejection. 'I thought you loved me.'

As she stood there, looking at his tall, dark silhouette against the pale sky, flakes of fluffy white snow floated down, danced for a while in the wind, then fell on their heads and shoulders. Meredith felt the flakes attach themselves to her eyelashes, making her blink. Logan became a blur as the snow fell faster and thicker. She expected him to turn and go, but he remained there as if rooted to the spot, turned to a block of stone by some kind of island magic.

She wasn't aware of him moving, but thought she heard a low animal growl as he pulled her roughly into his arms and ravished her mouth in a kiss that was so wild and urgent it frightened her. And yet she didn't want it to stop, didn't want him ever to let go. She was more than ready to offer herself up to him if it meant they could stay together.

But it was not to be. Logan ended the kiss as abruptly as he had thrown himself into it. Suddenly he was striding away from her, an ever fading dark shadow.

'Go, Meredith!' he called out over his shoulder in a voice ragged with emotion. 'You know what they say about me – like father like son. You deserve better than that.'

'You're not like him, Logan,' she shouted at his back. 'You could never be like him.'

Logan gave no sign that he had heard her response. Breathless and with her knees turned to jelly, Meredith sank to the frozen ground, unaware of the bruising stones and the sharp marine grasses beneath her. Her first thought was to run after Logan, beg him to change his mind, but then she discarded the idea as being useless. It was not in her nature to beg, but in the last few minutes she had shamefully done just that. It would be, she promised herself, the first and last time she did so.

She struggled to her feet, dry sobs tearing her body apart, and retraced her steps to Village Bay. There was work to be done and her father would be worried if she was not there to do it.

Josiah watched his daughter's return with an ache in his heart for his only child, whom he loved so dearly. Meredith was headstrong, but she was also vulnerable, despite her years. It had struck him recently that she had never had a meaningful relationship with anyone, which had filled him full of concern for her future. He would not wish her to become bitter and twisted like his sister-in-law, but history had a strange way of repeating itself in families.

There she was now, battling valiantly against the elements, but even so he could tell that she was also battling against her emotions, which had probably been stirred in a way that she had never experienced before. She had a strong liking for the big Scot, but Dr Jolly feared that Logan was a difficult customer, taciturn and set in his ways. It was unlikely that he would live up to Meredith's expectations.

When Meredith eventually staggered unsteadily through the door her clothes were caked with a thick blanket of snow. She closed the door behind her with difficulty and stood there, her back pressed against it, steaming gently in the heat of the cottage.

'Come and get warmed,' he said to her, not meeting her eyes, but turning to pour out a mug of hot tea, lacing it liberally with brandy. 'Come on, girl. Get that wet shawl off and sit here by the fire.'

She did as she was told, not saying a word until she had drunk half the contents of the mug, staring all the while into the flames and the smoke spiralling up the wide chimney from the peat fire.

'Well, aren't you going to ask me what happened?' she said eventually.

Dr Jolly pressed his hand on her shoulder and kissed the top of her damp head.

'I'm sure you'll tell me, if you want to,' he said. 'In your own good time.'

She stared some more into the flames, then tossed back the remains of the tea, the strong spirits in it hitting the back of her throat and making her cough.

'Have some more,' Dr Jolly encouraged, but she shook her head.

'I've been humiliated enough, Father, without you getting me drunk.'

'Logan humiliated you?' The doctor's hackles began to rise as he waited for her reply.

'No, not Logan. I humiliated myself.' Meredith glanced up at him, then swiftly averted her eyes. 'I belittled myself by begging him to come back to the mainland with us.'

'There's nothing very belittling in that, daughter.'

'That's not all. I … I told him that … that I wanted him … that I loved him.'

'Ah! And he turned you down. Is that it?'

'Not exactly. He said he could never go back and …' Her words seemed to get stuck in her throat. She dropped her head in her hands for just an instant, and gave a shuddering sob before composing herself sufficiently to meet her father's concerned gaze.

'My dear girl,' he said. 'He's not for you….'

'It was not you whom he kissed, Father,' she said in a low, determined voice. 'There, the subject is closed. I have work to do. I just hope that the amount of brandy you put in my tea will not prevent me from hitting the correct keys.'

'Oh, my love—'

'Please, Father, no pity. I couldn't stand it. Sympathy will only destroy what little pride I have left. Now, where are the notes you would like me to transcribe?'

Dr Jolly gave a wistful smile, gathered together a scattering of pages that were covered in his inimitable scribble, and passed them to her. She didn't look at him, not even when he affectionately stroked her cheek.

'Meredith ...' He started to speak, but then became lost for words and spread his hands in the air. Meredith turned her full attention to the work at hand, and her fingers were soon flying over the keys as if they were hot coals.

'Off you go, Father,' she said, tutting impatiently as the keys of the writing machine jammed annoyingly because of her haste. 'Go on. Leave me to work in peace. I'll get it done in half the time without anyone to distract me.'

Duly dismissed, the doctor wrapped up warmly and went to join the others who were out in the pastures with the villagers, rounding up the sheep that were not expected to live another winter. The animals would then be slaughtered, the wool woven and the meat salted to provide food at a time when there were few birds on the islands.

Meredith heard her father leave the cottage and gave a sigh of relief. She was alone, so she could afford to give way, just a little, to her bruised emotions. Resting her head in her hands over the temperamental machine, she drew in a shuddering breath. Closing her eyes was of no help. All she could see were those few minutes with Logan, playing and replaying in her head. Her lips still tingled from the passion of his kiss.

And yet he had sent her away from him, had refused her, even though he had admitted wanting her. Of course she could see the difficulties that he would face were he to go back to the mainland, but they were surely surmountable. And yet, she could imagine that it would be difficult to speak out against a man so revered and respected as was Professor Macaulay. Her own father was an admirer of the famous naturalist and had been for many years. And Josiah Jolly was not a man who was easily taken in.

Behind her a soft, scuffling footstep sounded. Meredith stiffened, feeling the hairs on the back of her neck rise and a prickling sensation creep up her spine. A hand descended on her shoulder before she had time to turn in her seat to see who was there.

'Don't be afraid my dear,' came the whispered words in a rasping voice that instilled in her a deep, cold terror.

The professor was standing directly behind her. She did not have to see his face to know it was him. She could smell him, smell the rottenness of him, the sourness of his breath, the staleness of his sick body.

'Professor Macaulay!' she said, jumping to her feet and dodging to the other side of the chair so that there was something solid between them. 'You are obviously greatly improved to be able to walk from your bed to my work table. Well done!'

'Here, girl,' he said, his speech only slightly slurred. 'Come. Let me lean on you a little. We can walk together.'

'I'm sorry, Professor, but I have work to do.' Meredith frowned down at the jammed keys of her machine and wished that he would go away. 'Perhaps Frazier ... or Johnny—'

She almost gagged on the words as his long arm reached out across her chair and his clawlike fingers latched on to her wrist.

'They are all out in the fields chasing sheep like naughty little boys,' Macaulay said, a disturbing twitch deforming the right side of his face. 'I'm tired of naughty little boys. Come, Meredith. Keep me company. I have been so lonely since my *malaise*.'

'Please, Professor ...' Meredith took a step back, but she was incapable of breaking free of his hold. It was unbelievably strong for a man so afflicted and she began to wonder to what extent he was fooling them all. 'Please sit down. I will talk to you as I work, but I must finish it or my father will be highly displeased.'

'Your father never thinks anything but good of you,' the professor said.

'He's a good man and a good father. I try to please him.'

'Perhaps you would be better off trying to please me.' His eyes were suddenly burning through her and Meredith felt something curdle sickeningly in the pit of her stomach.

'I ... I really don't know ... I mean ... I haven't the time to ...' Her throat was so restricted she could hardly speak, for he was slowly pulling her, drawing her towards him and fear rose like a solid object, ready to choke her.

'Don't play with me, child!' Macaulay's voice was becoming stronger by the minute, his eyes more scarily cruel. 'You know what you're doing to me, flaunting yourself, flashing those eyes of yours. Come! Come soothe my aching loins.'

Meredith's jaw dropped open in complete shock and disgust. She looked around her wildly, hoping, praying, willing someone to enter the cottage, but there was no one. She was alone with this monster who was so very different from his son.

'Damn you, Professor,' she screamed out at him. 'I'd rather die than soothe any part of you!'

But he wasn't listening. A smile was spreading crookedly across his face, a dribble of saliva was running down his bristly chin and the hand that tugged at her was gaining in strength.

Meredith looked wildly for something to grab, to hold onto, but there was nothing within reach and the professor was slowly but surely dragging her in the direction of his dark, lonely corner. She knew exactly what he had in mind for her when he got her there.

CHAPTER 12

SAVED! THANK GOD, she was saved! A clatter of feet and a chatter of excited male voices interrupted the horrible fate she was about to experience at the professor's hands. As the door burst open to admit the rest of their party carrying a poor dead sheep, Macaulay let her go. Meredith almost fell with the suddenness of the release, then, staggering as far away from him as possible, she stood there breathless and rubbing frantically at the red finger-imprints that encircled her slim wrist.

Peter was first into the room. He took one look at the little scene before him and his expression darkened.

'What's going on here?' he demanded, seeing Meredith's stricken face and knowing immediately that something was wrong.

Meredith slid crabwise around the table so that she had something firm and solid between her and Fergus Macaulay. Peter put his arm about her shoulders and looked at her questioningly, before his suspicious gaze returned to the professor, whose chest was heaving as he apparently struggled to get his breath.

'What is it?' Dr Jolly came in, followed by a rosy-cheeked Johnny, both brushing a glistening coating of soft snow from their shoulders and stamping their feet loudly. 'Meredith?'

Meredith could only shake her head, unable to form a coherent sentence in front of them all.

'Professor?' Peter's arm slid to Meredith's waist.

'Leave it, Peter,' she said quickly, glad of the reassuring pressure of his hold. 'It was nothing.'

'Ha!' Professor Macaulay threw back his head back and gave a dry laugh, then pushed himself upright, bracing himself unsteadily against the table. 'Yes, that's it. A slight accident, my friends. As Meredith says, it was nothing.' His voice rose and he gave another laugh. 'I stumbled, that's all. So damned clumsy of me!'

Then he shocked them all by flinging an arm out in a wide, angry arc, sweeping everything from the table on to the floor, typewriter included. It made a terrible noise that seemed to echo in their ears in the shocked silence long after the professor limped with ungainly steps out of the room.

'Is that what really happened, my dear?' Josiah Jolly hung up his outdoor clothes near the fire, where they steamed gently.

'Meredith, if the professor did anything to … to upset you….' Peter's voice trailed off.

'Yes, Peter, what would you do?' It was an unfair question. He was only being kind and she was glad he was still holding on to her, but she wanted no trouble. There had been enough on this bizarre trip to last her a lifetime. She shook her head. 'I'm sorry, Peter. I'm a little nervy today. I shouldn't have spoken to you like that.'

'That's all right.' As if he suddenly realized that he was still clasping her to him, he dropped his arm and took hold of her hand instead, rubbing it between his two hands. 'Are you sure you're all right, Meredith ? You're like ice and your fingers are shaking. Look, Dr Jolly. I hope she's not coming down with anything.'

Dr Jolly gave her an intense look and felt her forehead.

'Hmm. You do feel a little feverish, child.'

'Really, Father, I'm quite all right,' she insisted, knocking his hand away with a little show of impatience. 'You do fuss so.'

'I'm concerned for your welfare and you certainly look a little strange. Not yourself at all.'

Meredith was aware that all the men were staring at her, including Frazier, who had appeared out of nowhere immediately after the professor's departure.

'Professor Macaulay wouldn't do anything to harm your daughter, Dr Jolly,' the gillie now said in a low, gravelly voice. 'He's very fond of Miss Jolly. Unfortunately, unmarried women of a certain age are known for having … shall we say … fantasies. I think that's the word the professor would use.'

Meredith felt her chest fill out with anger as she rose to her full height and gave Frasier a hard look.

'I do not indulge in fantasies, Mr Frazier,' she informed him stiffly. 'That is something reserved for old maids and widows. The fact is ...' She glanced around the room at Peter, her father, and Johnny. 'I think it best if I am not left alone with the professor. He is quite deranged.'

Dr Jolly reached up to a shelf, took down his tobacco jar and began to fill his pipe. 'The man is still too afflicted by the stroke he suffered to do any harm, surely?'

'I don't think he's as frail as he makes out, Father.' The words were out of Meredith's mouth before she could stop them. 'Now, if you'll excuse me, I need to get a breath of fresh air. A brisk walk will do me good.'

'Not on a day like this, daughter. The snow has not stopped falling since you came in. There can be no brisk walking today.'

'Oh!' She looked despairingly at the white curtain of falling snow and heaved a sigh.

The doctor gave her a strange look, then frowned down at his pipe, which had refused to light. He pocketed the thing and rubbed the back of his neck as if trying to erase an uneasy thought.

'I think,' he said slowly, 'that this place is having a bad effect on all of us. We've all been working too hard for too long. It's high time we went home.'

'We all feel the same, Dr Jolly, sir,' said Peter, 'but how do you propose we do it? The boat isn't due to collect us for months, and even then it may not be able to get to us if the seas are bad.'

Dr Jolly nodded and studied the backs of his hands, still frozen from herding and catching sheep.

'Yes, it doesn't bear thinking about. Even I am beginning to doubt old Lachlan's method of sending a message in a bottle. For all we know the thing could have been washed up at the North Pole, or been swallowed by a hungry whale.'

Frazier chose that moment to make a derisive sound and, throwing cynical hands in the air, he marched off to join the professor in his chamber. It was time for him to massage his master with liniment and oils. If the professor had been annoyed in any way by the girl, it would not be an easy task. There was no dealing with the man when he was in one of his black moods.

'Peter, take Meredith back to her lodging, will you,' Dr Jolly said gruffly and pointed a chastising finger at his daughter. 'I want no argument from you, young woman! Back you go and try to rest. There's no work for any of us tomorrow, it being Sunday and there's another baptism, so the service will be infernally long if the pastor has his way. I think even God must get tired of the man's droning voice.'

'But Father...' Meredith looked miserably at the floor, which was covered with scattered sheets of paper and, worst of all, her typewriting machine, all broken in bits and looking far from repairable.

'You leave that, my girl,' the doctor told her firmly. 'Peter?'

'It's all right, Dr Jolly.' Peter was already shrugging back into his coat and winding a long muffler around his neck. 'I'll see that she gets back all right.'

'I'm perfectly capable of taking myself home,' Meredith protested, though she didn't feel nearly as confident as she sounded and it would be comforting to have Peter accompany her back to Flora's cottage.

'What really happened back there, Meredith?' Peter asked when they were walking together up the hill behind Village Bay, their faces full into the gusting flurries of snow that stung their cheeks and made their eyes blur.

'It doesn't matter, Peter,' she said, giving him her hand so he could haul her up a particularly slippery patch of steep ground. 'I was probably mistaken after all. I was working, but my mind was busy elsewhere.'

'You know, don't you, Meredith,' Peter said after a few minutes had gone, 'that you can tell me anything. Whatever you say will be safe with me. In fact, *you* will be safe with me. You do believe that, don't you?'

His remark brought a warmth to her heart and a smile to her face. She squeezed his arm and drew even closer to him, enjoying their closeness.

'You're very sweet, Peter,' she said, and then frowned at her own remark, for Peter deserved something better than being told he was 'sweet'. 'I do appreciate your friendship, I really do.'

'But?'

'But what?'

'You're not in love with me?' It was a rhetorical question, as if he thought he already knew the answer.

Meredith fell silent. The thoughts in her head just at that moment were jumbled. Had things been different, had she met Peter in Northumberland and had never come to St Kilda, maybe she would have fallen in love with him. It would have been so easy to do, and even now she felt him tugging at her heartstrings.

'Love is such a strange, complex word,' she said eventually. 'It carries so many meanings. I love life. I love my work. I love animals, the countryside, the sea. I love my father. They're all different kinds of love.'

Peter was nodding slowly, his eyes both wise and hopeful. 'And me? How do you feel about me, Meredith?'

'I'm fond of you, Peter. *Very* fond.' Meredith pulled her shawl more tightly about her as the sharpness of the icy wind cut through her to the bone. 'I think I may even come to love you ... some day.'

'But not yet?'

'No, Peter, not yet.' She stopped then, and he stopped with her, turning to face her, sheltering her from the wind with his lean young body.

'For that I'm grateful,' he said. 'I will try not to expect more for now, if you will only tell me that I stand a chance of winning your hand one day.'

She rose on tiptoe and planted a cool kiss on his flushed cheek.

'All things are possible, Peter,' she said huskily, trying not to see the image of Logan in her mind's eye. 'But don't ask me to make any promises. The future will take care of itself. As for the present ...'

'Yes?'

'Just now, Peter, what I need more than anything else is a good friend. Can you be that for me?'

He smiled a little sadly, but it was a genuine smile. 'I'll be proud to be your friend, Meredith. Now and ... and for evermore, whatever happens in the meantime.'

'Bless you!'

She kissed him again, sweetly, the kiss of a friend, and then hand in hand they headed for Flora's cottage.

The flurries of snow and the icy blizzards followed from November into December with high drifts everywhere. The islands looked beautiful in their white mantel, especially when the wind dropped, the snow stopped and the sky became that shimmering turquoise blue that only appears in winter.

Meredith spent as much time as she could walking the hills and vales of Hirta, recording the magical scenery with her sketchpad and her watercolours. At every turn she saw the place looking like a Christmas card. Through it all rows of villagers marched single file, knee deep in snow as they carried home the clods of peat for their fires. A sense of peace and tranquillity had come over the land and its people.

But the peace was not to last for long. It turned quickly to sadness when, just before Christmas, a child fell ill. The nurse was called, but claimed there was nothing to be done, for the child's jaw had already dropped and then the death rattle set in. Meredith happened to be passing and tried to persuade the nurse to call in Flora MacInnes, but the nurse would not hear of it. She gave Meredith a sharp tirade in pure Gaelic, which was obviously meant to convey the fact that she was a stranger and not expected to interfere in the lives of the island people.

It wasn't until Meredith saw a grim-faced Logan marching down the street and going into the cottage where the sick child was, that she realized it was the home of his young daughter.

She waited: an hour, two, wanting to go inside, offer her help and support. But when she knocked tentatively on the door, the nurse appeared and planted herself menacingly in the space, preventing Meredith from entering.

'You are not wanted here, miss!' Meredith was told. 'Go away and let these people grieve in peace and private.'

Meredith backed off, but only as far as the stone wall that lead down to the bay. She sat there, hugging herself to keep warm, until the cottage door opened and Logan reappeared. He had to stoop low to get out to the street. For a few seconds he seemed as though he was incapable of making a decision as to which way to turn, then he caught sight of her.

She got hastily to her feet and approached him, arms outstretched.

'Oh, Logan! Is it your little girl? Is she the one who has died?'

He looked at her through eyes that were dead and dry. His face was expressionless, as if turned to stone. He stared unblinkingly, then turned and walked away. Meredith followed two paces behind. What could she say, what could she do? She didn't know. Something inside her was dead too. Her brain refused to function, as did her heart. She felt Logan's pain and the frustration of knowing there was nothing she could do to help him through it.

Logan stopped at the edge of the water. Meredith followed him, willing the love she felt for him to reach out and comfort him. She could see his head thrown back, his chest heaving. What was going through his tortured mind at that moment was impossible to imagine.

Meredith waited, but when he continued to ignore her, she accepted that he preferred to be left alone with his grief. She turned and started to walk back, fighting to keep her balance so that the wind would not sweep her into the swirling water.

'Meredith!'

She heard the desperate note in his voice. She hesitated, then returned to where he stood, now facing her.

'Logan?' She put out a hand towards him and he clasped it tightly.

'The child had been sick for days and they didn't tell me,' Logan said. 'I could have saved her … Flora could have saved her. They preferred to call in the nurse, whose methods are so archaic they're criminal.'

'I'm so sorry, Logan. She was such a pretty child.'

'She was not strong. She inherited the weak genes of her mother who was an asthmatic and had a weak heart. The child caught a chill that turned to pneumonia. Her body could not cope with it. But she could have survived, if only …' Logan shook his head violently and rubbed a hand over his face as if to wipe away his thoughts, his anger.

'Is there anything I can do, Logan?'

'What is there left to do? She is already dead. I'll bury her beside her mother.'

'It must be terrible for you,' Meredith said, blinking furiously at the stinging tears that were fighting to be released. 'In such a short time you have lost your wife, and now your daughter.'

Logan's eyes glazed over. He swallowed deeply and gave a sharp intake of air.

'Fiona was not my daughter, Meredith,' he said, his voice ragged with emotion. 'She was my half-sister. I married her mother to save her from the ignominy of being treated like an outcast.'

'I don't understand,' Meredith said, though she feared that she did understand, even though it was inconceivable to her.

'During his first trip to the islands, the professor raped Fiona's mother. He let me take the blame when they found the poor girl brutally abused and in a state of shock. She barely remembered her own name. The islanders were all for lynching me, but Lachlan and Flora spoke up for me and it was agreed that I could live if I married Dorcas.

'That, of course, was after my father had ordered my execution at the hands of Frazier. The gillie was supposed to put a bullet through my heart and throw me overboard once we got out of the bay here. Frazier missed, but managed to push me overboard. He obviously thought that I couldn't possibly survive. It must have been quite a shock for both of them to find me still alive here on Hirta.'

'Oh, Logan! That's …' Meredith's voice stuck in her throat and she could do nothing but stare down at her slim white wrist being tightly squeezed in his big, work-worn hand.

Logan pulled her closer to him and lifted her chin with the tip of a finger so that he could gaze down into her eyes.

'Do you believe me, Meredith? I swear to you it's the truth.'

'I've always believed everything you've said, Logan. Now, even more than before, since the professor …' Her face twisted as her voice came to a halt, unable to continue.

'Has he ever touched you? Hurt you?'

'He has made certain … advances …' She drew in a deep breath and averted her gaze.

'When did this come about?' Logan's hands gripped her upper arms so fiercely that she cried out with the pain of it and he slackened his hold, but did not let her go.

'A few days ago, when I was alone with him at the cottage.' Meredith's voice trembled; she was afraid of what he might do. 'It was nothing, Logan. He claimed that he had stumbled. Perhaps he did. I'm afraid I'm beginning to imagine things the longer I stay here.'

'No,' Logan said, shaking his head. 'You're not imagining things, Meredith. No woman … no child, male or female, is safe where that bastard is concerned. The trouble is that no-one he has abused has the courage to speak out against him. He is too important a personage to have any accusations of that sort believed.'

'I would gladly speak out against him,' Meredith told him. 'I'm sorry, Logan, but I find your father utterly despicable.'

'Unless you have very strong proof, it would be your word against his. Whom do you think the authorities would believe?'

'Perhaps we could find the proof needed, Logan. Perhaps Frazier …'

'Frazier! He would sell his soul to the devil if the professor asked him to do so. No, Meredith, it's a losing battle.'

'I've never done battle with anyone before,' Meredith said, her head rising proudly, 'but I'm not prepared to lose to your father. I'll fight him, and Frazier too, to hell and back, if that's what it takes to put him where he belongs and wipe your reputation clean.'

Logan gave a sharp jerk of his head and started to walk away from her.

'You don't stand a chance,' she heard him say.

Well, she thought, *we'll see about that*!

CHAPTER 13

As Christmas approached, the St Kildans became busier than ever, largely because of a violent storm, which brought down roofs, destroyed barns and scattered the hay feed, blowing it into the sea, so that the animals went hungry.

Fuel was getting low so economies had to be endured, fires being lit only when the light turned to blue-grey in the early evening. For the party of Naturalists it was a hardship such as they had never known before. They went about their tasks clumsily, wearing numerous layers of clothing with just their faces and their fingertips exposed to the elements.

Meredith was almost glad that her writing machine was in pieces and couldn't be fixed, not even by Peter, who would willingly turn his hand to anything. It would have been physically impossible for her to type, since her fingers, even in the thick woollen gloves she had brought with her, were stiff and blue with the cold the whole day long.

The party tended to huddle together on the worst days. Even Professor Macaulay and Frazier gave up their preferred privacy in order to add to and share body warmth close to the often empty grate. On these occasions Meredith made sure she kept her distance from the learned professor and his gillie, usually with her father or Peter between them and her. She was thankful that Macaulay made no attempt to molest her a second time.

Logan had once again taken up the task of accompanying Meredith back to Flora's cottage. They spoke only of mundane things on the trek up hill and down dale. It was as if they had reverted to being strangers, although the silences that lay between them were laden with tension that could be felt in the very air they breathed. Meredith's heart felt heavy and cold, even though keeping up with his long strides was the only time she felt warmth in her body.

There had been no school for a week because the church was being cleaned for the Christmas Day service and Mr McEwan was required to lend a helping hand. It was an important day for the islanders: a day mixed with prayer and merrymaking when they would all come together in the factor's house. Mulled wine, laced heavily with spirits, would be drunk and there would be singing and dancing through the night.

'I think,' Dr Jolly said to Meredith, pocketing his pipe because he had long since run out of tobacco, though it helped his concentration to finger it from time to time, 'it would be best if you returned to Flora before it gets too dark.'

They had been sitting together for some time in amicable silence, their numb fingers clumsily manufacturing paper Christmas decorations to drape around the cottage. Meredith shook her head and gave him a smile, shivering as she did so.

'I prefer to wait for Logan,' she said, looking hopefully at the closed door, willing it to open and admit the big Scotsman.

'He's already late, Meredith.'

'Yes, but he always comes,' she said, frowning at her fob watch and wondering what had happened to keep Logan. It had never occurred to her that he might not come one day.

As the minutes ticked by she became concerned. What if he had had an accident, she wondered? No, no, he was too careful for that. There must be a more feasible reason.

Meredith looked around the cottage. Everyone was there, except the gillie. For some bizarre reason, Meredith's stomach lurched and her heart gave a little thud inside her chest.

'Where is Mr Frazier?'

The others looked from right to left of them, as if expecting to see the gillie sitting somewhere unnoticed in the shadows. He was almost as silent as the professor these days and it was hard to tell which one of them was the more sinister: Frazier with his slight limp that the broken leg had left him with, or Professor Macaulay with his staring eyes, twisted mouth and lumbering gait. Meredith did not trust either of them.

'Fergus?' Dr Jolly looked at the professor. 'Do you know where Frazier is?'

At first it seemed that the professor did not hear the doctor address him, for he neither flinched nor did he reply. They all stared at him and waited, wondering whether his stroke had brought on deafness as well as the other incapacities that were more evident.

The doctor opened his mouth to repeat the question, but Professor Macaulay drew in a long breath and his good hand jerked spasmodically, sending the book he was reading sliding to the floor.

'Not here,' he said thickly. 'Out … out there … with Logan.'

It was odd how easily he had slipped into the habit of calling his son Logan instead of his given name of Stuart. Perhaps, Meredith thought, it was a relief to do so. He obviously had no wish to acknowledge his son. Neither did Logan want to accept any part of the man whose seed had given him life. She didn't blame him for that, even though she knew little of the two men's history.

'With Logan?' Meredith's head now snapped up and again she experienced that awful lurching of the stomach as a feeling of foreboding descended upon her. 'What would he be doing with Logan?'

But the professor's head had sunk back, his eyes closed. He was either asleep or feigning it. She suspected the latter.

'Does anybody know where they've gone?'

'What's disturbing you, daughter? You've become as white as a sheet.'

'I want to know, Father.'

'Good heavens, girl! What does it matter? I hesitate to say it, but what Logan does every minute of the day should not concern you.'

Meredith swallowed with difficulty and looked from face to face in the room and all but the professor stared back at her curiously.

'Peter? Do you know?'

Peter started to shake his head, then changed his mind and looked sulky. 'Frazier left over an hour ago,' he told her. 'I saw him going after Logan.'

'Where?'

'What does it matter?' Peter's shoulders rose and fell. 'As your father says—'

'It *is* my business! I don't ...' She glanced towards the professor and lowered her voice to a whisper. 'I don't trust Frazier. I owe Logan a lot. He fished me out of the sea once. I might not be here today if it hadn't been for him.'

'That's putting it a bit strong, Meredith.' Peter gave her a stony look, then relaxed somewhat. 'All I know is they were walking along the sea edge in the direction of Dun.'

'Together?'

'No, Frazier was following behind Logan. With that game leg of his it would be impossible to keep up.'

'And you didn't see them together?'

'No, but then I have little interest in what those two get up to. Come on, Meredith, I'll see you home to Flora's hearth. God knows, it's a sight warmer in that old hag's cottage than it is down here.'

'Peter! Don't call Flora an old hag! She's a wonderful person, the salt of the earth.'

'Mad as a hatter,' Johnny muttered and the two young men sniggered like schoolboys.

'That's enough, boys!' Dr Jolly admonished, reaching for his tobacco jar, then cursing under his breath when he remembered it was empty and had been for some time. 'Peter, see Meredith back to her cottage and ...'

The handle of the old heavy door rattled as someone gripped and turned it. The door opened and a stream of pale-golden light filtered in, followed by Frazier and Logan. Each of them had their arms full of dark, splintery driftwood, which they let fall on to the rustic stone hearth.

'Logan! Thank God!' Meredith completely forgot herself in her relief at seeing him alive and whole.

He gave her a sharp, enquiring look. 'What's wrong?'

'Meredith was worried in case you'd got lost, Logan,' said Peter with a touch of uncharacteristic sarcasm.

'No I wasn't!' Now Meredith felt embarrassed and put her hands up to her flaming cheeks, half-expecting her icy fingers to sizzle on contact. 'I was just concerned that you were … well, a little later than usual.'

'Frazier had spotted some driftwood along the shore,' Logan said. 'We collected as much as we could and carried it to a place where it won't get washed back into the sea. These pieces here are dry enough for burning.'

'Oh, I see,' Meredith felt humiliated by her own suspicious mind.

'You didn't think I had forgotten to call for you, did you, Meredith?'

'No, of course not. It was just …' Her shoulders lifted and she stared into the pathetic flames of the fire that gave out so little heat. 'Never mind. It was nothing.'

Frazier was ignoring the whole scene and busying himself by pulling the woollen cover up to the professor's chin and tucking in the edges with as much care as a loving wife. As for Logan, he gave a wry smile and accepted the glass of whisky that the doctor put in his hand.

'I'm afraid it's watered down slightly, Logan,' Dr Jolly said, 'but supplies are awfully low.'

'In that case, you should keep this for yourself, Doctor,' Logan said, offering the glass back, but being refused by a wave of the doctor's hand. 'Thank you. It's very welcome.'

'I'll get my coat and shawl,' Meredith muttered, avoiding Logan's eyes.

Before she could wrap herself against the arctic conditions outside, a loud knocking sounded on the door timbers, startling them all. The noise of hard wood on wood sounded again and a voice they recognized shouted out.

'Josiah! Doctor Jolly, sir!' There was no mistaking Lachlan's fractured tones.

Peter, who was nearest the door, pulled it open and the old man entered, leaning heavily on his staff, his free arm clutching at a collection of hessian sacks.

'Lachlan, what on earth are you doing coming all this way yourself,' Dr Jolly exclaimed, concerned for the elder's frail, arthritic state. 'You could have sent a boy with a message.'

'Och!' Lachlan shook his head and let the sacks fall to his feet.

'Don't I know that, my friend. The thing is I wanted to see your faces when I delivered the news.'

'News? What news could it be to bring you all the way from your cottage to ours in the freezing cold?'

Lachlan fished a large handkerchief out of his pocket and wiped a dewdrop from the end of his long nose, and tears from his rheumy eyes. He looked around the room, as if counting heads, making sure that everyone was present.

'Well, now,' he said, speaking with infinite care. 'You'll be needing these here sacks for your belongings.' From his coat pocket he drew out a bottle of his famous firebrand whisky. 'And here's a little something for the journey, for it will be devilishly cold out at sea and the winds are blowing keenly and showing no sign of stopping. 'Tis my last bottle, so take care not to waste it.'

'What's this nonsense, Lachlan?' It was Logan who spoke and his dark eyes were piercing as he stared hard at the old man.

''Tis the miracle you've all been praying for,' Lachlan stated, still directing his gaze at Dr Jolly from beneath his bushy grey eyebrows. 'Didn't I tell you, Josiah, that it would work – our message in the bottle – it must have got to the mainland as we hoped it would.'

'What are you saying, man?' Josiah Jolly looked as if he dared not believe what he was hearing.

'Why, bless you, is there not a ship on yonder horizon come all the way from Harris or Uist or wherever and it will be here afore the morrow, I'd say.'

There were gasps all round. Peter and Johnny rushed to the cottage's one small window, which looked out over the bay. They pulled aside the heavy goatskin curtain.

'Where is it?' Johnny cried, his voice almost a squeak with the excitement of the moment. 'I can't see it!'

'Yes!' Peter said, looking over his shoulder and aiming his bright smile at Meredith, who hardly knew what to think or feel. 'Yes, I see a light. Not more than a pinprick where the sky meets the sea. It'll be here in no time unless the wind changes direction.'

'How wonderful,' Meredith heard herself say, half-heartedly and with a weak smile that faded when she caught sight of Logan watching her, his face a serious, unreadable mask.

Then the professor was pushing himself up out of his chair and taking a few staggering steps to the window, where he elbowed Johnny and Peter aside so that he could look for himself.

'Thank God!' he murmured, his voice rasping in his throat. 'At last I can be rid of this cursed place. Frazier!' He turned from the window and addressed the gillie, who was standing stony-faced at the other side of the room. 'Pack our bags.' He swallowed hard, struggling against the hemiplegia that made it difficult to speak. 'And see to any unfinished business.'

Frazier nodded, but remained where he was, unmoving, blinking at the professor as if waiting for further instruction.

'What are you waiting for, imbecile!' Fergus Macaulay lumbered forward, steadying himself by gripping the gillie's shoulder, making the man stagger beneath his weight. 'You know what to do.'

'Ay, Professor Macaulay,' Frazier said after a short pause.

'Then do it, man! Do I have to spell it out for you?'

Meredith couldn't help but notice the pointed way in which the two men spoke to one another, as if in ciphers, and wondered what it meant. Logan, too, had noticed, for he was now regarding his father and the gillie with suspicious eyes.

'I'll leave you to it, then,' Logan said eventually, nodding to each of them in turn. Then, without another word, he left the cottage.

Meredith followed him through the door, running after him in the dark.

'Logan!' she cried out. 'Logan, is that all you have to say?'

He stopped abruptly and she almost barged into him.

'What else is there to say, Meredith? I have said all that is necessary.'

'Come with us! You must!' Meredith gripped his rigid arms and gave him a tug, but it was like trying to move a pillar of stone. 'You must come back and clear your name once and for all. You'll never be happy unless you do.'

'It would need some brave souls to speak out against my father. I have my mother and my sister to think about. Their lives would not be worth much if the world discovered the truth behind the great Professor Fergus Macaulay. They've suffered enough. I wouldn't want to be responsible for more pain.'

'But Logan, I …' Meredith gagged on her own words as he pulled away from her and continued to walk into the darkness with long, urgent strides.

'Leave it!' she heard him say over his shoulder. 'Go home. Forget this place. More than anything, forget me.'

She mouthed his name, but the only sound that emerged from her constricted throat was a hoarse whisper. He had ordered her to forget him. How could she ever do that? If she never saw him again she knew she would love him for the rest of her life.

Someone came up to her from behind and draped a shawl about her shoulders, held her tightly in his arms for a brief moment. It was Peter. Judging by the expression on his kindly face he had overheard and fully understood what had passed between her and Logan.

'Oh, Meredith,' he said, his voice echoing the subdued emotion he was feeling deep down. 'I'm so sorry.'

Meredith sniffed and tossed her head proudly, desperately trying to demonstrate that she was braver than she felt.

'It would never have worked, would it, Peter?' she said huskily as she preceded him back to the cottage with brisk steps. 'Come on. There's work to be done if we are to be ready in time for that boat to set sail with the turning tide.'

CHAPTER 14

THERE WERE TEARS in Flora's old eyes as she helped Meredith gather together her belongings on that last morning. Meredith had gone to the cottage alone. She had scanned the hills for a sight of Logan, but he was nowhere to be seen.

'Och, I dinna know what's wrong with me,' Flora said, lifting her apron to wipe the moisture from her cheeks. 'I haven't shed a tear since I was a slip of a wee girl. There must be something strong in the air, is all I can think.'

'It's probably the wind,' Meredith said, giving the old woman a brief hug.

'Aye, indeed,' Flora said with a shake of her shoulders as if she were a hen fluffing out her feathers. 'There's ice in it like sharp needles. You wrap up warmly during the voyage, lassie.'

'I will,' Meredith promised.

'Here, take this,' Flora said, proffering a patchwork shawl that she had spent the last few months stitching by candlelight, each square of material filled with chicken feathers and goat's wool. 'It's not much, but 'tis all I have in the way of a gift so you won't forget me or this island.'

Meredith felt her throat constrict. Flora would not have been pleased with a further hug. She did not like displays of emotion. Instead, Meredith took the shawl and held it close to her heart, then pressed her cheek to it and tried not to weep, for every square encapsulated a memory of her time there on Hirta.

'It's the nicest present I've ever had, Flora,' she said huskily. 'Rest assured that I will never forget you, good friend that you have been to me.'

Flora flapped her hands in the air and tried to look nonchalant, but her chin quivered the tiniest bit and she had to bite down on her lips to stop them from doing the same.

'Get along with you now, child, or the boat will leave without you.'

'I don't think there's any fear of that,' Meredith said with a wistful smile. She took a last look about her and her eyes slid hopefully to the hills beyond in the direction of Logan's cottage.

'You won't see him,' Flora said, having guessed wisely what was in Meredith's heart. 'Logan doesn't like goodbyes.'

They walked together to the gate, and all the time Meredith kept hoping to see Logan's tall, rangy figure marching over the rise. Her hopes were, however, in vain.

She saw the others standing on the shore, surrounded by their bags and boxes. Peter and Johnny had carried the professor between them, then handed him over to the sailors from the boat, which was anchored further out in the bay. By the time her feet touched the shingle they were already boarding.

The St Kildan boat was waiting, with four islanders at the oars, ready to transport the remaining Naturalists to the steamship that was to take them back to the mainland. Her father, who had hung back, raised his hand in greeting.

'Come on, girl,' Dr Jolly called out to her, hastily turning the greeting into a beckoning gesture. 'The captain wants to get away in the next half-hour, before the weather turns about for the worse.'

He took her bundle of things from her and, grasping her hand, hurried her to where Jamie MacDonald was waiting to help them into the fishing boat.

'Go carefully, now, Miss Jolly,' he said, handing her over to her father, who had gone first.

'Jamie,' Meredith had her feet safely on the boat's timbers, but still she clung on to the young man's hand with both of hers as if she did not want to let it go, 'I haven't said goodbye to Logan.'

'He knows fine you're going, Miss Jolly,' Jamie said with a wry smile. 'Is there a message you would like me to take to him?'

'Yes … no … Oh, I—'

'Meredith, we must leave *now*,' Dr Jolly said from the other end of the boat.

'Yes, Father …' She looked beseechingly at Jamie. 'Tell him….'

She clamped her lips tightly shut and shook her head. Whatever she said now would make no difference. He would most likely have forgotten her by the time they were reinstalled at Northumberland. He had made St Kilda his home, where nobody could hurt him any more. On the mainland lay a past that he had no nostalgia for. It was, after all, best that he didn't return. Wasn't it?

Meredith let go of Jamie's hand and, in doing so, her eyes swept the high cliffs. Logan's dark silhouette, with the sunlight gleaming all around him, stood proudly erect on the highest promontory. She gasped at the sight of him, but he did not move, did not even raise a finger. She could not see his eyes, but she knew that they were fixed unwaveringly upon her. She liked to think that his heart still burned with the passion he had put into that last kiss. A passion, like an eternal flame that would never die.

She raised one hand and gave a slow wave, then let it drop back to her side. She turned to find her father looking at her, his expression full of concern.

'Come, my dear,' he said gently. 'It's time to go.'

Meredith settled herself beside her father and concentrated on the dark waters lapping against the boat. She studied the timbers, the men readying themselves at the oars. Anything rather than look back. If she looked back, she would be lost.

The sound of a gun firing twice in quick succession made them all look up sharply. It had come from above where Logan had been standing, but he was no longer there.

'Logan!' Meredith cried out.

'Now now, dear.' Dr Jolly held on to her, pulling her down beside him.

'Father, you don't think…?'

Before she got her words out there was a rattle of stones and the gillie, Frazier, came towards them with his limping run. He had a bundle under his arm and was carrying a long-barrelled pistol. He leapt into the boat as the helmsman untied the securing rope and they all smelled the hot, oily odour that the weapon was emitting.

'What on earth were you doing, man?' Dr Jolly demanded. The gillie gave a grimace that made him look menacing, yet his eyes seemed a little fearful as they darted this way and that.

'Just hunting our supper, Doctor,' he said, his voice even more rough-edged than usual.

He unwrapped what he was carrying in some bloodstained material and revealed a young goat. But it was not the dead goat that made Meredith put a hand over her mouth in order to stifle a cry of alarm. She recognised immediately the material it was wrapped in as being that of Logan's shirt. Unless she was very much mistaken, it was the very one he had been wearing earlier when he stood looking down on her.

'What have you done?' she asked, her voice barely above a terrified whisper.

'Why, only killed a goat, Miss Jolly,' he told her, again wrapping the poor animal so that it did not shed its blood all over the boat. 'They say that the Arabs consider goat to be a delicacy. I, for one, am looking forward to tasting it.'

'But what of Logan? What have you done to him?'

Frazier lifted his shoulders and gazed out at sea with half-closed eyes. 'What makes you think I've done anything to him?'

'The shirt. It's his.'

'I found it lying on the ground near where I shot the goat.'

'And did it already have Logan's blood on it?' Dr Jolly enquired.

Frazier gave a lopsided smile. 'Maybe. Come to think of it, yes. It looks like Logan has more enemies than he was aware of, don't it, eh?'

Meredith felt the world tilt. For a moment all consciousness seemed to drain from her and her skin prickled with a numbness that went deeper than her flesh, right down to the bone.

'Oh, dear God!'

'Don't listen to him, Meredith.' Her father was clasping her to him as the boat left, bobbing and lurching through the choppy waters of Village Bay.

'Ay,' said Jamie MacDonald, who was accompanying them. 'Logan will be all right, I'm sure.'

He meant his words to be reassuring, but his eyes said something different. He kept looking back to the rocks above the jetty as if willing Logan to reappear and prove him to be correct.

'How can you know for sure?' Meredith asked, holding back the tears that stung her eyes.

'Och, Miss Jolly, he's indestructible, is Logan.' Another glance at the rock where Logan had last stood. 'He'll be all right. Don't you worry about him.'

'Father...?' She threw a desperate glance at Dr Jolly and felt his hold on her tighten.

'Don't even think of going back, daughter. We have to leave now or face spending more months on this God-forsaken archipelagos.'

Meredith fell silent. The decision to leave the islands had already been taken. Whether Logan was dead or alive, she could do nothing to change the situation. He had not wanted her sufficiently to go back to the mainland with them. And she could not contemplate staying on Hirta.

'Come, Meredith,' Dr Jolly said. 'You have the rest of your life to live. Logan has chosen his own path and I doubt it will ever cross yours again.'

'Yes, Father. You are right, as usual.' She grabbed at the side of the boat as the agitated sea threw it about like a child's paper toy. She could see that they were almost upon the steamship. She could hear the engines whirring, ready to transport her out of this place and put her back where she belonged. And Peter was hovering anxiously close by, ready to catch her if she fell. She would feel so safe in his arms, and maybe she could learn to love him after all, once she could subdue the intolerable yearning she had for Logan. The pain of leaving him behind was almost too much to bear. Now she had to live in complete ignorance of whether he was alive or dead.

The crossing to the mainland was rough. For the first hour all they could do was hang on and pray while the sailors staggered about the deck like inebriated monkeys. At the halfway point the captain ordered the Naturalists down below with the cargo. Unfortunately, this proved just as dangerous. Some of the cargo, which consisted of rough wooden crates, had come adrift from their rope fastenings and was shifting about precariously. Twice, Meredith had to jump aside out of the path of one of the crates that seemed determined to crush her.

'Get to the back, Meredith,' her father ordered as he and Peter and Johnny wrestled with the loose cargo, trying to secure it more efficiently. 'It's not safe at this end.'

Meredith pushed her way through to the dark stern end of the hold where there were bunks that looked solid enough. She slipped into one and pulled a heavy, coarse, foul-smelling blanket over her to keep out the damp, penetrating cold that hung cruelly in the dank air. She did not know where Frazier and the professor were and cared less. Her thoughts were fixed unshakably on Logan and the shirt wrapped around the dead goat.

A sudden lull brought a welcome break from the fierce tossing of the merciless sea. Meredith lay still and prayed that the elements would now be kind to them. She struggled up on her elbows and breathed air that was only minimally fresher than that beneath the old blanket. Through the worn, timber slats beside her she heard a low mutter of voices. There was a scratching noise and light flickered into life through a crack, together with the distinctive odour of sulphur as someone struck a match.

The continuing flicker of light told her that a candle or a lamp had been lit. Meredith put an eye to the crack and peered through. She saw Professor Macaulay, his face stretched into his most fierce expression.

'Did you do the deed, Frazier?'

A second person came partly into sight, just the hands and forearms which belonged unmistakably to the gillie. He was holding up Logan's shirt as if offering evidence.

'Here you are, sir. See for yourself.'

Meredith pressed her face to the slats, trying to see more. The professor was now gone from her sight and Frazier was holding up the shirt, shaking it out, turning it until he came to the patch of blood that was still fresh. There was a hole in the centre of the patch through which he stuck a thick forefinger. Meredith clasped a hand over her mouth, not wanting to give away her presence.

'There you are, Professor, sir,' the gillie said in a gruff whisper. 'Is that not proof enough, or would you have preferred me to bring his body on board too?'

'There were two shots, but only one in the shirt.'

'Ay, and one in the goat.'

'So, this time you succeeded in your task? Stuart … *my infernal son*? *He is dead*?'

'Ay, sir. Stuart … or Logan as he is now known. A bullet through the heart, just like you ordered, and nobody saw it happen.'

'You did well this time, Frazier. I will see that you are rewarded.'

'Thank you, sir.'

'But if you say a word of this to any living soul—'

'I won't, sir, you can trust me.'

'See that I can, Frazier. Otherwise, you're a dead man.'

'Ay, sir. Don't you think that I know that?'

At this point there was a great howling of wind like the wail of a banshee, and a deafening lashing of rain. The steamboat was once more tossed high before slapping down hard on the boiling sea. They had passed through the eye of the storm and now worse was awaiting them.

Meredith, numb with shock, gave a spontaneous cry, though she could not hear her own voice above all that was happening around her. She tumbled from the bunk and tried to stand, but all she could manage was to crawl on all fours.

A hatch above her head was wrenched open, giving access to a cascade of seawater that soaked her to the skin. One of the crew appeared, head and shoulders silhouetted against a grey and indigo sky, rain falling in silver arrows all around him.

'Everybody on deck!' he shouted gruffly, reaching down with one hand to haul Meredith up the vertical ladder, which she was attempting to climb without success. 'There are ropes. Tie yourselves down.'

'Father!' Meredith shouted as she was pulled and pushed up on to the heaving deck which was now awash.

'I'm here,' came the response. 'Save yourself, girl. I'm all right.'

'Here, miss, I've got ye!' The sailor who had dragged her up from the bowels of the boat was now dragging her to one side, wrapping a coarse hemp rope around her and securing it to a rail near the centre of the vessel.

'Please help my father,' she begged, but the man had left her and was already out of earshot.

They limped into the port of Harris as the storm abated and the sky turned pale green and purple with gilt-edged amber clouds. The flat sea was a metallic blue and the land a shimmering iridescent green.

Meredith struggled with the knots of the rope that bound her, but it took the sharp knife of the captain to release her. She was relieved to see that her father and Peter, though exhausted, were none the worse for their experience. And Johnny seemed almost exhilarated. He obviously could not wait to get off the boat and on to the shore, where a welcoming party awaited them, including the local reporter who insisted on them posing while his associate captured their image on his plate camera with an explosion of flash powder.

All was confusion. Meredith stood on wobbling legs looking about her. In the middle of a crowd of journalists she recognized her father's white head. She struck out towards him, but the crush was too much. Luckily, someone took hold of her hand and led her around the outskirts of the crowd. It was Peter.

'Oh, Peter, I'm so glad to see you ... these people ... I didn't expect such a fuss....'

'Are you all right, Meredith?'

'It'll pass,' she said through shivers and rattling teeth. 'I need to sit down, that's all.'

Peter pushed her gently down on a low wall. He sat beside her and slid a protective arm about her shoulders. Some kindly soul from a nearby house came and draped a heavy woollen blanket over them. Another produced two cups of steaming tea sweetened with too much sugar, but it helped revive them.

'Peter ...' Meredith gave a sob, 'I think Logan is dead.'

'What? Meredith, what are you saying? What makes you think that?'

She told him everything she had witnessed, including the conversation between the professor and his gillie over the bloodstained shirt.

'There was a bullet hole in it, Peter,' she said. 'Right where it would find Logan's heart.'

'And you think…?'

'Frazier. Following the professor's instructions. They tried to get rid of Logan five years ago, but failed. This time … Oh, Peter! Poor Logan! Now he can't even clear his own name.'

'Then we must do it for him, Meredith,' Peter said, squeezing her hand.

'You would do that, even though…?'

'If it would make you happy, yes. I'd do anything in the world to make you happy, Meredith.'

Before she could reply to his touching words, Meredith saw her father bearing down upon them, followed by one or two of the townsfolk.

'Meredith, Peter! These kind people have offered us accommodation,' Dr Jolly called out, then he was standing before her, arms outstretched, ready to embrace her.

'Oh, Father!' she cried as she threw himself at him.

He held her tightly to him, kissing the top of her head and pressing a hand on Peter's shoulder. They had been through hell together and had come out the other end unscathed.

'Dr Jolly?' The captain of the steamship in which they had endured the storm was approaching, grim-faced and flanked by two officers of the law.

'What is it, my good fellow?' Josiah Jolly turned to greet the men, though he still held on to his daughter as if he would never let her go, as did Peter on her other side.

'Bad news, I'm afraid.' The captain scraped his fingers through his grizzly beard and looked uncertain of what to say

'Oh, look!' Meredith interrupted, pointing along the beach where four men were carrying a stretcher, the occupant of which was obviously dead.

'Yes,' the captain said. 'I'm afraid your Professor Macaulay did not survive the voyage.'

There was a short, startled silence. They watched as the men and the stretcher approached. Dr Jolly lifted the blanket that covered the body of Fergus Macaulay.

'He was in very poor health,' he said. 'He suffered a major stroke while we were on St Kilda. It is a miracle he lasted so long.'

'His death has nothing to do with his failing health, sir,' said the more senior of the two policemen. 'He was stabbed through the heart.'

'Good Lord!' Dr Jolly dropped the blanket and took a staggering step back.

'Two of your party seem to be missing, Dr Jolly. That blond-haired boy and the gillie.'

'Dear God, not Johnny!' Peter murmured in Meredith's ear. 'Surely not!'

Meredith said nothing. She was too worried about how she could prove to the authorities that Logan was innocent of any crime of which his father had accused him. The two most important people who could give evidence against the professor had taken flight.

CHAPTER 15

MEREDITH HEARD THE familiar rustle of pages as her father walked down the hall, already reading his daily journal. His footsteps halted and he gave a loud gasp as if something had displeased him.

'What is it, Father?'

They had been back in Northumberland for less than a month, so the islands and all that had happened to them there were still fresh in their minds. They had been questioned rigorously by the police on the murder of Professor Macaulay, but eventually they had been allowed to go home. There was no doubt in anybody's mind that he had been stabbed, either by the gillie or by Johnny, and a search was under way to find both men.

What had been heartening on their return home was the fact that Aunt Agnes had miraculously cast off the accustomed black bombazine and had taken to wearing purple taffeta, albeit with black-velvet trim. They had yet to discover the reason for this, for Agnes was not exactly forthcoming, despite the unusually bright glint in her small, blackcurrant eyes.

"This newspaper journalism,' Dr Jolly said, coming into the room, holding the paper open before him. 'So many facts wrong.'

Meredith could read the headlines of the front page, printed in heavy black capitals: *The world of science mourns brutal slaying of famous naturalist.*

'What are they saying now?'

'Oh, they still maintain that young Johnny stabbed the man. They even suggest that he threw the gillie overboard. Everyone, of course, knows how devoted the fellow was to Macaulay.'

'Perhaps it isn't so far from the truth, Father,' Meredith told him and saw his eyebrows rise in astonishment.

'If you know anything, daughter, you must tell the police.'

Meredith shook her head and went back to her tapestry, keeping her eyes fixed on the sharp needle threaded with wool.

'It's not what I know, but what I feel,' she said. 'Frazier wouldn't have murdered the professor. If anything, he needed to keep that horrid monster alive. As for Johnny, impossible though it seems, I think he is more likely to have wielded the knife.'

'That would surprise me.' Dr Jolly bunched up the sheets of news and threw them to one side. 'The boy was terrified of his own shadow. How Macaulay came to choose him for the expedition I shall never know.'

'He chose him because he was too scared to stand up for himself.'

'You don't mean…?'

'He was the kind of boy who was easy prey for men like the professor.'

The doctor frowned deeply and scratched at a sideburn. 'Ah! And here I was thinking that my daughter was the innocent one.'

Meredith gave a pained smile. 'Peter explained everything to me, Father. He knows about things like that.'

'Ah!' Dr Jolly repeated again. 'Dear Peter. I like that boy, Meredith.'

'Yes, Father. So do I.'

'Is that all you have to say about him?'

Meredith knew what her father was doing. Since taking their leave of Peter in Edinburgh, the doctor had never ceased trying to sing Peter's praises and to get Meredith to admit that she could perhaps feel more than just a liking for him. And she thought that perhaps she could, sometime, have more than sisterly feelings for Peter. But he was not Logan, and it was Logan that still filled her heart with hopeless longing. It would be a long time before the gaping wound that he had left her with healed.

'What is it you are writing?' Meredith redirected the conversation away from Peter and looked at the pieces of writing-paper on her father's desk. He had been scribbling away fervently, but without much success, judging by the number of sheets he had crumpled up and discarded.

The doctor followed her gaze and gave a sigh. 'I was trying to write a letter of sympathy to Macaulay's widow,' he said. 'I'm finding it damnably difficult. We really should have called on her when we were still in Edinburgh.'

'I'm glad we didn't, Father,' Meredith said. 'All I could think of was to get home and put the whole business behind me.'

'It wasn't all bad, daughter.' Josiah sifted through the morning mail that had been placed on a side table earlier.

'No, I suppose not.'

'It was a good expedition. We came back with more new information than I thought possible.'

'Will you still write the book? Even though…?'

'Yes. Yes, I will. In fact I have been asked to do so. You will, I hope, do the illustrations, Meredith?'

Meredith inclined her head. She had a doubtful smile on her face.

'Oh, Father, I don't know. I'm in a strange mood….'

'You are grieving, my dear. It will pass in time. You and Logan … it was never meant to be.' Her father picked up a letter from the top of the pile and held it out to her. 'Look here. A letter from Edinburgh already. If I'm not mistaken, that is Peter's handwriting.'

Meredith took the letter, turning it over and over in her hands, which trembled slightly. The very mention of Logan's name had made her grief harder to bear. She could see him still, standing on the rocks, strong and silent and her heart swelled as if it might burst with love for him, even though she knew him to be dead.

She had told the authorities what she had witnessed but, since the professor and most probably his gillie were also dead, there was no one left to punish.

Slowly and almost reluctantly she slid her thumb beneath the red wax seal and withdrew the creamy sheet of stiff vellum on which Peter had penned a few lines in his neat, sloping hand.

'It is from Peter,' she said softly, her eyes skimming again and again what he had to say. 'He sends you his best regards, Father.'

'Well, that's all very nice, but what else has he to say for himself?'

'He …' Meredith had to stop and clear her throat. 'He is asking for my hand in marriage, Father.'

'Splendid! Of course, he has already spoken to me on the subject. You know well my sentiments on that matter.' He came to her, his arms open wide, and hugged her to his chest. 'It would give me the greatest pleasure, Meredith, to see you happily settled with a good husband.'

Meredith drew in a deep breath. A lump had arisen in her throat and she was fighting to control her emotions, so speech was out of the question. Fortunately, her aunt chose that moment to enter the room with a rustle of silk petticoats and a waft of Devon Violets.

They both stared at her in surprise. This was completely unexpected, for she rarely entered the parlour and they hardly saw her except at mealtimes. However, there she was in a new lilac frock with frothy cream lace at her neck and amethysts in her ears.

'Agnes!' Josiah Jolly exclaimed, unable to keep the amazement from his voice. 'Are you quite all right?'

She threw him a reproachful look, one thin eyebrow raised. 'For what reason do you ask me that, Josiah. Do I appear ill in your eyes?'

The doctor shook his head and looked to his daughter for support. It was always too easy to get on the wrong side of his sister-in-law. Any upset now might send her back into her black bombazine and anxiously rattling jet beads.

'Why, Aunt Agnes, you look quite radiant!' Meredith blurted out. 'That colour suits you so well.'

'Come now, child, hardly that!' Aunt Agnes looked embarrassed and her cheeks glowed pink. Although her words suggested otherwise, it was obvious how pleased she was.

She settled herself in Josiah's favourite chair by the window and stared out at the winter sunshine. They couldn't help noticing that she played nervously with her fingers and at every sound she pulled herself upright and seemed momentarily to stop breathing.

'Hmm,' said Dr Jolly, frowning first at his pipe and then at his sister-in-law, stubbornly occupying his chair, but Agnes ignored him and continued to sit where she was.

Twenty minutes passed with the three of them sitting in silence, then Agnes jumped to her feet and clasped her hands to her heart, looking for all the world like the young girl she must once have been.

'He is here!' she pronounced in a breathy whisper and her pink cheeks turned to crimson. 'Oh, dear!'

A very smart, bewhiskered gentleman with a top hat, pince-nez, pale-kid gloves and a silver-handled cane, which he swung with barely disguised pleasure, came sauntering across the road towards the house. He hesitated at the gate to adjust his appearance with a tug here and a flick there, then approached the house in a march so stately that he must have spent some time in the military.

'Are you expecting a visitor, Agnes?' Dr Jolly enquired, bristling with a mixture of curiosity and amusement, for he had never seen his sister-in-law in such a state of anticipation.

'Oh, dear me!' Agnes kept repeating as she dodged away from the window so as not to be seen by the presumed visitor, who was regarding the house as if looking for a sign of occupation.

'Shall I let him in, Agnes, since it is Daisy's day off?'

'Oh, dear, oh my goodness!' The good lady seemed to be on the verge of hysterics and was, indeed, searching frantically for her smelling salts, but her fingers were too jittery to cope with the stopper of the tiny blue bottle of sal volatile.

'And who might our visitor be?' Josiah Jolly demanded, quizzical eyebrows raised in Meredith's direction.

Agnes cleared her throat noisily, and had to do it again before she found her voice.

'It is a dear friend,' she said, patting imaginary wisps of hair into place and smoothing out her voluminous skirts. 'A Mr Lionel Crabtree ... *Major* Crabtree, actually, though he is no longer in active service.'

'I didn't know we were acquainted with any of the military,' Dr Jolly said, peering curiously at the man who was hovering in slight impatience outside the front door.

'He ... um ... he ...' Agnes stuttered and fanned her face frenetically with a lace-edged handkerchief hardly bigger than a postage stamp. 'He fought alongside my own dear George ... the young man I was to marry. Apparently, they were the best of friends. He has been calling on me every week since the first of August.'

'In that case, we'd better bid him enter,' said Dr Jolly, a slightly bemused smile sliding into place. 'Unless you intend to keep him standing on the doorstep?'

Even as he spoke there was a light rapping on the door. Agnes drew in a deep breath and pulled herself up to her full five feet, puffing out her chest like a proud peacock. She took a further moment to compose herself, then went to receive her visitor.

'My dear Major,' they heard her say in a voice as light and as soft as they had ever heard her employ. 'Do come in. How nice to see you.'

'Agnes, how lovely you look!'

'Why thank you, Major—'

'Oh, come now, I'm sure that you can call me Lionel, having said you would do me the honour of becoming my wife.'

Dr Jolly and Meredith exchanged open-mouthed glances. Meredith bit down hard on her lip so as not to disgrace herself by laughing out loud. Her father kept a straight face, but betrayed his amusement by the twinkling of his eyes.

'It seems to me, Meredith,' he whispered, 'that we should go away more often, if this is the effect our absence has on your aunt.'

During the second week of February Meredith approached her father with the news that she was to travel to Edinburgh at the weekend.

'On your own?' Dr Jolly looked at her disapprovingly over his reading spectacles and puffed with vigour on his pipe. His sister-in-law was out walking with her fiancé, so he was taking advantage of her absence.

'Oh, Father, it's not such a huge undertaking,' Meredith said, smiling at his concern. 'I'm all grown up now. Besides, Peter will meet me at the railway station.'

'I see.' A cloud of blue pipe smoke rose into the air and he looked down into the bowl of the pipe reflectively. 'Might one ask the reason for this sudden return to Edinburgh?'

'I was going to tell you, Father.' Meredith took a deep breath and pulled at the lace trimmings of her tight bodice. 'It's to do with Logan … No, hear me out! I know he's … well no longer with us, but …'

'Go on, child, I'm listening, though I have the distinct impression that I will not like what I am about to hear.'

'No, you probably won't like it, but it's something I'm driven to do.'

'And what exactly is that, Meredith?'

'I want to try and clear Logan's name. He should not have his reputation blackened because of the evil deeds of his father.'

Dr Jolly started pacing the room, running an agitated hand over his head. 'And how might you do that, with Fergus Macaulay just as dead as his son? If the man was as devious and as sinful as you say he is, he will have covered his tracks well. There are people in this world, my dear, who think he was a saint. Try to blacken his name and you will end up facing their wrath.'

Meredith stamped a foot and folded her arms in front of her. She stared at her father with an unmistakable expression of bold determination.

'I've got to try, Father. It's the least I can do for the man I loved. Or would you rather I donned black like Aunt Agnes did and waste the years that I have left mourning a man I can no longer have?'

'What nonsense you do talk at times, daughter.' Dr Jolly knocked out his pipe in the fire grate and replaced it in the rack on the mantelshelf. 'What, pray, do you have in mind?'

Meredith really didn't have anything in mind. She had thought that she would just make some enquiries in Edinburgh and see what she might be able to make of the answers.

'I will occupy myself with the details on the long train journey to Edinburgh. It will help to while away the time.'

'Hmm.' Dr Jolly was staring out of the window, his back to the room. 'You know, I still feel guilty at not calling on Mrs Macaulay to offer my condolences.'

'It was a little difficult with the police milling around asking so many questions.'

'She must think us thoughtless and ungrateful. I could, of course, send a letter of sympathy, but I feel it would be better to go and see her, don't you think, Meredith? It's not too late, is it?'

'Does that mean you'll be going with me?'

'If that will not upset your plans, my dear.'

She went over to him and planted a light kiss on his cheek.

'I shall be more than pleased to have you as my travelling companion, Father, and I know that Peter will be delighted to see you again. His family lives just outside Edinburgh and he has already said that we are welcome to stay there at any time.'

'In that case I'd better go and pack my things.'

'What about Aunt Agnes?'

'Something tells me that she will put up no argument whatsoever.'

CHAPTER 16

THE TRAIN WHEEZED into Edinburgh on a freezing January afternoon. The sun that shone down from a clear blue sky was without warmth and icicles hung from the buildings like transparent daggers dripping coldly on the heads of passers-by.

Peter had been on the platform to meet them, blowing on his hands and stamping his feet to keep the circulation going. Misty clouds of human breath floated all around as people laughed and talked while they made their way tentatively on the frozen ground to their respective destinations.

They received the warmest of greetings from Peter and his family and Meredith was surprised at how pleased she was to see him again. As for Peter, he didn't have to put his feelings into words, for his eyes glowed with love at his first sight of her.

'You must make yourself at home,' said Mrs Lewis, her plump, rosy-cheeked face beaming a warm welcome.

'You're too kind, dear lady,' Dr Jolly said, accepting a tot of warming whisky from Peter's father with an appreciative nod. 'We shall not be putting you out for too long. We have just come to pay our respects to Professor Macaulay's family, which we should have done earlier, but—'

'Ah, yes, Peter has told us all about that business. What a tragedy for a family to lose both father and son in such terrible circumstances. The papers, of course, have been full of the story.'

'There's worse,' Peter said, handing over the morning newspaper. 'You probably haven't seen this.'

'What is it?' Meredith asked while her father fumbled for his reading spectacles.

'It's Johnny. They've arrested him for the professor's murder.'

'Johnny! Oh, no! They can't possibly think that… ?'

'It's true, I'm afraid.' Peter spread his hands. 'Of course, the news-papers have labelled him a coward, stabbing a poor, defenceless man. There's quite an uproar in the professor's circle of friends and colleagues.'

'Hmm,' grunted Dr Jolly, his eyes skimming the article. 'I was afraid this might happen.'

'Oh, poor Johnny,' Meredith said. 'I don't condone murder, but I do believe he had suffered enough to drive him to a desperate deed.'

'And you would be right,' Peter said. 'I just wish he had waited and let Nature take her course. But then, he had been through so much at the hands of our famous professor. His emotions were never much in control.'

'Dear me!' Peter's mother went pale and clutched at her generous bosom. 'Did he … the professor, I mean … Peter, I hope he never…?'

Everyone looked slightly embarrassed, including Peter, but he shook his head vehemently and gave his mother a reassuring hug.

'No, Ma, he didn't. I wasn't the sort he fancied, thank God.'

Meredith took a deep breath and frowned deeply before speaking out.

'If he liked boys in that way,' she said slowly, 'then why did he show an interest in me? Why did he abuse that girl on Hirta … the one who bore him a child?'

It was Dr Jolly who answered her.

'There are some men, my dear, who can't draw the line. They seek only bodily satisfaction. It doesn't matter to them how they get it. Carnal desire excites them, the more unnatural the better. They are animals, the worst beasts there are. I suspected as much of Macaulay when I saw how he seemed to indulge young Johnny, but I didn't want to admit it.'

'Me too,' said Peter. 'Johnny was always too scared to speak out. I don't think he was the only one, but his victims are outnumbered by the professor's rich and influential friends. Whom do you think the grand public will believe, eh? Even in death Fergus Macaulay still wields a rod of iron.'

Meredith's forehead creased deeply as she tried to come up with some kind of solution that would help lay the blame squarely at the professor's door, but it seemed an impossibility. Logan was dead and could not speak out on his own behalf, and the one man who probably knew the truth, the gillie Frazier, was missing. He would hardly come forward voluntarily, for it would undoubtedly mean the gallows for him.

'There must be a way to clear Logan's name,' she said. 'Peter, you must talk to people, find someone, anyone with enough courage to speak out.'

'I've tried, Meredith, believe me,' Peter said with a resigned sigh. 'But what is the word of a poor student or a prostitute against the reputation of someone like Fergus Macaulay?'

'Please try again,' Meredith pleaded, her eyes round and as big as saucers. 'If you do nothing else for me, promise me that you will do this.'

'He's dead, Meredith. Nothing can hurt him now.'

'I know that, but I don't want him buried with the stigma his father gave him. He doesn't deserve that. He was a good man.'

Peter nodded slowly. 'Yes, I tried to dislike him, especially when I thought he was stealing you from me, but … you are perfectly right to say that he was a good man.'

'Aye, lad,' Dr Jolly said. 'I felt much the same as you but, truth be told, he was a good and brave soul soured by his past, and what man wouldn't be with a father such as Fergus Macaulay. Do what you can, Peter my boy.'

'I will, Dr Jolly,' Peter told him. Then, taking Meredith gently in his arms, he placed an affectionate kiss on her lips. 'If I fail, I hope you will not throw me aside, Meredith?'

She smiled and tenderly stroked his cheek. 'I won't. You will always be my own, dear Peter.' The words coming out of her mouth surprised her, for she had said it from the heart.

'Good luck, laddie!' Dr Jolly slapped his shoulder and looked pleased at witnessing such a scene between Peter and his daughter. He felt encouraged that Meredith was at last on the verge of settling down, and with a young man who was worthy of her.

*

Meredith and her father stood pensively on the doorstep of the Macaulay household, listening to the fading chimes of the bell after the third time it had been rung. Only an eerie, echoing silence followed. Not a voice, not a footstep, nor the creak of a floorboard sounded, neither was there a tweak of the creamy lace curtains that blocked out the view from the street.

Meredith leaned across her father to give the bell pull another tug, but he stayed her hand and shook his head.

'I'm sure,' he said, 'that if the family were home they would have answered by now. And if they are in there, not wishing to see anybody, it would be impolite to insist.'

Meredith, whose mind was far from thoughts of being polite, frowned at him and gave an impatient sigh.

'We can't just give up, Father. Somehow or other we must—'

'Meredith, Meredith!' Dr Jolly gripped her arm and pulled her gently but firmly away from the house. 'Come, my dear. I fear there's nothing we can do. I shall write a letter to Mrs Macaulay and her daughter.'

'What good is that, Father? We need to speak to her face to face. The daughter too. I'm sure we can get them to admit the truth. After all, the professor is no longer here to make them suffer his abuse.'

'Did Logan mean so much to you, daughter?' He looked at her sadly and she felt her eyes prick as tears formed, which they did every time she thought of the big, brusque Scot who had made her girlish heart beat like a woman's.

'I know you find it difficult to believe, Father,' she said, her voice a small croak in her throat. 'But I knew the moment I set eyes on Logan that he was the man for me, even though he himself did not see it at first.'

'Oh, I think he did, lassie.' Josiah stroked her flushed cheek and gave her a tight hug as they walked down the path together. 'The man did everything in his power not to have feelings for you, because he knew how impossible his situation was. Logan was a man of honour. I have to respect him for that.'

'I thought you didn't like him.'

'Ay, you're right, but that was because I had the belief deep inside me that he would hurt you sooner or later and I didn't want that. You're my darling daughter, Meredith, and all that I have. I love you dearly.'

Meredith stiffened slightly and pulled away from him, making him study her face with some trepidation.

'Perhaps you have loved me too much, Father. After all, you have kept me close by your side since Mother died.' She shook her head at his worried expression. 'Oh, I've enjoyed being with you, working under your direction, but ... well, it wasn't until I met Logan that I realized that I could have so much more in my life than just ... friendship.'

She heard his intake of breath and was glad that he did not repeat the question that had seemed always to be on his lips since they left St Kilda. Her answer would forever be the same. Yes, she was fond of Peter and they would probably marry one day, but she could not say, not yet, that she was in love with him. Not the desperate, all-consuming love she had felt for Logan.

They were almost through the gate when the big front door swung open and a plump figure with ruddy cheeks and lace-trimmed cap all askew on her grey head, came slithering down the frosty path towards them, arms flailing.

'Sir, sir! Miss!' She skidded to a halt and stood wobbling there, blinking furiously as the cold air struck her. 'Madam says would you like to come in?'

They entered gladly, though the house did not seem much warmer than it had been outside. The plump woman bobbed and smiled nervously as she tried to adjust her cap and introduced herself as the housekeeper, Mrs Robertson.

'We thought that perhaps there was nobody at home,' the doctor said and the woman bit down on her lip and nodded.

'I'm sorry about keeping you waiting, sir,' she said, pressing a hand to her heaving chest. 'I was upstairs changing beds and I had to run all the way down to tell Mrs Macaulay that she had visitors. There's no-one else, you see, sir. Just the mistress and me and normally she doesn't see people who call.'

'But she will see us, I hope?' Meredith asked.

'She said no at first, miss,' the housekeeper said, 'but when I told her who it was ringing the bell ... I recognized you from the last time you came to see the professor, you see ... well, she said in that case she would see you.'

'Is she well?'

The housekeeper's face crumpled and she dabbed at her small eyes with the edge of her apron.

'Oh, sir, she's not at all right in her head since ... well, you know ...' She blew her nose noisily. 'Doesn't eat, doesn't sleep, doesn't do anything but sit there in the parlour like some forgotten soul that lost her way to Heaven. I fear for her mind, sir. You'll see what I mean.'

'But isn't there a daughter?'

'Yes, sir. Miss Marion.' Tears welled up again in the housekeeper's eyes. 'With all this business of the professor and young Mr Stuart dying, she took really bad and the doctor sent her to some kind of hospital to convalesce. I do fear she might go off her head. People do, you know, when they goes in to them asylum places. Look at little Miss Janet, her sister ...' The woman pulled herself up and stood rigid before them as if she had been found out in a misdemeanour. 'There now, I shouldn't be talking out of turn to strangers. I'll take you to see Mrs Macaulay now.'

She led them across the wide hall and tapped lightly on a door, opening it without waiting for a reply and beckoning to them to enter.

'Dr and Miss Jolly to see you, madam.' She dipped a knee and whispered to them before hurrying off: 'Be gentle with her, won't you, sir ... miss? Well, I'll leave you and go and fetch some tea.'

Anne Macaulay was sitting by the fire, which gave the only light in the room, for heavy curtains were now drawn across the casement windows, though the lamps were unlit. She seemed like a shadow of her former self and her clothing hung limply on her as though they covered a skeleton. One would have been forgiven for thinking she was no longer a warm, breathing, living being.

It was a long moment before Mrs Macaulay showed any sign of being aware that she was no longer alone. She reached for the poker that rested close to her chair and stoked the fire, coaxing a black coal back to life. It crackled and flames leapt up the chimney, bringing instant warmth into the room.

'Allow me, Mrs Macaulay,' Dr Jolly said, coming forward and taking the liberty of adding more coal from the brass scuttle in the hearth.

Ann Macaulay lifted her head and her dark eyes, sunken and shadowed searched the doctor's face; then she turned to Meredith.

'I'm sorry,' she said, her voice cracked and weak. 'I've been rather ill, you see …' She made a feeble effort to rise, but gave it up and sank back against her cushions.

'I'm Josiah Jolly, Mrs Macaulay,' the doctor announced. 'And this is my daughter, Meredith. We met last year before accompanying your husband to St Kilda.'

'Ah, yes, I remember now.' Her face twisted as if the woman had been visited by a spasm of pain. 'My husband … my son … so tragic …'

She stared intently into the fire, her visitors momentarily forgotten until Meredith approached her and sank down on her knees before her, one hand touching the cold hand that gripped the arm of the chair.

'Mrs Macaulay, we are sorry if our visit upsets you, but it is imperative that we should talk to you,' Meredith said, ignoring the warning glance of her father. 'There are things that perhaps only you and your daughter know about Professor Macaulay.'

'What things?' The question was sharp-edged and the woman drew back as if suddenly afraid. 'I don't understand you, girl. I know nothing! Nothing!'

'You must know! It's time that the world knew the truth about Fergus Macaulay.' Meredith brushed off her father's hand as it gripped her shoulder. 'He was an ogre, a monster! He preyed on weak boys and young girls and—'

'How dare you speak of my husband like this!'

'I dare because I want to clear the name of a good man and I will do everything I can to do just that.' Meredith gripped Anne Macaulay's hands in hers and squeezed them until the woman winced with the pain of it. 'The good man I speak of is your son, Logan … I mean, Stuart. The professor had him murdered rather than allow him to return to the mainland and spread the word that his father was a vile and wicked man, a wife-beater and an abuser of children.'

'No! It's not true!'

'It is true, I tell you,' Meredith cried out with all her might, 'and if you will not speak out I'll find another way to inform the world of his despicable nature. I loved your son, Mrs Macaulay, and he loved me. But he is dead now, though he might still be alive today if you had not kept quiet years ago. Your daughter Janet might also be alive and well, but she is dead because of what her father did to her. And what about Marion? You stood by and allowed it to happen. Don't you feel any responsibility at all for your husband's ill-doings?'

Meredith gave Mrs Macaulay a shake, then let go of her wrists. The professor's widow put her hands up to her face and screamed, shaking her head from side to side.

'Enough, Meredith!' Dr Jolly hooked a hand beneath his daughter's arm and pulled her back to her feet. 'This is cruelty!'

'There are all kinds of cruelty, Father,' Meredith said as he half-pulled, half-pushed her out of the room. 'Silence can be the worst cruelty of all. Mrs Macaulay is distressed, but I'll wager that her distress is caused by the guilt she feels right now. A guilt which will haunt her for the rest of her days.'

'Come.' Dr Jolly marched her across the hall as Mrs Robertson appeared, her face distraught at the sound of her mistress's screams. 'I think we've done enough harm for one day.'

'You're not going, are you, sir?' The housekeeper dried her hands on her apron and glanced towards the parlour where Mrs Macaulay's screams were subsiding into snuffling sobs.

'I'm afraid it was a mistake to come here today,' Dr Jolly said. 'Mrs Macaulay can't help us. Not when she is in such a deplorable state.'

'You might try asking me your questions, sir,' Mrs Robertson said, lifting her chin up high and folding her arms across her chest in a businesslike manner. 'If it's about the professor, there's not a lot I don't know. He wasn't a man, sir, he was a devil, and it's no wonder his family came to grief. I'm just sorry that the laddie didn't survive, for he was not of the same blood as Fergus Macaulay, much as he looked the spitting image of the man.'

CHAPTER 17

Meredith and the doctor could not believe their ears. The housekeeper glanced cautiously down the hall, but there was no longer the sound of weeping from the parlour. The elderly woman touched a work-worn finger to her lips and signalled for them to follow her.

She led them to a warm kitchen, where the air was laced with the appetizing aroma of freshly baked bread. A cauldron of broth bubbled on the black-lead stove. Mrs Robertson gave it a quick stir and moved it away from the heat.

'I hope you will forgive me for bringing you in here, Dr Jolly … Miss Jolly …' She gestured for them to sit down at a scrubbed white-wood table and joined them. 'Madam never comes in here, so I can speak to you in confidence.'

'I wish you would, Mrs Robertson,' said Meredith and was hastily admonished by her father for being so impatient.

'It's quite all right, sir,' the housekeeper said. 'I have been waiting for the opportunity to get this knowledge off my chest and ease my conscience. I know I should have spoken out long ago, but I have no husband, and a family to take care of. Besides, I honestly thought that no one would believe me. He was such a famous and a well-liked man, you see.' She hesitated, looking undecided for a few moments, then went on: 'I suppose it doesn't matter any more now. You see, Mrs Macaulay has given me my notice. She is selling the house and moving to Canada, where she has a sister.'

'I see,' said Dr Jolly. 'In that case, my dear lady, we would very much like to hear anything you can tell us.'

Meredith leaned forward eagerly. 'What did you mean when you said that Logan ... Stuart, that is ... wasn't of the same blood as his father?'

The housekeeper shifted uneasily in her seat and stared at her hands, spread out before her.

'I've looked after Mrs Macaulay since she was a beautiful young bride full of joy and hope for the future. Her happiness didn't last long. Her husband soon found pleasure in beating her when the mood took him. It was a blessing that his work took him to all four corners of the world, so he had long absences from home. It was while he was away ... in India, I think it was ... that a distant cousin of his visited. The physical resemblance was remarkable, but he had all the good qualities that the professor lacked. It was wrong, what they did, but I couldn't blame poor Mrs Macaulay for falling in love with the man, and he adored her.'

'What happened?'

'There was a child. That was Stuart ... the man you now know as Logan. It was the name of the professor's cousin as well as the boy's grandfather, God rest their souls. Logan Macaulay stayed around for a few years. He and the boy were inseparable. The professor hated him. He knew fine what went on behind his back, but he was away so much in those days. Then one day, after the two of them had fought – like mad dogs in the street they were – Mr Logan left and never came back. It was about that time that the professor took on that gillie person.'

'Frazier?'

'Yes, sir. Nasty piece of goods he was, but he was like a little puppy dog around the master. Did all the professor's dirty work, I suspect.'

The housekeeper pulled out the table drawer and took from it a slender notebook that was well-worn and curled at the corners.

'Take this, sir. Everything I know is written in there. I kept a diary, you see. The beatings, the abuse ... it started a long time ago. There are names and addresses noted, but I can't guarantee that any of them will speak out. It's all too shameful, you see.'

'What about the daughter, Mrs Robinson?' Dr Jolly asked, quickly pocketing the book before the woman could change her mind.

'There were two daughters. Janet was the favourite. Pretty little thing she was. That is, until her father started … well, you know … misbehaving with her. When she was found to be with child, they packed her off to an asylum. She died in childbirth. The whole situation was just too much for Marion, the other daughter. A nervous breakdown, the doctor said. Thankfully, he got her into a decent institution or she might have ended up like her sister. I pray to God she will come out of it whole.'

'Where can we find her, Mrs Robertson?' asked Meredith.

'She's in the Burnside Convalescent Home on the other side of Edinburgh,' the woman told them. 'I doubt she'll see you, but you could try.'

They found the convalescent home without too much difficulty. The cabbie of the hansom they rode in told them he knew it well, but emphasized that it was a pity that only the rich could afford to stay there and be looked after.

'Not that I'd fancy them there nuns praying over me,' the man said with a grimace, then quickly apologized for being disrespectful.

'Not at all, my good man,' Dr Jolly told him. 'I'm not the most pious of individuals myself.'

'How long will it take to reach Burnside?' Meredith wanted to know; anxious to get on and get the business over with.

'Not too long, miss. Twenty minutes at best, as long as it doesn't snow.'

Fortunately, it didn't snow and they reached their destination well within the twenty minutes the cabbie had estimated.

Burnside Convalescent Home was a surprisingly attractive building nestling in rolling green lawns with long ponds reflecting conifers and decorative statuary. Despite its being winter, with a freezing mist hanging in the air, it was easy to see how relaxing a place it must all be for the patients.

'How beautiful it is, Father.' Meredith gave a gasp of admiration as she let her gaze wander over the grounds and beyond, to the distant hills.

'Indeed,' Dr Jolly agreed. 'I can't think of a better place to recover one's strength and to revive the spirit.'

The cabbie dropped them off at the front entrance, which was imposing, with white columns and grey marble steps.

'You'll wait for us, I hope?' the doctor enquired. 'We shouldn't be too long.'

'Ay, I will an' all, sir. You take all the time you want.'

A pink-cheeked nun in a soft grey habit and flowing white veil opened the door to them. Her smile was warm and welcoming, and her eyes twinkled good-humouredly.

'How can I help you?' she asked gently with a slight bow of her head.

'Good day to you, Sister.' Dr Jolly inclined his head respectfully. 'I am Dr Josiah Jolly and this is my daughter. We have come to visit one of your patients. A certain Miss Marion Macaulay.'

At the mention of the name the nun seemed to flinch and the light left her eyes as her smile faded.

'I'm not sure that that will be possible, sir. She is a very sick young woman.'

'We realize that,' Meredith said as calmly as she could manage, 'but we really do need to see her. It's of the utmost importance.'

'Are you of the family?'

'No, but I ... we knew Miss Macaulay's brother very well and it is on his behalf that we are here.'

The nun looked from one to the other of them, then backed into the hallway and beckoned to them to enter.

'If you would wait here please, I will enquire, but Miss Macaulay has been in a very low state these last few days. She suffered a setback after the news of her father's death.'

'Who told her?' Dr Jolly asked, his eyes full of concern.

'It was the family solicitor, sir. We begged him not to, considering her delicate state of health, but ...' The nun seemed to realize suddenly that she was being indiscreet and shook her head, touching her fingers to her lips. 'I'll just ...'

Leaving the words hanging in the air behind her she hurried off down a long, dark corridor, habit rustling, feet tapping. It was a good five minutes before she returned, smiling uncertainly.

'I have had a word with the Mother Superior, sir, and she is agreed that you can see Miss Macaulay, on the understanding that she must not be upset in any way.'

'Sister, I have to be honest and tell you that we are here on something of a mission.' Dr Jolly glanced swiftly at his daughter before carrying on. 'We hope to clear the name of a good man accused of vile crimes of which he is innocent. Unfortunately, he is now dead … we believe murdered, though it cannot be proved.'

'Who is this man, sir?' The nun seemed to be holding her breath in anticipation of his answer.

'Logan!' Meredith blurted out the name, then pulled herself up short, aware of her error. 'Stuart Macaulay, Sister. Miss Macaulay's brother. They were very close, I believe.'

'Indeed.' The nun was recovering her composure and pressed a hand to her bosom. 'Oh my, yes! The poor soul has talked of no-one else since her admission here. She obviously loved him dearly.'

'We will be as tactful as possible,' Dr Jolly assured her. 'I cannot guarantee that she will not be upset, but she may want to help us, nevertheless.'

The nun nodded uncertainly and touched the crucifix that hung heavily around her neck. 'You seem like an honest man, sir. I will trust you to do your best for Miss Macaulay.' She smiled at Meredith. 'She doesn't normally receive visitors, but perhaps she will gain strength from what you have to tell her.'

'Where is she, Sister?

'You'll find her in the conservatory. She likes it in there, with its views over the gardens. Come this way. I'll make sure you are not disturbed, though few patients go in there at this time of year.'

The thin young woman with the dark hair and the lost expression gave no indication that she was aware of their presence. Neither Dr Jolly nor Meredith felt confident about how they should approach her. The last thing either of them wanted was to upset the young woman and they knew well that this might be their only chance to speak to her.

'Sister Marie-Thérèse tells me that you knew my brother.' She did not turn her head, but continued to stare out of the window where a few snowflakes were beginning to float down like fluffy white feathers.

'Miss Macaulay …' It was Meredith who took the initiative and placed herself where Logan's sister could see her. There was no more than a minute flicker of the darkly ringed eyes in her direction. 'Your brother was very dear to me. My father and I spent some months on St Kilda with him. We have only recently returned.'

'That is not possible. Stuart died five years ago.'

'That's what you were told.'

'Are you saying that my father lied to me?'

'No. Professor Macaulay truly believed him to be dead.'

'At his hands?'

Meredith suddenly felt that the interview was going the right way. They would not have to convince this woman of her father's guilt and her brother's innocence. The difficulty would be to get her to admit to the truth in a court of law.

'At his command,' came the reply.

'The gillie? Frazier?' There was no trace of doubt in her voice.

'Yes,' said Meredith, recalling the conversation she had overheard between the two men on the boat.

'My father was an evil man. I'm glad he's dead.'

After this remark there was a heavy silence. Meredith saw Marion Macaulay's long, bony fingers grip the arms of her chair. She exchanged glances with her father, who was trying to signal to her to go carefully forward, but she was too impatient. Besides, the woman seemed willing to talk, and she felt she must seize the moment.

'I doubt that you are the only one to think that, Miss Macaulay.'

'Is it wicked to hate one's parent?' Marion Macaulay's haunted eyes looked searchingly at Meredith. 'I feel it must be, but … when they told me he had died I … I felt nothing but relief. Then I was overcome by the most awful guilt.'

Meredith went down on her knees and took the woman's chilly hands in hers, holding them tightly.

'We do not choose our parents, Miss Macaulay, any more than they choose us.'

'But are we not taught that love for our parents must be uncondi-
tional...?'

'Yes, and vice versa, but we only follow the rules that are laid down
by strangers. We do not make those rules and what is good for some
is not always good for others. It is no sin not to love. Love is something that comes naturally from deep within our being. It's a spiritual
thing, felt only when it is right.'

'Like when you find someone you will love for the rest of your
days?'

A fleeting image of Logan swept through Meredith's mind. She
gulped and nodded, but for a moment she was unable to speak. She
felt her father's hand press her shoulder and she blinked rapidly,
anxious not to show too much emotion, but Miss Macaulay was
watching her closely.

'My daughter lost someone recently to whom she was rather
attached,' Dr Jolly said quickly, doing his best to intervene between
the two young women.

'How lucky,' Marion said, surprisingly. 'I have never had anyone to
lose, except my brother, whom I loved dearly.'

Meredith sniffed and blinked some more. She still held on to
Marion Macaulay's hands, afraid that if she let them go the woman
would clam up and refuse to talk to them any further.

'Then you must know how I feel,' she said softly.

'Meredith, my dear, I don't think ...' Dr Jolly frowned down at her
but both women ignored him.

'You lost a brother too?' Marion said.

'No, Marion ... I may call you by your given name?' Marion
nodded briefly and Meredith continued, her voice trembling with
emotion. 'I lost a man I loved with all my heart. I knew him by the
name of Logan, but his real name was Stuart Macaulay.'

'Stuart ... I don't understand. Not my brother, surely? As I have
said, he has been dead these past five years.'

'That's not so,' Dr Jolly said softly. 'Your brother died a few weeks
ago only.'

'We came face to face with him on the island of Hirta, where he
preferred to be known simply as Logan.'

'Logan was the name of our grandfather,' Marion said, 'And a distant cousin – nice men, both of them.'

'The distant cousin whom you recall bore a strong resemblance to your father,' said Dr Jolly. 'Is that not so, Miss Macaulay?'

The young woman nodded. 'Yes, the likeness was uncanny, but all the Macaulay men bear the same physical features.'

'So we are led to believe. However, it is almost certain that he was your brother's father, not Professor Fergus Macaulay.'

Marion Macaulay's mouth dropped open and her face seemed to turn to stone with the disbelief of what she was hearing. She stayed like that for a long time, then shook herself and lifted her shoulders and chin so that she looked much taller than the tiny, slumped woman they had found only a few minutes ago.

'So that's why my father hated Stuart, and why, obviously, my brother was such a different person from the man he believed to be his father. I always wondered how such a terrible man could father such a good son. I heard my father and Uncle Logan arguing one day. At the time, I couldn't understand what it was all about, but now it all makes sense. It came to blows. My father was a brilliant orator, but only in public. In his private life he had more use for his fists than for words. The next day Uncle Logan was gone and my mother cried for weeks and would not be comforted.'

She stared from Meredith to Dr Jolly and then back again, her eyes glassy, her lips quivering.

'Stuart is still alive, you say? All this time he's been alive and he's never been in touch with me?'

Meredith's eyes slid fearfully in the direction of her father. The situation was becoming precarious now that they had entered into the subject of Logan.

'I'm very sorry, Miss Macaulay,' Dr Jolly said, taking out his dry pipe and fingering it for something to do. 'We have reason to believe that Logan … that Stuart was killed as we left the island. In fact we know he was. Meredith overheard the gillie, Frazier, confirm that he had shot your brother and assured your father that this time there was no mistake.'

'Oh, no, dear God! How can I bear it … to lose my dear brother a second time, just when I thought … oh, how cruel that is!' Whereupon

Marion Macaulay set to weeping in the most heartfelt way, so that Dr Jolly's own eyes became moist and Meredith had to struggle not to join in.

They were suddenly aware of the scuffing of soft leather slippers. They turned to find Sister Marie-Thérèse coming down upon them with a very stern expression.

'Now, didn't I tell you to be gentle with the child!' she admonished. She directed them to the door. 'Please leave. I cannot have my patient upset in such a way.'

They hesitated, holding their ground, but the nun was adamant and kept indicating the door while regarding them with reproachful eyes.

'No! Please, Sister Marie-Thérèse!' Marion swallowed back her sobs and rose unsteadily to her feet. 'These good people have asked for my help and I will do anything they want, for the sake of my brother's good name.'

Dr Jolly smiled with relief. Meredith ran to her and gave her a sisterly hug, which made them both cry and cling to one another. The nun's eyes widened perceptibly at the sudden change in her patient's demeanour. She dropped her astonished gaze and moved back to the corridor, muttering to herself, or perhaps praying.

As the two weeping young women dried their tears and exchanged quavery smiles, Marion took Meredith by the arm and guided her to the door.

'Come to my room,' she said hoarsely. 'You too, Doctor. It is more private there and we can talk in peace without being overheard.'

'Are you sure you are well enough to do this, Miss Macaulay?' Dr Jolly said as they walked slowly together down a corridor of plain, numbered doors. 'We can come back some other time if—'

'No! It must be done now. It will be difficult, but I will tell you everything. The truth must come out, so that my brother's name can be cleared. For as long as I can remember, my mother has lived with the strictest rule that all things must be brushed under the carpet and not talked about or the shame would kill her. All that silence and secrecy! None of it is worth the deaths of the two people I held most dear in this world … not to mention those poor souls I never met. My mother will have to live with it alone, because I can't any longer.'

'We're so grateful, Marion,' Meredith said.

'There is just one thing I must ask of you.'

'Anything, my dear Miss Macaulay.' Dr Jolly nodded.

'I want to visit the grave of my brother. Will you take me there?'

CHAPTER 18

I T WAS WELL into spring before they could get a passage on a steamship heading for the islands of St Kilda. Josiah Jolly, deeply engrossed in the writing of their previous field trip, declined to go. He had made his decision only when he heard that Peter was to accompany the two young women.

In the time since they had first met Marion she had grown in strength, though any beauty remaining after her unenviable life was considerably faded. It was doubtful that anything would bring it back, for she must carry with her the dark memories of the past and they would haunt her for evermore.

However, her eyes shone brightly and her smile was warm and genuine now that the world knew the truth behind the now infamous Professor Fergus Macaulay. Anne Macaulay had taken the whole affair badly, unable to live with the shame. She had removed herself swiftly from Edinburgh and gone, as planned, to live with her sister in Canada, where she would not be known. It would be some time before she would allow her daughter to visit her, if ever.

With so many gruesome details being dragged out into the daylight and people having the courage, at last, to come forward, the police had made short work of the case. The gillie, Frazier, had been arrested and charged with murder. So tired was he of being on the run that he confessed all and turned out to be a star witness. It was as if he thought that since he was going to be hanged anyway, he might as well go to his death with a clear conscience. And that included revealing the truth as he knew it about Fergus Macaulay, even though the man was dead.

Strangely enough he had also confessed to the murder of the professor, thus freeing Johnny of the charge. No one doubted his word and Johnny was released from prison, a hairsbreadth from being hanged. He was a broken man, but with a small promise of a better life stretching out before him.

Three passengers were leaning on the rail of the ss *Hebrides*. It was a bright May morning with a clear blue sky and a full yellow sun that was trying its best to warm the frosty air. There was no wind and the sea was mirror calm. Everyone aboard was hopeful of a smooth voyage.

Marion moved away, edging her way along the rail to get a better view of a pair of otters that were playing on the port side of the boat. A family of wealthy tourists on board were throwing bread and laughing at the antics of the two delightful creatures.

Peter moved closer to Meredith and covered her hand with his, then lifted it to his lips in a surreptitious kiss.

'Are you all right, Meredith? Are you sure you can cope with this voyage?'

With one accord they both stared down at the diamond engagement ring she wore on her finger. A cluster of diamonds winked and blinked back at them in the sun. Meredith had loved the ring when Peter offered it to her, but she was awed by how expensive it looked. After all, Peter was only just serving his apprenticeship as a botanist in a large museum of natural history in Newcastle.

He had wanted them to be married quickly, afraid that he would lose her if they waited too long. However, she had persuaded him that it was more prudent to wait until he was earning sufficient money to pay rent on a house of their own rather than live with her father.

'Of course I can cope.' she said, smiling a little too broadly to hide her innermost fears that it was perhaps a little too soon to revisit Hirta and the past that had hurt her so deeply. 'Have you ever known me not cope with anything?'

He smiled at her quizzically and shook his head. 'No, but you've just reminded me of how little I do know about you.'

'You'll have a very long time to acquaint yourself with all my foibles,' she said humorously. 'I hope you won't find them too tiresome.'

'Never.' He laughed softly and kissed her cheek, making them both blush when they realized that Marion was watching them from a few yards away. 'But I am concerned that this trip might upset you.'

She thought about that and took a deep breath, deciding that it was best to be honest. After all, they were to be married one day and honesty between a man and his wife was of the utmost importance. She might as well start here and now.

'Peter, I won't deny that seeing Hirta again ... and Logan's grave in particular ... well, yes, it will hurt deep inside. However, it won't change how I feel for you. I'm so very fond of you.'

Peter gave a sigh. 'But will you ever come to love me the way you loved Logan?' he asked.

'That's not a fair question,' she told him and turned her face to a light breeze that was blowing now that the boat was pushing away from the land and heading out to sea.

'I don't care what the answer is just now,' he replied. 'As long as you are mine I shall be the happiest man in the world and I will spend my lifetime making you love me.'

'Oh, Peter, you are ...'

'Funny?'

'Very sweet, and I do love you, so there.'

They drew apart slightly as Marion approached with a look of concern.

'For goodness sake don't mention my name when there are people around,' she said in a whisper. 'These tourists are all going to Hirta because of the newspaper reports on my father. If they find out who I am ...'

'Don't worry, Marion,' Peter assured her. 'We'll be discreet.'

'There will be a grave, won't there? I mean, the people on the islands ... they're not primitive, are they? They don't bury people in unmarked graves, surely?'

Meredith couldn't help flinching at the thought, but she held her expression rather than allow Peter to see how she really was being affected by this pilgrimage to Logan's grave. Even if Marion had never asked to go there, Meredith would have made the journey. It was essential that she should do it before she got married. Without standing at the place where Logan lay and placing flowers or something personal on his grave, she could not go ahead with her marriage to Peter.

'No, they're not that primitive,' she said. 'They are good Christians. Don't worry about it, Marion.'

The sea remained calm until they came in sight of St Kilda. It was as if they had passed from one world to another in seconds. The wind picked up, the waves reared like blue-grey horses with flying white manes. Even the air tasted more salty and the boat began to rock and to roll in an alarming fashion.

There was a call from the captain for all passengers to get below decks as the sky darkened and the weather grew squally. It was not only a familiar request to Meredith, it caused her a certain sense of *déjà vu*. Marion, it being her first time on a boat of any kind, was the first to leave the deck.

'Come on, Meredith. It's safer to go below,' Peter said, but Meredith shook her head and continued to hang on to the bow rail.

'No, Peter, I'm all right here,' she shouted as the wind moaned and screamed up to gale force. 'I need to see Hirta.'

'Is this one of your foibles that I have to learn to live with?' he asked, trying to smile but looking too anxious for comfort.

'What?' She was hardly listening, much more determined to see the boat's passage and still be there on deck when they reached Village Bay.

'You won't listen to me, will you?' Peter tried again.

'No! I'm determined to stay here and see out the end of the voyage.'

'Stubborn! Your father warned me.' He put one arm about her shoulders and with his free hand, clung on to the rail as the boat tossed precariously. 'In that case, I'll stay with you.'

She turned her head, pulled her hair back from over her eyes, and squinted at him with a pained smile.

'All right,' she said, then her attention returned to the islands, which were gradually getting bigger, though they were shrouded in mist. They looked hauntingly lovely and unreal at the same time.

The *Hebrides* docked without incident, despite the choppy seas, though many of the tourists were suffering from *mal de mer*. It dropped its dinghys, carrying those passengers who were brave enough or well enough to disembark and they struck out for beach.

There was a party of rich Americans on board. One man in the group looked rather green, but his wife was too excited to sympathize and repeated over and over again that she couldn't wait to tell the 'folks back home' of their adventure.

'Gee, I hope the ghost of that terrible professor doesn't haunt the island! I'll just die! Come on, Brody! Help me out of this damned boat and then you can go vomit till the cows come home.'

All along the main street of Village Bay the locals were already out and waiting with their produce, hoping to make a profit that would pay their next few months' rent. Meredith recognized most of the faces, but the islanders were too busy to notice her pass by with Peter and Marion, for which she was grateful.

They dodged around the produce being offered for sale: dried and salted fish, wool, preserved seabirds, knitted and woven garments. The St Kildans were posing for the tourists, who had cameras and were clicking away at what must seem to them to be sights unseen by the rest of the world.

'We don't have much time,' Peter reminded the two women who were marching ahead of him. 'The captain said that a storm is on the way and if we don't get off the island in half an hour we may be forced to stay.'

Meredith and Marion took no notice of him. They strode out and soon the graveyard was in sight. Meredith felt a cold shudder work its way through her body and wondered whether Logan's sister felt the same.

There were one or two new graves, but although they had a stone erected at the head, there were no names, there being no stonemason on the island.

'Which is his?' Marion cried, throwing her arms wide and turning in a circle to encompass all the unnamed graves.

Meredith shook her head. There was only one way to find out.

'We'll ask Lachlan,' she said. 'He'll know.'

Marion and Peter followed her breathless trek to Lachlan's cottage. The door opened before they reached it and Lachlan hobbled out on to the street, leaning heavily on his cane. He looked older and sadder, Meredith thought, shrunken in size because of his age and his rheumatism.

'Lachlan!' she called to him and saw his white eyebrows rise in consternation. 'It's me! Meredith Jolly! Don't you remember me? And here is Peter and ...'

She stopped, for Lachlan's gaze had fallen on Marion and he appeared not to like what he saw.

'Why have you come back here, Meredith Jolly?' he asked in a slow, deep voice. 'You belong to a different world. There is no place for you here. The tourists, that's different. They bring money ...' He spat in the dry dust at his feet. 'You have not come as a tourist, I trust?'

'Of course not, Lachlan,' Meredith told him gently, her throat tightening. 'We have come ... we have brought Logan's sister to mourn at his graveside, but we are unable to find where he is buried.'

Meredith felt her voice cracking dangerously as she spoke of Logan. Lachlan noticed it and gave her a piercing stare.

'You should not have come back here. This is a place of bad memories. Go back to your homeland and have a good life.'

'Lachlan...!'

'There is nothing for you here.'

Meredith couldn't believe that he was speaking to her in such a manner.

'If you won't help us, Lachlan, I'll go and find Flora. She'll tell us—'

'Flora MacInness, is it?' Lachlan bellowed. 'The old witch lies in the graveyard at long last. She always said she would not go until she could dance on my grave: Well, I'm still here and not a day passes that I don't do a bit of a jig over her resting place, just to let her know she was wrong. Fortunate she is that we buried her on hallowed ground and didn't plant her in that apothecary's garden of hers.'

Meredith's shoulders slumped downward at the news of the death of her old friend.

And if the dead could speak, Flora would be objecting loudly that her wishes had not been carried out.

'It's to be hoped she will not choose to haunt you, Lachlan,' she said haughtily. He gave her a withering look such as only Lachlan could give. He looked, for all the world, like Michelangelo's depiction of an angry God.

'She already has, the old witch – and her not yet my age! She probably died just so she could get to Heaven before me.'

It was all Meredith could do not to smile, for she knew how fond the old man really was of Flora. But the thought that was uppermost in her mind came tumbling out, and with it tears that welled up in her eyes.

'Lachlan, we've come all this way to visit the grave of Logan. This is his sister, Marion. Can you tell us where it is?'

Lachlan looked perturbed at the question and fell strangely silent. Through the silence came the eerie sound of a warning hoot drifting across the bay from the SS *Hebrides*. The captain was getting impatient to leave and was calling to his passengers to make haste back to the boat. On the beach the tourists, clutching their purchases were lining up ready to get back on board.

'Meredith,' Peter tugged urgently at her arm, 'we must go. I don't want to be stranded here on Hirta. It might be months before another boat can come in.'

'Oh, but we can't go yet!' Marion gave a cry of despair. 'I must see my brother's grave. I can't leave without …'

Meredith took over her plea as Marion burst into helpless tears.

'Lachlan, quickly. Where did you bury him?'

She could see the old man's jaws clenching and unclenching. He rubbed a gnarled hand over his grey forest of a beard and sniffed.

''Tis not here, child,' he said, dragging the words out as if they were difficult to pronounce. 'I canna show ye. Nobody can. Now go before the boat sails without ye.'

'But …' Meredith stamped her foot in outrage. 'How can you not show us? Lachlan, I thought you had more heart than this. You know how I loved Logan …' She closed her eyes momentarily, aware that she was admitting her feelings in front of Peter, he would be dreadfully hurt to hear what she said, even though he knew it to be true. 'And … and Logan loved me. We need to pay our respects, say goodbye….'

'Please!' begged Marion, her face awash with tears. 'Show us where he lies.'

There was a moment's hesitation, and then Lachlan slowly shook his head and backed into his cottage.

'I cannot help you,' he said, waving his hand before his face as though he would hide behind it. 'Please go now, before it is too late. There is no point in you staying.'

He shut the door in their faces with a decisive click. Meredith fell forward, arm raised and was about to beat on the wooden panels with her clenched fist, but Peter stopped her.

'No, Meredith,' he said. 'You know Lachlan as well as I do. Wherever Logan is buried, it is not here, that is certain.'

'But why?' Meredith gave another stamp of her foot. 'This was where he belonged. He was a part of these islands.'

'I'm sure there were good reasons for him to be buried elsewhere.' Peter drew the two women away from the cottage and urged them down the path in the direction of the shore, where the last tourists were anxiously clambering into the second dinghy. The *Hebrides*'s hooter sounded again, more persistently and distant figures could be seen with arms waving urgently. 'Come. We must hurry.'

Two burly sailors stood ready, arms akimbo, as they watched the party of three hurry over the stony path. Behind them the *Hebrides* was bobbing up and down in the sea like a cork as the rising wind stirred the waves. The sky that was bringing the storm clouds towards the islands was deep indigo and thunder rumbled in the distance.

Marion was first into the dinghy. Meredith hesitated, ignoring the impatience of Peter, who was ready to carry her on board if necessary. She had to have just one last look at the place where she knew her heart would always remain.

'Meredith! For God's sake!'

'It's all right, Peter,' she said, giving herself a little shake. 'My father taught me that when there was nothing that could be done, it was best to do just that.'

They struck out towards the *Hebrides* as the first flash of lightning spliced through the sky, the oarsmen pulling manfully, their muscles swelling with every stroke. A squally rain began to fall, but Meredith was oblivious to it. Peter stayed by her, gripping her hand as if he was afraid to let go.

'It will pass in time, Meredith,' he shouted in her ear as the noise of the storm rose in a great crescendo.

'What, Peter?' She could not take her eyes away from Hirta.

'The pain in your heart.'

He understood. Of course he did. He couldn't help but know that the pain of her loss was every bit as profound as her love for Logan had been. Right now she felt that she would never recover, but she knew deep down that she would. She had to, for life went on and if you didn't go with it, you were lost. Meredith had no wish to emulate Aunt Agnes for the next forty years.

She shaded her eyes, not because of the blustery storm, but because she wanted to hide the tears that sprang there coursed down her cheeks, where they were washed away by the rain.

'Do you remember, Peter,' she said thickly, memories rushing back, 'the day we arrived here, nearly a year ago?'

'How could I forget? We all nearly drowned.'

They had almost reached the steamship. Somewhere in the background, the noise of the weighing anchor rattled metallically. The captain was shouting orders, ushering the passengers below decks. Meredith barely noticed anything but the fact that she was being transported further and further away from Hirta. Her gaze skimmed the bay, absorbing every contour, every tiny dwelling place, every moving figure as villagers gathered to wave them off. Her eyes blurred as she followed the outline of the land, the undulating rocks that rose up high where she had had her first sight of Logan. He had stood there, like a statue, before coming to rescue her. In just the way that a figure was standing there now, silhouetted against the stormy sky.

There was something familiar about the man's shape, about his stance. Was she seeing things, hallucinating because he was so strong in her mind and in her heavy heart? It couldn't be!

'Logan!' His name escaped her lips, but was whipped away by the howling wind and Peter did not hear it.

Her heart gave a leap. He was not dead after all! For the second time, he had been saved. Yes, it surely was him, larger than life itself, standing watching her as before, but this time she was leaving and he had no reason to rescue her from the boiling sea.

CHAPTER 19

'Stop!' Meredith cried as loudly as she could, making Peter beside her jump. 'Stop the boat!'

'Meredith, what is it?'

But before Peter could get a grip on her, Meredith hauled herself up on to the rim of the boat. As Peter's hands shot out, grappling with the hem of her coat, she leapt into the agitated sea. Screams rang out from ship and shore. It appeared, for a moment, that Meredith was drowning, weighed down by her clothes. She sank once, twice, but then she kicked out and started swimming back towards the island.

Behind her, she could hear Peter calling to her, and a backward glance showed that the dinghy had turned and that he was hanging over the prow, a lifebelt in his hands, ready to throw it over her.

'Forgive me, Peter,' she cried, choking on the icy salt water that washed over her and threatened to pull her down into the murky depths.

She raised herself as best she could, coughing and spluttering, fearing that she was almost certainly going to drown unless she headed back to the boat. But Hirta beckoned and she was drawn to it like a piece of metal is drawn to a magnet. Her lungs were bursting, but she still called out to Logan, even though she could no longer see him, the briny sea stinging her eyes so that everything was a blur.

A shout went up from the island. Somehow, Meredith managed to open her eyes sufficiently to see the irregular shape of the dinghy, with Peter still at the prow. By some weird miracle, she was getting further and further away from it, the flowing tide dragging her closer and closer to Village Bay. Through half-closed eyes she could see a shaft of sunshine beaming on the pebbly shore. But closer to her there was something else in the water ploughing through the rise and fall. There was much splashing, but it was not a boat. It was a man.

Someone was in the sea, muscular arms slicing through the waves, feet kicking up a foamy plume behind him. They collided, breath expiring from their lungs, and then strong hands were gripping Meredith, holding her in a vicelike grip.

'Meredith! Little fool! Hold on!'

'Oh, Logan! Logan!'

They were going to end as they had begun. If they were both to die now, Meredith would die happily in the arms of the man she loved. One last time, she let her eyes rest on his beloved face, then the sea came up and swallowed them in a dark surge too powerful to fight against. She relaxed against Logan's chest and everything went dark as the life was washed out of her.

Josiah Jolly could not keep still. He paced, he twitched, and he pulled out his pipe and immediately pocketed it again. It was midsummer, but the day was grey and morose, the rain streaming down the windowpanes like rivers of glycerine, turning the garden beyond into a distorted watercolour palette.

At last there was the sound of hoofs and the rattle of carriage wheels on the road; then, two minutes later, came the sound of voices. The little maid, Daisy, was flushed and nervous and as excited as Dr Jolly as she announced the arrival of Mr Peter Lewis.

'He's alone, Daisy?' the doctor barked out and she shrank back from this unaccustomed manner.

'I ... er ...' She looked about her desperately, but was saved from further embarrassment by Peter coming into the room, brushing rain droplets from his shoulders.

'Where is she?' Dr Jolly fixed Peter with a piercing eye, his fists clenching and unclenching, and his whole body rigid with tension. 'Where is my daughter? How dare you keep her away from me so long with not a word of your safety or your wellbeing? I had reports of an accident at sea ... the SS *Hebrides*. A young woman was said to have jumped overboard, but the papers did not name her. Don't tell me it was Meredith. I won't believe you. No daughter of mine takes her own life!'

'Please, Dr Jolly, calm yourself.' Peter was uncertain how to continue, the doctor was in such a frenzied state. 'Obviously you did not receive my letter. We got here as quickly as we could....'

There was a rustle of silk and Marion Macaulay appeared behind Peter, smiling shyly. The doctor looked at her, disappointment clouding his face. There was, after all, only one person he longed to see, and this woman before him was not his beloved daughter.

'Letter? What letter? I received no letter.'

Further noises and rustlings and whisperings drifted down the hall, followed by two pairs of footsteps, one heavy, one light. Peter and Marion turned to greet the newcomers, while Josiah Jolly waited with bated breath and eyes as big as saucers. A man and a woman entered, both looking slightly self-conscious.

'Hello, Father,' Meredith said, her face suddenly lighting up at the sight of him.

'Meredith, my own dear girl!' He held out his arms and she ran into them with a little sigh of pleasure. 'I thought I had lost you!'

'So did I,' Peter said, his smile crooked and wobbly.

'Peter, my boy, did I say how pleased I am to see you ... both of you...oh, and you too, Miss Macaulay—'

'I'd like you to meet my husband, Father,' Meredith said.

'Good heavens, Peter, why did you not say right away! Congratulations, my boy!'

Meredith's laugh was full of joy as she hugged her father and kissed his cheek, then she beckoned to the tall, clean-shaven man with the eyes like polished ebony who was still hovering in the hall. Dr Jolly's eyes grew even wider still as he looked at the dark young man waiting to be introduced. 'I feel, sir, that we have met before?'

'Father, *this* is my husband,' she said, linking her arm lovingly through that of the stranger. 'You will remember Logan better if you picture him with his fierce black beard.'

'Logan! But yes, of course ... *husband*, you say! How can that be? First of all, the man is supposed to be dead ... that makes twice now he's been resurrected. Am I turning senile, or what? Meredith ... you were supposed to marry Peter. Oh, dear boy, I am so sorry! I...' His mouth clamped shut and he looked embarrassed as his eyes travelled from Peter to Logan, then he turned away and went to stare again out of the window.

'It's quite all right, Dr Jolly,' Peter said and received a smile of gratitude and affection from Meredith, and a nod of appreciation from Logan. 'I have already given them my blessing. I always knew I wouldn't stand a chance as long as Logan was alive. Once we thought he was dead, the way was clear for me, but to be honest, I knew Meredith could never be more than just fond of me. Logan won her heart and ...' He looked at Logan and held out his hand in friendship. 'You deserve it, Logan. As long as you make her happy, I will be honoured to be your friend.'

'Well, this is all too much to take in,' said Dr Jolly, sitting down heavily in his favourite chair and mopping his brow. 'I don't know what to think, apart from being hurt not to be at my only daughter's wedding.'

Meredith laughed lightly and went to kneel by his chair, taking his hand in hers.

'I'm sorry about that, Father, but the sea was so rough there was a chance that we would all be lost on the way back to the mainland. We thought it a good idea for the captain of the *Hebrides* to marry us, you know, just in case. But now that we're here and safe, we'll plan a proper wedding, just to please you. Isn't that so, Logan?'

Logan looked at father and daughter. They were so easy together. He wondered how long it would take the doctor to accept him as his son-in-law. Would he ever be fully accepted? Josiah Jolly was a good man, but like many fathers, he wanted the best for his daughter and Peter fitted the bill far more appropriately than the once exiled Stuart Logan Macaulay, son of a murderer.

'Dr Jolly,' he said, ill at ease in his mainland town suit after the six years of rough but comfortable St Kildan woollen garbs. 'I know I am not the man of your choice for your daughter, but I swear by all that you and I believe in that I will do everything I can to keep her safe and happy.'

The doctor mulled over his words and his jaw worked as if he were grinding his teeth.

'Would ye jump into the sea for her?'

'He already has done, Father,' Meredith chuckled. 'Twice!'

'And Meredith jumped into the sea for me,' Logan said, his face cracking into a wide, attractive smile. 'Though I think I'll be giving her some swimming lessons before she plans to do it again.'

He pulled Meredith gently to him and held her in a close embrace, planting a tender kiss on her forehead.

'Och, laddie, I just hope you know what you're taking on in marrying my daughter.' The doctor, too, was smiling as he got up and went to the sideboard to pour a celebration drink. 'Meredith has the strength and constitution of a horse and the head of a mule.'

'That is something I have already discovered,' Logan said. 'I think we're well matched on those scores.'

'Aye, you should produce good healthy children between the two of you.' Dr Jolly grinned broadly. 'Now, sherry for the ladies and brandy for the gentlemen, and perhaps, Meredith, your Aunt Agnes might like a drop of gin.'

'Gin! Aunt Agnes?' Meredith showed her astonishment. 'Where is she?'

'I do believe she is in the morning room with her fiancé. They announced their engagement yesterday and today she is wearing a dress of fuchsia silk and planning on a wedding gown of blue satin with cream lace.'

It was a long time before any of them retired to their beds. There was so much to be discussed, so much to plan, and nobody wanted to leave the family gathering before all the gaps had been filled, all the knots untied.

'What are you thinking of, Meredith?' Logan took the silver-backed brush from Meredith's hand and continued stroking it through her hair while she stared out of their bedroom window at the moon-bathed moors that stretched to the horizon.

'I'm reliving it all,' she told him, dreamily. 'Every precious moment from beginning to end.'

'Even the bad moments?' He bent and touched his lips lightly to her temple.

'Yes, even the bad moments. They make the good times seem even more precious.'

'I thought I'd lost you for ever the day you left Hirta. I never dreamed that you would return.'

'You didn't really want me to leave, did you, Logan?'

'No, but I knew it was best for you, that being with me would ruin your life. I couldn't bear to be responsible for your unhappiness.'

Meredith sighed and leaned her head back against him, feeling the soft beating of his heart and knowing that soon their hearts would be racing together as they made love on the soft feather mattress of the bed where she, herself, had been conceived.

'I still can't understand why Frazier only pretended to shoot you. He was a horrid man, almost as vile as the professor.'

'He told me that he owed me for healing his broken leg and that he felt bad about the first attempt at murdering me. It was all at my father's ... I mean, at Fergus Macaulay's behest. He was already wanted for murder, so would be hanged anyway if caught, so it didn't matter one way or the other. Luckily, he decided to shoot the goat and pretend that the blood was mine.'

'It seems to me, my love, that luck follows you around. Are you invincible perhaps?'

Logan laughed softly and kissed the top of her head as he put the hairbrush down and slipped his arms about her.

'Perhaps. Come, Meredith. I'm tired of brushing and talking. I want to make love to my wife.'

'And are you going to take that job at the hospital that my father intends to put you forward for?'

'If they offer it, yes.'

'Oh, they'll offer it, but will you...?'

'Enough!' He lifted her from her chair and carried her to the bed, showing amusement at the fact that she still blushed furiously at any form of intimacy.

'Logan...?'

'Tomorrow, my love!' And he effectively prevented her from saying anything further by covering her mouth with his own and all the questions that had been floating through her brain now floated away on a cloud of happiness that she had never thought possible.

'Yes, Logan,' she whispered against his lips. 'And all the tomorrows after that.'